MAIL ORDER BRIDE

Montana Orphan

Echo Canyon Brides
Book 8

LINDA BRIDEY

First Printing, 2015

Dedication

This book is dedicated to all of my faithful readers, without whom I would be nothing. I thank you for the support, reviews, love, and friendship you have shown me as we have gone through this journey together. I am truly blessed to have such a wonderful readership.

Contents

Chapter One

Running through the forest, she ignored the tree branches that slashed at her arms and the sharp stones that cut her bare feet. The moonlight helped her see where she was going, but she had no idea where to go. She was tired and hungry and lost. She was also terrified. The trees ended and she almost ran into a barbed wire fence. Avoiding it at the last moment, she turned to her left and followed it until it ended.

Where there was fence there were barns, and where there were barns there were people. *Good people.* She didn't know what they were after all this time, not in any real sense. Vague images and scenes played through her mind every day, but they weren't real. Still, she'd hoped that one day she'd see kind people again.

The fence seemed endless, but fear drove her onward over the rough ground. It evened out as she encountered a lawn and saw a house. Racing across it, she was dismayed to discover that it was dark and looked deserted. The huge, two-story, red brick structure was daunting to her; she'd never seen a house that large.

She tripped running up the front stairs onto a wide veranda but righted herself. Pounding on the door, she looked around frantically to make sure no one was coming after her. No one answered the door and no lamps were lit in response to her knocking. Maybe they couldn't hear her because the place was so big.

Running around to the back, she knocked on another door, but with the same result. There was a third door on the east side of the house and she beat on that one, too. Everything stayed quiet and dark. Desperation made her try the doorknob. To her disbelief and relief, it opened and she went inside the house, quickly shutting it behind her.

The hallway she stood in was lined with several doors. She knocked on a couple of them, but no one answered. Because there was no movement from anywhere in the house, she knew then that it was completely empty. She'd knocked loudly enough that someone would have surely heard her.

Going back to the door she'd come in, she figured out how to lock it. This was as good of a place to hide as any. She wasn't going to risk traveling on and being caught. Tentatively, she walked through the hallway until she found herself in a big room with a lot of furniture in it. Very fine furniture.

She felt dwarfed in the room, but it didn't get much better as she traveled through the dining room and into the kitchen. It was easy to see that the people who lived there were very rich. The marble kitchen counters gleamed in the moonlight. The silvery light glinted off an eight-plate cook stove that, although well-used, was clean.

Where there was a kitchen there was food. There were so many cupboards that she didn't know which one to open first. Finally choosing the one directly in front of her, she found a jar of pickles and a tin of sardines. She had no idea what they would taste like, but she recognized them as food. She'd eat them no matter what.

Unscrewing the jar lid, she attacked the pickles, stuffing them in her mouth and chewing them as fast as she could. The sweet-sour taste was to her liking and she ate several of them. Then she opened up the sardines and the scent of them gave her pause. She'd eaten worse, so she ate all of them, alternating them with the pickles to help drown out their taste.

Sated for the time being, she put the pickles back, but had no idea what to do with the empty sardine tin. Looking around, she found a pail that seemed as though it was used for trash collection. She put the tin in the pail and yawned. Leaving the kitchen, she went back through the hallway, searching for a place to sleep.

She found a room that was really two rooms, but it looked used. In her memories, she saw a yellow house and remembered that there were several bedrooms in it. One had been unused, but she couldn't remember what it was called. She'd look for a room like that. At the back of the hallway, she found a staircase and went up it, hoping that she might meet someone. Gaining the second floor, she found no one as she knocked on doors and opened them.

The first two rooms were used, but the third room was a bathroom with a large tub, wash basin, and commode. Using the house in her memory as a reference, she remembered what one was for. Knowing that she needed to wash up, she decided to do that first thing in the morning— if no one came home that night.

The next room was devoid of belongings in the closet or lying around on the dresser or bureau. Not wanting to get the pretty floral comforter dirty, she curled up on a corner of the nice rug. Feeling relatively safe, she dropped off into a fitful sleep.

As their family carriages arrived in Billings, Montana, Nick Terranova turned the one he drove left onto the street that led to the hotel where his family and Arrow would be staying. The early April weather was mild and perfect for a wedding. He could hardly believe that his little sister, Vanna, was getting married in two days.

Her betrothed, Arrow Flies Swift, was excited and nervous about their upcoming nuptials. The Cheyenne brave had worked hard over the winter months to learn about Catholicism in preparation for his conversion. He and Vanna had met and fallen in love the previous October and Arrow had declared his intentions to marry Vanna on the first day he'd met the Terranovas.

He'd saved her from a bear, killing the huge animal, and had carried her home since she'd sprained her ankle. Her father, Alfredo, had been resistant at first to a relationship between the brave and his daughter, but once it had become clear that Arrow wasn't going to give up and that Vanna was smitten with Arrow, he'd given in.

Although Alfredo and his wife, Sylvia, would have preferred their children to marry Catholics, they'd been lenient when their youngest son, Sal, had married Lulu Johansson, who was Protestant. Since marrying in late December, Lulu had converted, knowing that it was important to Sal's family. They hadn't expected her to, but it had been her choice.

Arrow had felt the same way. Even though he'd been a medicine man's apprentice with his tribe, he had decided to overcome the religious obstacle of conversion so that he could marry Vanna. Again, the Terranovas hadn't made this a true condition, but Arrow had taken it seriously and he wanted to please his future in-laws as well as share Vanna's faith.

Her family was also respectful of his religion's traditions and they didn't mind him mixing the two religions, which had similarities, such as the belief in the Creator. Sometimes before dinner, he offered a Cheyenne prayer, which he said in English. He'd studied the new language diligently, engaging his new friend, Adam Harris, Echo Canyon's new schoolteacher, to help him with it. He was now essentially fluent and had also learned some mathematics and history.

Arrow was an intelligent young man and once he'd started learning, he enjoyed studying all sorts of things. Nick, who had been a seminarian at one point, had been one of Arrow's main teachers concerning Catholicism. He'd helped to prepare him for the Catechism classes necessary for converting to the new religion. Arrow had also been baptized.

Nick slowed his team, smiling as he thought about how fun teaching Arrow all these months had been. Arrow's dry sense of humor and mostly calm demeanor was in stark contrast to Nick's Italian family's boisterous personalities; the brave was a skilled instigator who often worked backhanded compliments into a conversation in a way that fooled the object of the taunt into thinking it was genuine at first. He liked to keep a fight between the other members of the family going while he calmly sat at the dinner table or in the parlor at night. It only took a minimum of words for him to do it, too.

Pulling his team to a stop in front of the hotel, Nick jumped down from the seat and stretched to work out the kinks in his back from driving. He'd driven his parents and Arrow and Vanna while his other brother, Gino, had taken turns with Sal driving Lulu and the majority of the family's luggage. Alfredo had spelled him here and there, but Nick liked driving, so he'd been at the helm most of the time.

Alfredo alighted from the conveyance and helped Sylvia down. "We made good time, Nicky. I'm glad you found that quicker route."

"Me, too. You feelin' ok?" Nick asked.

"For the millionth time, I'm fine," Alfredo retorted. "I haven't had any problems since last year, so quite askin'."

"Ok, ok," Nick said.

Arrow jumped down from the carriage, also glad to be able to move around. He had never ridden such a long way in a vehicle before and, were it not for his companions, he would have been bored to death by the tedious journey. Instead of helping Vanna from the carriage the way Alfredo had Sylvia, he merely lifted her down.

Alfredo frowned at him. "Way to show up the old man, Arrow."

"You're not old," Arrow said, smiling. "Just lazy."

He moved quickly away from Alfredo, who made a grab for him.

"You're supposed to respect your elders," Alfredo said. "It's not too late for me to cancel this wedding."

"Oh, yes it is," Sylvia said. "We've already paid the deposits and I didn't travel all the way here just to have the wedding canceled. You'll have to find another way to punish him."

Arrow grinned. "I look forward to it."

The rest of the family joined them and they went to check in at the Golden Lion, a popular hotel in the city. Once they were situated, they met down in the dining room for dinner. They were a lively bunch, alternately teasing and arguing with each other. There would be more of them the next day when Arrow's brother, Wild Wind, his wife, Roxie, and more friends of the family arrived for the rehearsal dinner.

Gino sat next to Nick as they ate. He leaned closer to Nick. "So Chelsea will be here tomorrow. Are you looking forward to seeing her?"

Nick almost rolled his eyes, but he wasn't going to give his younger brother any ammunition. Lulu's cousin had made it clear in December that she was interested in Nick. She'd given him her address, inviting him to write to her. The brown-eyed blonde was fun, smart, and beautiful—every man's dream—but Nick was hesitant about starting a relationship.

The deaths of his wife, Ming Li, and their son, Jake, three years ago had left Nick a broken man and he still grieved for them. Sometimes he thought he would like to find someone and other days he felt as though he would never be ready to move on. He'd even considered going back to seminary, but in his heart, he knew that he would be doing it for the wrong reasons. Being a priest was about helping to solve problems, not hiding from them.

"This roast is terrible," Nick said, cutting the tough meat. "The potatoes aren't done and the beans are mushy."

"I agree," Gino said. "But you're avoiding the question. You've been writing to her for a while now. Aren't you excited to see her?"

"Honestly, it'll be nice to see her, but I'm not excited about it, Gino," Nick said. "I like writing to her, but only as a friend. I made that plain the last time I wrote her. I was very nice about it, but firm."

Gino attacked his roast angrily. Normally he was almost as even-tempered as Nick, but the situation aggravated him. "I don't understand. A beautiful woman practically throws herself at you, but you don't want her. I would *love* to write to her and *I* would be excited to see her, but she's made it clear that she's not attracted to *me*. What's so wrong with me?"

Nick said, "There's nothin' wrong with you."

"I'm a good-looking guy, right?"

"Yeah."

"I make a good living; I'm not Sal, who used to chase anything in a dress; and I'm funny," Gino said.

Nick nodded. "Smart, too, especially about money."

"Right. So why haven't any of the women I've written to wanted to meet? I've offered to go to them or to pay for them to come here. I can't figure it out. I've written to Catholic girls, too, so that isn't it. I wrote to a couple of Protestant girls and even a Jewish girl. Hey, Arrow! You know any nice Cheyenne girls looking for a rich, white husband?"

"Shh!" Nick admonished him. "Knock that off. Have some patience, for Pete's sake."

"I've been patient. Very, very patient," Gino said. "I'm not a monk or a priest."

Nick just stared at him.

Gino smiled. "Sorry. I sometimes forget that you're not a regular guy. I don't know how you do it. Don't you miss it?"

"I don't think this is a good place to discuss that, Gino," Nick said, irked. "It's called control."

"Well, if you married Chelsea, you wouldn't have to control it," Gino said.

"That's not a good enough reason to get married and you know it," Nick said.

Gino said, "You shouldn't lock yourself away like this, Nicky. It's not good for you."

Nick gave up on eating the horrible meal, not only because of the poor food quality, but because Gino wasn't going to let the subject go. He set his silverware down and wiped his mouth.

"I don't want to talk about this," Nick said. "Especially not here."

"You never want to talk about it. It doesn't matter where we are. You shouldn't keep it bottled up like that," Gino said.

"Everyone deals with things in their own way," Nick said. "What's right for one person isn't always right for another."

"From what I can see, you're not dealing with it at all," Gino said.

Nick barely kept from pounding the table. "I'm going for a walk."

Gino said, "I'm just worried about you, that's all."

Rising from the table, Nick strode away before he clocked Gino.

Chapter Two

Sylvia watched Vanna gaze at her engagement ring, smiling as she did so. It was the morning of the wedding and she was breakfasting with her daughter and daughter-in-law, Lulu. It was hard to believe that her little girl was about to become a married woman.

Vanna glanced up and caught her mother's scrutiny. "What?" she asked.

Sylvia smiled. "I was just remembering when you were born. You were such a pretty baby, and now you're a beautiful young woman. Don't look at me that way, Giavanna Theresa Terranova."

Vanna smiled a little, but kept her thoughts to herself. She was still sensitive about her curvy, fuller figure. While it was popular for a woman to have an hourglass figure, her hourglass was somewhat bigger than what was considered fashionable. Sylvia wasn't the only one who scolded her about her negative feelings.

Arrow didn't like hearing her put herself down, either. On a couple of occasions, he'd shown her how beautiful she was to him, but she was still plagued by self-doubt.

"Vanna, you would think you'd be over this by now. Look at the man you're marrying! I've always told you that men would find you attractive, but more importantly, they'd see your inner beauty," Sylvia said.

Lulu said, "Sylvia's right. I know how you feel, Vanna. I never thought anyone like Sal would want me because I kept seeing all my faults instead of focusing on all of my good qualities. He saw all of those good things about me, not the bad. You have so many good qualities and you're a very pretty girl."

"But all the boys in Echo snapped up all the thin girls and none of them ever talked to me much," Vanna said. "None of them wanted anything to do with someone my size."

Sylvia remembered having the same problem when she was Vanna's age. However, she hadn't been much older than Vanna when she'd met Alfredo and fallen in love with the handsome man with the beautiful blue eyes and brown hair. Unlike Vanna, however, Sylvia had been a little forward for the time and had been determined to capture Alfredo's heart.

Having been taught by her older sisters, Sylvia had known how to flirt with a man and had wasted no time letting Alfredo see her appreciation of him. She'd instructed Vanna on a couple of the more chaste methods, but Vanna was too shy to employ them.

"That's because they were too stupid to see what a beautiful girl you are," Sylvia said. "Arrow certainly thinks so, but that's because he's much smarter than they were. Any man who tries to trade bear meat for a woman on the first day he meets her and her family obviously thinks you're beautiful."

Vanna laughed. "I wish I could have seen him trying to trade with Pop for me. Some women might not think that's very romantic, but I do. And then he carried me all the way home. I still can't believe it."

"When I saw him carrying you up the steps, I thought I was seeing things," Sylvia said. "But there was something about him that made me like him right away. Maybe it was the way he looked at me for permission to shake your hand when you thanked him. Or the fact that he gave you one of his eagle feathers. I know how precious those are to Indians, so for him to give you one showed how much he thought of you."

"I can't wait for him to see me wearing it today. He doesn't know that I am." Vanna sighed. "I miss his hair. I cried the whole time Win cut it. I could tell that it hurt him, too, even though he tried to hide it. I can't believe Father Carini made him cut it."

Sylvia pursed her lips. "I wasn't happy about that, either, but at least he agreed to marry the two of you. He was against it at first until he knew that Arrow was converting, and once he passed his Catechism classes so well, he approved even more. At least it's still a little down past his collar. It won't take too long for it to grow back."

"I know, but it's not right for him to be changing so much," Vanna said. "He shouldn't have to."

Lulu said, "Vanna, he knew that he wasn't expected to, but, like me, he wanted to show how much he loves and respects you and your family. Besides, in his culture, the husband often does things the way the bride's family wants. He goes to live with her family, remember?"

Vanna said, "I know. I'm being silly. Besides, after we're married, he can grow his hair back and do everything the way he normally does. It just seems like he's making all of the sacrifices."

"Vanna, he doesn't see it that way," Sylvia said. "Wouldn't you do the same thing if you were living with his tribe? Wouldn't you follow their traditions because you love him?"

"Yes, I would. Without hesitation."

Lulu said, "That's what Arrow's doing, Vanna. Now stop worrying and concentrate on the wonderful day ahead of you. Soon you'll be Mrs. Arrow Swift."

"Giavanna Swift," Vanna said. "Doesn't that sound romantic?"

Sylvia chuckled. "I felt the same way when I married your father. It does have a nice ring to it." She grew a little misty-eyed. "By this afternoon, you won't have our last name anymore."

"Oh, Mama, don't cry. You'll make me start and I don't want my eyes all puffy and red for the ceremony," Vanna said.

Blinking her tears away, Sylvia said, "I'll try, but it's hard. Now, if you're finished eating, we should start getting you dressed."

Vanna said, "I'm done. Nick's right. The food here is terrible. We're all spoiled by you and Nick's cooking, though. Nobody cooks like you, which is why your restaurant is doing so well already."

In February, Sylvia and Nick had realized their dream by opening a restaurant together and it had taken off. Between the traditional Italian dishes they made, they also served down home cooking, as well as a few French and Mexican dishes. As result, Alfredo had hired Toby Lockwood as their new ranch foreman since Nick now ran Mama T's full-time.

Sylvia helped open and went home around two in the afternoon. They'd stolen their friend, Allie Alderman, away from the diner, which had been the only restaurant in town until the Terranovas had opened theirs. Mama T's was becoming so popular that sometimes people had to wait to be seated. Allie's mother, Jessie McIntyre, also worked a few hours over the busy dinner time four nights a week.

Jessie's son-in-law, Keith Watson, had been hired as a part-time dishwasher and general worker. He usually worked Friday and Saturday nights. Since he was a very muscular six-foot-five man, he was able to do a lot of the heavy lifting that the waitresses couldn't do, which came in handy.

Silvia smiled. "I'm thrilled with how successful we are so far. I just hope it continues that way."

Lulu said, "I've no doubt that it will. Your meals are superb and your prices are reasonable."

"Thank you, dear."

Vanna rose and said, "All right. Time to get started. My stomach is in knots."

Lulu hugged her. "It's going to be all right. You'll see."

Lulu's cousin, Chelsea, joined them. "Hello, ladies."

"Hello," Vanna said. "How's Nick?"

Chelsea pursed her lips. "Not interested is how he is."

"I'm sorry," Sylvia said. "Don't take it personally. He's just not quite ready. I'm not sure that he ever will be. But I have another son who's very interested in you."

"I know, and I feel so badly, but I just don't feel that way about him. What a mess this is. I'm interested in Nick, but he's not interested in me. Gino is interested in me, but I'm not interested in him. It's nothing

11

personal against him, either." Chelsea sighed. "Oh, well. This day is about Vanna, not me. So, what can I do to help?"

The women were getting Vanna ready when Molly McIntyre, Keith's wife, came into the room. "Hi, everyone. I'm here. I got caught up in a story I'm working on and lost track of time."

They smiled indulgently at her. Molly was the co-owner, editor, and reporter of the *Echo Express*, the newspaper in Echo. She often forgot everything else when she wrote.

As they began dressing, the women chatted gaily about the wedding, laughing and teasing Vanna, who was glad for the diversion from her anxiety. She tried to focus on the man she was about to marry and felt a warm rush of love for him. Soon, they'd belong to each other forever.

Arrow finished with his tie, making sure that it was straight. He'd tied his hair back, glad that Father Carini had let him keep some of the length. As he made sure it wouldn't come loose from its thong, he saw Wild Wind frown as he watched him. He knew that his brother disapproved of him being married in a Catholic church.

Wild Wind and Roxie had been married in their unusual tipi/house by Andi Thatcher, Echo's preacher, but it had been a much more relaxed ceremony—a far cry from the ceremony about to take place. Andi hadn't made Wild Wind cut his hair and he'd been able to wear his Cheyenne ceremonial garb.

Arrow had been required to wear a traditional tuxedo, cut his hair, and convert to Catholicism—all of which angered Wild Wind. He didn't understand Arrow's willingness to do these things. He felt as though Arrow was turning his back on his heritage and faith.

"Do not look so disappointed, brother," Arrow said in Cheyenne. "Be happy for me on my wedding day."

Wild Wind said, "I am happy that you are marrying the woman you love, but you are giving up far too much of yourself to do so. There are times when I do not recognize you."

"I do not know why that should be so," Arrow responded. "You used to wear white man's clothing and you even tried courting Andi. Just because you were not able to combine the two faiths does not mean it is wrong of me to do so. There are many similarities and I am able to accept the differences and follow both. You were not in love with Andi or you would have done anything to be with her."

Their friend, Lucky Quinn, also spoke in Cheyenne. "That is true. You were meant to be with Roxie and Arrow is meant to be with Vanna. I was able to combine the two religions and I was raised Catholic. It can be done."

Wild Wind nodded. "You are right. I just do not want to combine them. I am happy with my religion and have no need to learn another."

"I understand," Arrow said. "I do not expect you to. I only ask that you respect my decision the way that you respect that Roxie is Christian. You did have a Christmas tree, after all."

Wild Wind and Lucky laughed, remembering the sight of an eight-foot Douglas-fir tree festooned with all manner of decorations and ornaments standing in the huge lodge. Presents had filled the space underneath it. Roxie had also hung mistletoe over the doorway from the main room into the kitchen. The effect had been festive, beautiful, and exotic.

"I have to admit that it was fun," Wild Wind said. "Roxie was funny when she opened her gifts."

Arrow nodded, but his mind turned to his bride. He was filled with anticipation to see her and become her husband. He knew that it was traditional for the bride and groom to greet the guests at the front door of the church as they arrived and then walk down the aisle together accompanied by their parents. However, the couple had decided to have Alfredo walk Vanna down the aisle to Arrow.

When Arrow didn't respond to a comment Wild Wind had made, he and Lucky smiled at each other, understanding that the younger man's thoughts were elsewhere. This was further confirmed when Arrow closed his eyes, mentally going over the order of the ceremony. He would have done the same thing if the wedding were taking place in a Cheyenne village.

Nick came into the room, saw Arrow's closed eyes, and stayed silent as he smiled at the other two men. He remembered doing the same sort of thing on his wedding day. A pang of grief ran through him followed by anger. He sometimes became frustrated with himself over his inability to move on.

Arrow opened his eyes and greeted Nick. "I wondered where you were. Thanks again for doing the readings and singing for us today. I know it will be beautiful."

Nick's baritone voice and evocative singing were sought after in Billings and people from St. Michael's often hired him to sing for their weddings and christenings. "You're welcome. It's an honor to be singing for you and Noodle," he said, using Vanna's nickname.

Lucky's gray eyes shone. "I'm lookin' forward to hearin' ya sing. I haven't had the pleasure yet. I'm also excited about the ceremony. It's been years since I was to a weddin' mass."

Nick said, "It's nice to have another Catholic in Echo who understands."

"Aye. I do. I have nothin' against any religion, but I can't help but miss the way I grew up worshippin'," Lucky said.

They were joined by Father Carini, who smiled at the four men. "Gentlemen, it's time for you to come to the altar with me. Are you ready, Arrow?"

"Yes, Father," the groom said.

Father Carini nodded. "Good. Do you want a last prayer before we go?"

"Yes, Father," Arrow repeated, figuring that one more prayer couldn't hurt. It would help calm his nerves.

As they bowed their heads, Father Carini saw Lucky cross himself.

"Are you Catholic, my son?" he asked.

Lucky smiled. "I am. Born and raised."

The priest chuckled. "An Irishman. It's been a while since I've met one. We don't have a whole lot of them around here."

"Right. I've not met another Irish soul since I came to Echo," he said.

"Well, it's nice to meet you."

"Likewise, Father."

Once the prayer had been said, the men filed out to the sanctuary, lining up at the altar. Arrow smiled at the congregation that had gathered, nodding to several people. Father Carini caught a couple of resentful looks from Wild Wind and smiled inside. He couldn't say he blamed Arrow's brother for being upset.

Most likely he saw the requirements Arrow had been expected to meet as offensive. He knew that Wild Wind had worn his long hair flowing loose on purpose as an act of defiance. Arrow had warned him that would probably be the case, telling the priest about the attack on Wild Wind by a large group of men from Echo. Since then, Wild Wind had reverted back to wearing only his native clothing and staying more true to his heritage.

The only reason Father Carini had asked Arrow to cut his hair was so that he fit in a little more while he was in Billings. It was a safety measure, not something he required for the wedding. He knew that Vanna and Arrow were going to be staying in Billings for their honeymoon and there were a few Indians there, but they all had their hair cut short as a symbol of their assimilation. If Arrow did, too, he wouldn't stand out from the others, thus lessening the chances of any trouble breaking out.

As a Cheyenne brave, protecting their women was paramount and Arrow would do whatever was necessary to protect Vanna. He could live with a haircut, which was temporary. He couldn't live without Vanna, so if having short hair kept her safe, it was a minor sacrifice.

The organist began playing *Canon in D Minor* and the congregation stood. Arrow's heart lurched as he saw Vanna standing with Alfredo at the entrance to the sanctuary and sent her a quick smile before resuming a proud expression. However, his eyes held a happy light that everyone could see.

Father Carini had enjoyed having Arrow as a Catechism student, having never spent much time with Indians. It was interesting to find out that Arrow had also been a medicine man's apprentice and they'd had many conversations outside of their classes about the differences and similarities in their religions. It had also given him a greater insight as far as whether or not Arrow was genuine about learning and practicing the Catholic religion. He had found Arrow to be honest, respectful, and inquisitive—all good things in a student.

Alfredo couldn't keep the tears out of his eyes as he looked down at his little girl before starting down the aisle. He loved his sons dearly, but he'd been so happy to have a little girl, and he'd doted on her from the beginning. With her black hair, deep brown eyes, and slightly olive skin, she was the picture of Sylvia but with Alfredo's milder temperament.

"Ready, Noodle?" he asked, wishing she was a baby again.

He was proud of the woman his daughter had grown to be, but hated giving her away. It was comforting that she and Arrow would be living at the Terranova estate so that he could still see her every day. He would've missed Arrow, too. The brave technically didn't live there yet, but he was there so much that he might as well have. It was rare that he didn't eat breakfast or dinner there.

Vanna nodded and smiled. "I'm ready, Pop."

I wish I was, he thought. "Ok. Here we go."

Walking Vanna down the aisle was an honor for Alfredo and he took the duty very seriously, especially because it was the only time he was going to have the chance to do it. Vanna tried to contain her smile, but it was hard, especially when she saw Arrow's smiling eyes. The heat in them also reassured her that he thought she was beautiful. Suddenly something occurred to her; God had saved her for Arrow. He was her destiny and God had known what He was doing when He'd created her. Her insecurities fled in the face of this revelation and she concentrated fully on her groom.

The smile in Arrow's eyes lessened when Alfredo gave him Vanna's hand. The two men stared at each other for several moments before Alfredo nodded and smiled a little. He gave Vanna a one-armed hug, kissed her cheek, and went to join Sylvia as he tried to keep his tears at bay.

After Father Carini greeted the congregation, they sang the *Gloria*, which was followed by the opening prayer. The guests sat down at its conclusion and Nick went to the lectern to give the first reading. His deep

MAIL ORDER BRIDE: *Montana Orphan*

voice carried well and his delivery was flawless. Father Carini listened, thinking what a fine priest Nick would have made.

All through the ceremony, Arrow stared into Vanna's eyes. Some Catholic grooms and brides found the long wedding tedious, but Arrow enjoyed every part of it. Vanna, too, found it deeply moving and relished each moment of the momentous occasion. Both of them said their vows carefully and with the utmost seriousness. When they exchanged rings, they felt drawn closer together than before, the symbols of their unending love giving them great joy.

Wild Wind performed his best man duties perfectly, genuinely happy for his brother and Vanna. He'd become friends with the Terranovas and he knew that they were good people. Alfredo wasn't the only man moved to tears. They trickled from Lucky's eyes off and on throughout the service, especially when Nick sang *Ava Maria*.

Vanna's brothers were also emotional, especially Sal, who was the next oldest Terranova child. He and Vanna had always been exceptionally close and he was thrilled to see the way Vanna had blossomed since meeting Arrow. She was more confident, happy, and mature. Sal knew that it was because Arrow constantly encouraged her and reassured her when her insecurities surfaced. He was grateful to the man who was becoming his brother-in-law for loving his little sister so much.

Nick had known from the first day they'd met Arrow that he and Vanna would marry someday. He'd had a good time watching his parents fight it at first, but quickly give way when they realized that it was impossible to dissuade the young couple. Despite Arrow's different race and culture, they had liked him right away. Arrow had also liked the family despite his previous negativity towards white people that had been left over from his dealings with the military on the reservation.

From the beginning, he'd called Sylvia and Alfredo Mama and Pop. This was because no one had formally introduced them and told him their given names. Arrow's understanding of the English language had been very limited at the time, so he didn't know that these were familial terms and not names. However, even once he knew the difference, he kept calling them Mama and Pop, and the elder Terranovas hadn't been able to refuse him much of anything. So in many ways, Arrow had already become another son to them.

After the ring exchange, Father Carini gave the couple permission to kiss and although it was kept brief, as was expected, it was no less moving to them. After the communion and blessing, the priest dismissed the congregation and Vanna and Arrow processed from the sanctuary followed by the rest of the wedding party and Father Carini.

The newlyweds received their guests as they filed out of the church. They'd hired a photographer from Billings to take their pictures and once that was accomplished, they set out for the banquet hall.

While the wedding had been a mostly somber affair, the complete opposite was true for the reception. Laughter, music, and high spirits reigned throughout the event. Almost everyone had some liquor and the five-piece band played a wide repertoire of music that hardly anyone could resist dancing to.

Vanna was a good dancer and had taught Arrow to dance, a pastime they'd come to enjoy immensely. Holding Vanna in his arms was always sheer pleasure for him, but having her in his arms as his wife was doubly joyous. The new Mrs. Swift thought that her husband was the handsomest man God had ever made and dancing with him filled her heart with happiness.

Watching them, Sylvia said, "I remember looking at you like that at our reception, Alfredo."

"And I remember looking at you like that, Syl," he said. "I still do."

Sylvia looked in his blue eyes. "So do I."

Alfredo smiled. "Well, c'mon, Mrs. Terranova. Let's go dance and keep looking at each other like that."

She laughed and gladly followed him to the dance floor.

Nick watched his parents dancing and smiled, happy to see them still so much in love after thirty years of marriage. Looking at Vanna and

Arrow, he hoped that they would have the same sort of happiness. He wished the same thing for Sal and Lulu, too. Chelsea came over to him.

"Mr. Terranova, I know this is incredibly forward of me, but I would like just one dance with you. As friends," she said, smiling.

He returned her smile. "I'd like that. I'm glad there aren't any hard feelings."

"No, there aren't," she said.

As Nick danced with Chelsea, he wondered why he didn't feel anything for her. Then he put that out of his mind and let himself have a good time.

Chapter Three

"Hold still," Arrow commanded Vanna.

"I don't believe this is happening on our wedding night," she lamented. "I'll bet no other bride in the history of the world has ever had so much trouble getting out of her wedding dress."

Arrow smiled. "I'm sure that some bride has."

"I should have worn a Cheyenne dress. You'd have had it off me in no time."

His laugh made her smile. "I don't think that would have gone over well with Father Carini."

She giggled. "It would have been funny to see his face, though."

Arrow was as eager to get Vanna out of her dress as she was to be free of it. They had waited a long time to be together and they were both more than ready. Finally, he freed the knots in the lacing of her high-necked, long-sleeved dress and loosened them. Tamping down his impatience, he removed the dress slowly, kissing her soft skin as he did so.

Her breath came more rapidly with every caress; she let out a delighted gasp when he bit her shoulder as he stood behind her. It felt primal, and it made her forget that her dress had just dropped to the floor. Arrow knew that she wouldn't want the dress wrinkled, so he had her step out of it and she hung it up quickly in the closet of the honeymoon suite in which they were staying.

She came back to him and he kissed her urgently while she undid his shirt buttons. The mental pictures of his muscular, golden-bronze torso had her make quick work of them. As he had on a couple of occasions when their attraction had gotten the best of them, he wordlessly showed her how much she excited him.

When they were both completely bare, he picked her up and laid her down on the bed, stretching out beside her. Taking her left hand, he kissed her rings.

"You are finally my wife," he said. "I want you so much, but there is no need to rush."

She ran her right hand through his shorter hair, "I know how you feel. I want to remember every minute of our first time making love."

"Then it shall be so," he said, claiming her lips in a slow kiss that made her insides melt.

As time passed, they treasured each kiss, reveled in every caress, and knew that through this sensual act they were creating a bond that would never be severed.

The young woman spent the next couple of days roaming through the huge house, afraid to go outside and be seen by the men she saw working around the place. Although at first she had wanted someone to help her, she'd had second thoughts about it; she didn't know if anyone might know her captors. She knew that the owners of the estate were sure to come back at some point, but she decided to stay there for the time being. At least she was safe, had food to eat, and a comfortable place to sleep.

The first morning after she'd entered the residence, she'd bathed in the big tub in the bathroom. Even though the water had been cold, the soap had smelled heavenly and being clean made her feel human again. She would have heated water, but she knew that the smoke from a fire in the cook stove would have given her away.

When she'd dried off, she had been loath to put her dirty things back on, so she'd looked through the closets for something to wear. In the little suite on the first floor she had found an older, simple calico dress that fit her fairly well. This was the only garment she allowed herself, knowing that she had trespassed more than enough already.

Down in the cellar, she'd found plenty of canned fruit, vegetables, and even some sort of jerky to eat. Now that she was clean, she slept curled up on the bed in the empty room, but didn't get under the covers. Instead, she covered up with an afghan that had been draped over the wingback chair in the room. When she was awake, she occupied herself by looking at the family pictures and paintings on the walls.

She found some books to read and tried to remember the words she used to know. A few of the books contained mostly pictures and she enjoyed looking at the beautiful places depicted in them. She would have been happy to stay in the lovely house forever, but she knew that the time was coming when she was going to have to take a chance on appealing to someone for help.

"I'm so glad we pushed on," Sylvia said as Alfredo unlocked the front door. "I can't wait to sleep in our own bed. I'm spoiled by how nice it is."

"Me, too. The hotel beds were all right, but they don't compare to ours," he said, going inside. He lit a lamp in the parlor so they had light to see by. "I'm gonna get the stove going. I could use some coffee before we hit the hay. How about you?"

"I'd love some. I'll come make it," Sylvia said.

"I can make it," Alfredo said.

"That's all right. I don't mind."

"Which means that you don't like my coffee as much as yours," he said.

Smiling, she replied, "I didn't say that."

"You didn't have to."

The rest of the family, minus the newlyweds, came into the house, talking and arguing noisily. Sylvia loved listening to the younger people. One of her greatest joys was hearing the house full of life. And now with two of her children married, there would be grandchildren to look forward to.

Nick and Gino trooped up the front stairs, each carrying suitcases, while Sal and Lulu went down the hallway that led to their suite. They heard Lulu laugh about something Sal had said and Alfredo shook his head. "Nothing changes there."

"Shush, Al. They're going to make us some grandbabies," Sylvia said.

He chuckled as he sat down at the table.

Sylvia got out a tin of crackers and opened the cupboard for a tin of sardines, but found none. "Did you eat all of the sardines before we left?"

"What? No. There were three or four things of them," Alfredo said.

"They're all gone," she said.

"Maybe Nick did something with them?"

Sylvia shook her head. "We didn't cook much the day before we left—certainly nothing with sardines."

As she walked across the kitchen, she noticed that there was something in the garbage pail when it should've been empty. Three sardine tins were in it.

"Alfredo, someone ate the sardines. The tins are in the garbage pail."

"Why are you so worried about it? We'll buy more," Alfredo said, tiredly. "Someone else must have eaten them."

"Well, it wasn't Gino or Sal. They don't like them. Lulu only eats them cooked in with something and she wouldn't eat them all, anyway," Sylvia said.

Going over to the sink, Sylvia saw an empty Mason jar in it. "Al, someone ate all the pickles that were up in the cupboard by the sink."

Alfredo got up and looked in the sink with her. "What the heck's goin' on here? Toby's the only ranch hand who has a key to the place. He wouldn't come in here and eat our pickles and sardines."

"Someone has been in our house, Alfredo. They might even still be here," Sylvia said as a chill of fear tripped down her spine.

Male voices woke the woman and her heartbeat accelerated as fear flooded her body. She'd been so sound asleep that she'd never heard anyone come into the house. Doors on either side of the room opened, shut, and reopened.

"I'm just saying that I understand how Chelsea feels," one man said.

"Gino, I'm too tired for this. I don't want to hear any more about it. Ever," the other said.

The one called Gino said, "Ok, ok. You're right. Goodnight, Nick."

"Goodnight," Nick said.

Things quieted down until another male voice said, "I'll ask the boys if they've seen anything. Sal and Lulu said they hadn't and their side door was locked."

They knew that someone had been—or was still—in their house. It wasn't that she understood what they said, but the alarm in their voices made her suspect that they knew someone had trespassed. She scooted off the bed as a door was knocked on. When it opened, the third male voice asked, "Gino, have you noticed anything out of place up here?"

"No, Pop, but I was only in the bathroom and my room. Everything is fine. Why?"

"Someone ate all our sardines and pickles that were in the kitchen," Alfredo said. "Someone's been in the house."

The woman folded up the afghan and put it back on the chair and stood by it, undecided about what to do. She heard more doors open and close and she knew that they were going to find her. What would they do to her then? Did they know the people who'd had her? Tears sprang into her eyes as her fear intensified.

Going to the door, she opened it a tiny fraction, trying to see out into the hallway. Opening it a little more, she saw that the hallway to her right was clear. She could go down the back stairs and out the door there. Pulling the door open slowly, she streaked from the room.

"Hey!" one of the men yelled. "Get her!"

Strong arms closed around her and she was tackled. Immediately, she began fighting with all of her strength, but the man was too powerful for her.

"I'm not gonna hurt you," he said in her ear. "Who are you?"

She remained silent and stayed still.

"I'm gonna let you go, but there's no sense in running. There's too many of us and we don't mean you any harm. We just want to know why you're in our house."

The kindness in his voice eased her fear a little and she relaxed slightly. His hold on her loosened and he got up, pulling her gently but firmly to her feet.

"Good God, look at all of that red hair," Gino said.

Alfredo looked at him. "There's a strange woman in our house and you're worried about her hair?"

"I'm not worried about it," Gino said. "I just couldn't help noticing it."

The woman kept her head bent, afraid to look at anyone. Her terror touched the motherly side of Sylvia.

"Who are you? Why are you in our house?" she asked kindly, approaching the girl.

The friendly female voice made her chance looking up through the thick curtain of her wavy, flame-colored hair. The dark-haired woman's brown eyes held a mix of fear and curiosity, but also the same kindness as her voice.

She pulled her arm from her tackler's grasp and backed away from him until her back hit the wall.

Another woman's voice asked, "Who is she?"

"We don't know, Lulu," Nick said.

Lulu said, "She's wearing one of my old dresses. She must have taken it from my closet."

Sylvia moved closer to her. "Is there anyone else in the house?" she asked.

Sal had just come up the back stairs and he'd heard his mother's question. "No. I checked everywhere, even the cellar. Where the heck did she come from and how did she get in here? All of the doors were locked."

Alfredo said, "I don't know. She won't talk."

"What are we gonna do with her?" Gino asked.

Sal said, "Give her to the sheriff. She's trespassin'. She might be dangerous or know dangerous people. Maybe they left her here and they're gonna come back."

Nick said, "I doubt she's dangerous, but you might be right about someone possibly coming back for her. We'll guard her tonight and then take her to Evan in the morning."

She'd recognized the word "sheriff" and it filled her with dread. The last sheriff she'd dealt with had treated her with anything but kindness. Looking up, her eyes met the man's who'd caught her. They were the same color as the older woman's and she surmised that they were related.

Vehemently, she shook her head and opened her mouth, but nothing would come out. She closed her mouth again and sank to her knees, bowing before Nick and throwing herself on his mercy.

The family looked around at each other, completely at a loss.

Gino said, "I don't think she likes the idea of a sheriff."

Nick was shocked when she grabbed his ankles and shook her head. He could feel her hands trembling against his legs. He bent over, grasped her wrists, and shook them a little.

"C'mon and let go," he said. "It's ok. We won't hurt you."

She looked at his large hands. While he was very strong, his touch was gentle. Releasing his legs, she allowed him to pull her to her feet, but she still kept her eyes cast down.

Sal frowned. "Why's she actin' like that? Why doesn't she talk?"

Nick said, "I don't know why she doesn't speak, but someone only acts like that when they're used to being subservient. I saw that when I was a missionary. There are places where women are taught to never look a man in the eyes and when they prostrate themselves like that, they're asking to be spared from something. She's afraid of the sheriff."

"Evan? Why would she be scared of him?" Gino asked.

Sylvia said, "I don't think she's scared of Evan. I think she's scared of any sheriff."

Panic rose up in the woman and she tore free from Nick, running for the back stairs, but he easily hooked an arm around her waist, stopping her progress. Realizing that escaping was impossible, she docilely let Nick guide her back into the upstairs hallway. Tears of fear and frustration rolled down her cheeks. She felt Nick's fingers pressing under her chin and although she tilted her head up, she still tried to avert her eyes from his.

"Hey, look at me," he said.

She understood what he wanted and slowly raised her eyes to meet his gaze. His dark brown eyes were filled with concern and kindness.

"No sheriff," he said, shaking his head. "No sheriff."

He saw her brown eyes fill with more tears and his heart went out to her. Her level of terror went far beyond a trespasser being caught. His mind filled with questions as he saw what a beautiful girl she was. Her dark eyes were set in a heart-shaped face. Her creamy, pale complexion complemented her hair coloring and her pink lips were shaped like a Cupid's bow.

Even though his touch was insistent, it was still gentle. He wore his black hair in a short style that emphasized his handsome features. His slightly hooded dark eyes, aquiline nose, and strong jaw were a compelling combination. His naturally light olive skin tone would soon darken from whatever time he spent outdoors.

Nick was the tallest of the brothers, standing six-foot-three. Since he'd been getting around for bed, he was barefoot and bare chested. Years of ranch work had honed his body into a lean, muscular condition. While she recognized that he was a very good-looking man, his strength scared her.

Unless she could catch him off guard, there was no way she'd be able to get away from him. It was far better to submit to him to avoid bodily harm. She would go along with whatever he wanted her to do so she wouldn't anger him.

Sylvia said, "Well, we can't stand around here all night. What are we going to do with her?"

Lulu said, "We don't want her to run off. She might get hurt. We can't tie her up, though."

Alfredo asked, "Nick, she bowed to you. Do you think she'll listen to you if you tell her to stay?"

Gino smiled. "She's not a dog, Pop."

"You know what I mean," Alfredo said.

"Yeah, I know," Gino said.

Sylvia said, "Give it a try, Nicky. She might as well stay in the room she was in."

With a shrug, Nick said, "Ok." He made her look at him again. "What's your name?"

Her brow puckered and he could tell that she didn't understand him. He tapped his chest and said, "Nick. My name is Nick." He tapped her shoulder. "What's your name?"

She understood what he wanted now, but she wasn't sure she could manage it. After learning to stay silent, it went against her nature to speak. But there was no other way to tell him.

Pointing to herself, she whispered, "Maura."

"Maura," Nick said. "Good. At least we have a name. Maura, come with me."

She followed him into the room in which she'd been sleeping and stood uncertainly while he walked back towards the door. When she would have followed him, Nick stopped her.

"Maura, you stay here, ok? This'll be your room—at least until we figure out what's going on and where you belong," Nick said, making a staying gesture with his hand.

Maura halted, but she was perplexed. Where was he going? She was his now and should go where he did. Maybe this was a test. As he backed towards the door, she followed him.

"No, Maura. You stay here," Nick said, gesturing again. "I don't understand this. It's like she doesn't know English. It reminds me of Arrow when we first met him."

Sylvia said, "I think you're right."

Nick said, "I want to try something. Back up, everybody."

The rest moved out into the hallway and Nick exited the room, striding down the hallway. Maura went right after him, keeping her head bowed as she followed him. The Terranovas exchanged incredulous looks.

Casting a glance over his shoulder, Nick saw that Maura was behind him. He stopped and she stopped. He turned around and instead of staying facing him, she scooted around behind him. Nick didn't like this at all. Walking back to what he now thought of as Maura's room, he took her back inside it and again bade her to stay.

"Maura, stay," he said, closing the door.

Sylvia said, "Was she someone's slave or something?"

"Humph," Alfredo said. "Sure seems like it. The poor thing is scared to death."

Sal said, "Whoever she belongs to can't be good people. I know a lot of Indian tribes require women to walk behind them, but Arrow said that's for the women's protection. The men can shoot whatever danger might be ahead, especially if they're walking through tall grass. I don't think that's the case with Maura."

Gino said, "I agree. She's afraid of making Nick mad. Do you think she could have been with Indians at all?"

Nick said, "There's one way to find out. Let's see if she knows Indian sign since Arrow and Wild Wind have been teaching us." He knocked on Maura's door, but she didn't answer it. He opened it and saw Maura sitting stiffly on the bed. He gave her the Indian sign gesture for "come here".

Her eyes lit up and she immediately came to him.

In sign, Nick asked, "Where did you come from?"

Although she followed his hand movements, Maura didn't look at him directly. "I came here with my master. He bought me three moons ago."

Nick's eyebrows rose and his brothers, Lulu, and Sylvia made noises of dismay.

"Who did he buy you from? What tribe?"

"I was raised by the Comanche. The woman to whom I became a slave said they captured me when I was five winters old and I was allowed to live since I was quiet and kept up with them," she signed.

"This woman and her husband did not adopt you?" Nick asked.

"No. They did not want a daughter, just a slave. They had children."
Maura burned with shame. Her new master must think that she was
unworthy since her original captors hadn't wanted her in their family.

Nick's teeth ground together as righteous anger roared through him.
"Who bought you?"

"A fur trader from far to the north."

"Where is he now?"

Maura said, "I do not know. I ran away a few nights ago and found
your lodge. I sometimes remember things from my first life and I
remembered a lodge like this. You have a very fine lodge, Master."

"Did she just call you 'master'?" Gino asked, his blue eyes wide.

"Yes, and she'll never call anyone that again," Nick said tersely.
Speaking in sign again, he said, "Maura, you will never call me, or anyone
else, master ever again. I am not your master."

Maura didn't want to question him, but she was confused. "Please do
not become angry, but you captured me. That makes you my master."

"No, it does not. I—we—will be your friends, but no one is your
master. You are no longer a slave, Maura. You are free. Slavery is not
allowed in this country any longer."

This concept was beyond her comprehension. "But who will I live
with? I have no one. I do not know who my first family is. You seem like a
nice mas—man," she corrected herself. "Why do you not want me? I have
been told that I am pretty and pleasing."

The meaning of this was not lost on any of them. Nick flushed with
fury and embarrassment that she would think he would require that of her.
"It is not our custom to have slaves. Slavery is not allowed any longer. We
will offer you protection and friendship, but you are no one's slave."

"How will I earn food or be allowed to live in your lodge if I do not
work?" she asked. "I am sorry. I should not question you. You have been
kind. I do not want to go back to my old master. He and his men are cruel."

Nick frowned. "You will not go back to them. I promise you that."

Maura chanced a few glances at Nick and his family and saw the same
earnest expressions on their faces. Dare she hope that her suffering was
over? It didn't seem possible. She merely nodded.

"This is your room now, Maura. Your own space in our house. Tomorrow we will show you around more, but I am sure that we are all ready to sleep."

"I will not stay with you?" she asked.

"No," Nick said emphatically.

She nodded her understanding.

"Go on to bed and get some rest," Nick said, motioning towards her room. "Goodnight."

"Goodnight."

Maura entered her room, closed the door, and returned to the bed. With a tiny smile, she pulled down the covers. If this was truly hers now, there was nothing wrong with her sleeping under the fine blankets. Getting into the bed, she snuggled down and tried to calm her nerves. She was scared that her old master would find her and take her back. As she grew sleepy, Maura became determined to do whatever was required of her so that Nick wouldn't let that happen.

Chapter Four

Monday morning found Echo's pastor, Andi Thatcher, hard at work on her sermon for the next week. She had to strike while the iron was hot and she liked getting a jump on sermons. Something small hit her on her head, startling her. It fell onto her desk and she saw that it was a piece of peppermint candy, which was her favorite.

She looked up at the doorway, but no one was there. Smiling, she said, "R.J., get in here."

Her three-in-one man came in, a broad smile on his face. "How did you know it was me?" R.J. asked, coming around the desk to her.

"Because you have the best aim. Arliss and Blake have good aim, but they usually miss my head."

His warm chuckle made her smile. "You know us so well," he said before kissing her briefly. "Now, you have plans this evening."

"I do, do I? And just what are these plans?"

R.J. sat down in one of the chairs on the other side of the desk. "Oh, here's the rest of your candy." He put a small bag of it on her desk.

"Thank you. I can always count on you to keep me supplied. What plans do I have?"

"Dinner with us. I made reservations at Mama T's for seven. Does that suit?"

"Yes. That will be very nice," Andi said. "And what kind of trouble are you causing today?"

This was a standard question Andi asked of R.J., and he always had creative answers.

"Well, after I filched your candy from the store, I chopped and stacked more wood, hence the old clothing. Then I threw some rocks at Mrs. Lindstrom's nasty little thing she calls a dog. God forgive me, but I'd sooner stomp on the thing than look at it."

"R.J.!" Andi admonished him. "Don't you dare."

"I didn't say I was going to, I just said I'd like to. It would be a different story if the dog was nice, but it ruined two pairs of my dress pants by tearing the legs."

Andi tried to hide her smile. "I'm so sorry about that."

He leaned forward. "No, you're not. Look at you smiling, and don't tell me you're not because preachers aren't supposed to lie, Miss Thatcher."

She laughed and R.J. frowned as he stood up.

"Just for that, you owe me a short walk."

"I can't right now. I making headway on this sermon," Andi said regretfully.

He gave her a curt nod. "Very well. I shall exact my revenge—"

The church door opened and the sound of several pairs of boots interrupted R.J. As he looked at Andi, she saw R.J. fall back and Arliss take over. Other people didn't recognize his transformations as quickly as she did when it happened. Her eyes widened when three military officers appeared in the doorway.

"Good morning, ma'am. Are you Pastor Thatcher?" one of the men asked. His dark eyes roamed over her and he smiled at her in a friendly manner.

"Yes, I am," she said. "How can I help you?"

"Allow me to introduce myself," he said. "Lieutenant Finnley, at your service."

Smiling politely, Andi said, "Pleased to meet you, Lieutenant."

"Likewise. I have it on good authority that you're a very ethical, honest woman and preacher," he said. "Is that right?"

Andi's pulse jumped, but she kept her head. "Yes, I am." She grew a little more alarmed as she saw Blake take over for Arliss. That only happened when he perceived a threat.

"I'm glad to hear that. We have a report that there are a couple of Indians living in Echo Canyon. Is that true?" he asked.

Keeping her sudden fear reined in, Andi said, "Yes, that's true. They're all assimilated and peaceful, though."

"Would you call killing seven men peaceful?" Finnley asked.

"Of course not, but if twenty men came to your home for the express purpose of killing you, what would you do, Lieutenant? I've been honest with you, now please give me the same courtesy," she said with great poise. "You are in a house of God after all and in the presence of a pastor."

"Well, ma'am, I would certainly protect myself, but I'm not an Indian. I'm going to need you to tell me where they live, especially that one," the officer said.

"Blake, would you please excuse us?" she asked. "This doesn't involve you and I know you have a busy day ahead. I'll see you at services on Sunday."

Blake nodded. "Sure, Pastor. I'll get out of your hair. Gentlemen," he said, easing by them and leaving the church.

Andi turned back to Finnley. "He's married and his wife relies on him for a livelihood. Other than defending himself when under attack, he's never broken the law. He was also almost mortally wounded that night."

Finnley smiled. "I can see that you're a friend of his and I can see what a good person you are. However, this isn't a trial. I'm simply here to collect him and take him to the reservation."

"You can't do that. He doesn't belong there," Andi said. "He belongs here with his wife and friends. He's made a life here and I believe under the Dawes act, the fact that he's an agricultural worker means that he's met their requirements."

"Well, that's true, but has he become a United States citizen or has someone adopted him?" Finnley asked.

Andi's heart dropped into her stomach. "No, I'm afraid not."

"Well, then, we're taking him to the reservation," Finnley said.

The church door opened and Sheriff Evan Taft and his two deputies, Shadow Earnest and Thad McIntyre, met the soldiers.

Finnley smiled at them, noticing their badges. "Well, you must be Sheriff Taft."

"That's right," Evan said.

"Lieutenant Finnley."

The two men shook hands.

"What's the trouble?" Evan asked, even though he knew. Blake had already alerted them to the situation.

"We're here for Wild Wind. I've been ordered to take him to the reservation," Finnley said.

"There's no need to do that," Evan said. "If this is about what happened last winter, that was an isolated incident and there's been no trouble since then."

"That's none of my concern, but I am curious about why he wasn't arrested," Finnley said.

Evan smiled calmly in response to Finnley's implied criticism of his job performance. "Well, maybe you're not familiar with how law enforcement works, but he acted in self-defense. They threw Molotov cocktails through his windows while he was still in his cabin and when he came outside, they opened fire on him. They just happened to mess with the wrong man, that's all. I wouldn't arrest anyone for defending themselves against a mob of racist jackasses."

"All right. I'll concede that point. However, the fact remains that I've been ordered to bring him in. I was actually going to stop to get you next. You see, I'd like to do this peacefully, if possible. Since you're the law and obviously his friend, maybe you can make him see reason," Finnley said.

"I'd like to see these orders," Evan said. "You could be anyone, for all I know. I'm not gonna let you take anyone without some sort of proof of your identity and that you actually have the authority to arrest him."

Finnley smiled and reached into his uniform pocket and pulled out a thin packet of papers, which he handed to Evan. The sheriff opened and read them. Thad looked over his shoulder. He'd seen plenty of military papers in his work as a bounty hunter and he knew Finnley's papers were genuine.

Evan came to the same conclusion. Handing them back, he said, "Seems like everything's in order."

Finnley put them away. "Now, how about you make this as easy as possible on everyone and go with us?"

Anger, resentment, and grief made Evan's stomach ache. As the sheriff, his hands were tied. There was only so much he could do against the might of the United States military. At least he could prevent Wild Wind or Roxie from being injured if nothing else.

His green eyes glittered with restrained fury. "Sure. I'll go with you to take a good man into custody just because of his race," he said, sarcastically.

"We don't want just him. We're also after a Billy Two Moons and Wild Wind's brother, Arrow."

Shock pierced Evan's chest. "Now just wait a damn minute. Billy's adopted and assimilated. You can't take him. I know the law concerning that. He also co-owns a sheep farm, so he's covered under the Dawes Act. You're not touchin' him."

Finnley frowned, angry that his superiors hadn't known those facts. "You're right. All right. He's safe. Now about this Arrow?"

Shadow said, "He's out of town at the moment and we have no idea when to expect him back."

Finnley looked at Andi. "Is that right, Pastor Thatcher?"

Meeting his eyes, she nodded. "Yes. He left about a week ago and hasn't been back. I don't know him all that well, so I wouldn't be privy to his plans." All of this was true, so Andi had a clear conscience.

"Well, we'll have to send someone back to get him later," Finnley said. "So he's not adopted?"

Andi said, "I don't know that, either. As I said, I don't know him all that well. Someone could have."

Finnley sighed. "All right. Thanks for your help, Pastor. Shall we, Sheriff?"

"After you, Lieutenant," Evan said. "Andi, I'll see you soon. Pray for Wild Wind and Roxie."

"I will," Andi said, tears gathering behind her eyes.

As they trailed behind the military men, Shadow used American Sign Language to tell Evan to stall the officers. Evan gave him a questioning look, but Shadow just smiled at him. Evan smiled back, knowing that his deputy had something up his sleeve. He was happy to play a part in whatever Shadow had in mind. However, he wouldn't ask Shadow any questions. That way he had plausible deniability.

Evan always looked at the greater good and was willing to look the other way when it benefited innocent people. It was his own brand of justice. Wild Wind and Roxie were good friends and he would do whatever he could to help them.

"I'll go with these gentlemen. You two keep a watch on things around town," Evan said.

"Yes, sir," Thad said, tongue-in-cheek.

Shadow did likewise. Once outside, Thad and Shadow quickly left Evan with Finnley and his men and headed for the sheriff's office.

"I won't run," Wild Wind told Arliss. "I would be found eventually no matter where I went. I won't have Roxie living a life on the run. At lease here she'll be with her family and friends."

Roxie said, "Wild Wind, I don't care about myself. As long as I'm with you, that's all that matters." Terror flowed through her at the thought of Wild Wind being taken from her. "I need you. We've just started our life together. Let's go before they come. You should be free, not stuck on a reservation where there's not enough food and they've taken away your right to hunt. Your soul will wither and die."

He took her in his arms. "I need you, too. I appreciate your loyalty, but I won't have you living like that. And I wouldn't want to have any children while we're running. Arliss, get word to Arrow not to come back to Echo. They'll want him, too."

Arliss said, "I will. Are you sure about this? Thad could take you both to the Lakota camp where he took Avasa."

Wild Wind shook his head. "There's no guarantee that they haven't been captured. We would travel all that way for nothing and maybe still get caught. I won't risk Roxie's safety. This is what's best for everyone."

She grabbed his arms, her blue eyes filled with dread and anger. "This isn't just about you! What about what I want? Doesn't that matter to you?"

"Of course it does, but where will we go? If I wasn't turned in here, someone somewhere else would turn me in."

Someone knocked on the door of the unusual tipi/house and they quieted instantly.

"Wild Wind! It's Shadow!"

Relieved expressions passed over their faces and Wild Wind opened the door.

"We already know," Wild Wind said. "I'm not running."

Shadow smiled. "No, you're not. You're hiding. Pack some things and make it look messy. There's no time for questions."

Roxie asked, "Where would you hide us? They'll search everywhere."

Shadow's grin gave her chills. Even though the deputy and his twin, Marvin, were becoming somewhat redeemed, they still made many people uneasy. "Don't worry. Where we'll hide you, no one would ever think to look. Now hurry."

Wild Wind said, "How long can you hide us?"

Shadow laughed. "I lived there for almost two decades without anyone finding me. Now, *hurry!*"

Wild Wind made a snap decision. If there was even a slim chance that they could pull one over on the military, he would take it. If worse came to worse, he would turn himself in to spare anyone any more difficulties.

"Ok. Let's pack, Roxie," Wild Wind said.

She immediately ran to their bedroom with him and they hastily stuffed clothing and a few belongings into a couple of large buckskin bags and a satchel. They left some of their other things strewn around to make it look like they'd gone on the run in a hurry. Shadow had kept a lookout and just as the brave and his wife came to the door, he held up a halting hand to them. A rider was approaching and Shadow recognized Lucky Quinn.

Shadow said, "It's just Mr. Quinn."

They exited the tipi as Lucky jumped down from his horse.

"They were just out to our place," Lucky said, his gray eyes wide. "Ya have to get out of here," he said to Wild Wind.

Shadow said, "No, they don't. I'm going to hide them."

"Where?" Lucky asked.

"You don't need to know that. It's safer if you don't. You won't be lying when they ask you," Shadow said.

"Now look, Shadow, yer not takin' them without someone else knowin' where they are," Lucky said. "What if I need to talk to them?"

Arliss said, "Lucky, the fewer people that know their location, the better. I don't even want to know. If we need to talk to them, we'll get word to them through Shadow."

"Or Marvin," Shadow said.

"Fine," Lucky said. "They're headed over to yer place, Shadow, so if yer goin' there, you'd better not."

"That's great," Shadow said. "We'll come with you to your farm and go to our place from there. I'll take them in the secret entrance. Evan should have them out of there by then. Of course, the way we'll go, it won't really matter if they're there or not."

Wild Wind said, "Lucky, this is what I want to do. We'll be safe."

"Aye, but I can't help worryin'," Lucky said, grasping arms with his Cheyenne brother. "Let's go then."

Arliss said, "We better go back to town another way. We don't wanna run into them since they've already seen us. If they catch us out here, they'll know that I tipped them off."

Arliss and his counterparts usually spoke collectively about their selves. He'd been diagnosed with Multiple Personality Disorder when he'd been a teenager. The only time they usually said "I" or "me" was when they did something that only one of them would do.

Lucky said, "Aye. Don't incriminate yerself."

Wild Wind and Roxie had caught two of their horses and mounted up. The other three did the same. Arliss said goodbye to them, turned his horse in the opposite direction, and galloped away.

Chapter Five

As Gino walked from their first barn to their second one, a horse and rider came tearing up their lane, dust flying behind them. He stopped, knowing that there was something wrong from the speed they traveled.

Arliss pulled his horse to a halt. "Hi, Gino."

"Arliss?" Gino guessed. He didn't have a whole lot of dealings with Arliss, but he knew that he changed personalities. Most of the people in Echo knew that he did, but there were only a few who could usually tell which personality was in control at the moment.

"Yeah," Arliss said, his Alabama accent giving it away. "Listen. You gotta get word to Arrow and tell him to stay put in Billings. The military just came to town after Wild Wind. He's being hidden, but if Arrow shows up in town, they're gonna nab him. I'm sure they've got lookouts and scouts out, too. They won't care if he's married. He's not adopted and he doesn't work in agriculture. They won't think twice about taking him."

Alarmed, Gino said, "How did they know he was here?"

Arliss said, "My hunch is that one of the people who were in on the attack on Wild Wind last winter turned him in. Get word to him right away."

"I'll go to Dickensville and send a telegram," Gino said. "Thanks for tellin' me."

"Don't mention it," Arliss said, putting his horse into a canter.

Gino ran to the house to tell the rest of the family members who were home what was happening.

⌒

After riding to Lucky's sheep farm, they left him there after saying a brief farewell. Shadow took them through the woods along a trail that led to the Earnest ranch. Keeping silent, they traveled for about fifteen minutes before Shadow stopped and dismounted.

"You'll have to leave your horses here," Shadow said. "I'll put them in the barn later on."

Wild Wind looked around the forest. "Where are we going? There isn't anything out here."

Shadow gave him a mysterious smile and said, "Follow me."

They got off their horses, looping their reins around a couple of tree branches before gathering their belongings and trailing after Shadow. He walked over to what looked like a solid rock wall at the base of a low mountain. Running his hand along a hidden seam, Shadow unlatched the secret door that led down to his lair. From the time he'd been sixteen until three years ago, he'd lived there, undetected by anyone.

Wild Wind and Roxie were surprised to see a door-sized section of the rock wall open outward, revealing the entrance to a tunnel.

Shadow still enjoyed shocking people. "Allow me to show you to your temporary accommodations." Stepping inside, he picked up a couple of lanterns, lit them, and handed one to Wild Wind.

Wild Wind said, "You're right. I don't think anyone would ever think to look here for us."

Shadow said, "The only one who ever thought to look here for me was Evan. That's how he, Thad, and Win caught me. He figured out that there had to be a secret entrance hidden around here and they laid in wait for me."

"Is that how it happened? Not many know the whole story," Roxie said.

"No, they don't. Perhaps one day we'll tell you more," Shadow said. "Come. Let's get you hidden."

He waved them ahead of him into the tunnel. Then he swung the door shut again and sent the bolt home, thereby locking the secret door. Moving past them, he said, "This way."

Although Wild Wind felt trepidation, he was also curious. Shadow and Marvin had helped him the previous winter when he'd come to their ranch after he'd been shot the night of the attack. He'd arrived on their property barely able to crawl. The twins had carried him inside and Marvin had helped patch him up until they could get him to the medical clinic.

Roxie put her fear aside and followed Shadow while Wild Wind brought up the rear. As they traveled, she noted how chilly it was in the passageway and knew they must be underground. They came to another door and Shadow took a set of keys from his pocket and unlocked it.

"I'm sure things are a bit dusty down here—Bree and I moved upstairs shortly before the twins were born. We do clean on occasion, but we've been busy lately and haven't gotten around to it," he said, leading them onward.

He lit a couple of wall sconces and they illuminated a small sitting room. It was beautifully decorated with deep, wine colored wallpaper that met rich oak wainscoting halfway down the walls. The furniture was excellent quality, too.

Roxie looked around in wonder. "What is this place?"

Shadow said, "My lair. At least that's what Marvin and I have always called it. This is your bedroom."

He took them into a large bedroom done in the same colors as the sitting room, lighting a candelabra there. As the furniture came into view, he felt a pang of nostalgia for the space. He'd been happy here, especially once Bree had come into his life. This was where they'd made love for the first time and where the twins had been conceived. Although he'd adjusted to living in the upstairs house, there were times when he missed his lair.

"You can leave your things here for now while I show you around the rest of the place," Shadow said.

They put their bags down on the bed. Shadow led them out through the sitting room.

"Down here on the right is a full bathroom. You can heat water in the kitchen here. I'll bring some wood down here for you."

The bathroom and kitchen were as beautiful as the other two rooms they'd seen. There were more surprises, however. A short passageway led to a large, high-ceilinged dining room with a beautiful, mahogany table and sideboard. Beyond that was a huge parlor filled with more expensive furniture.

Wild Wind and Roxie stared around at amazement.

Roxie said, "I can't believe all this has been down here for so long. It's like stepping into some magical world."

Shadow grinned as he stepped over to a door. "It's precisely like that. This door leads into the actual cellar. I'll show you the other way out just in case you need to use it."

They went through the doorway with him and as he closed it, they saw that on that side, it was a shelving unit stocked with filled canning jars. They didn't fall as Shadow swung the door shut, so they surmised that they must be fixed to the shelves somehow.

Shadow tipped a jar of pickled red beets that was two shelves down from the top. The door opened again. "This is how you get back in."

"Amazing," Roxie said. "I have to admit that this is sort of fun."

"That's the spirit," Shadow said. "Outwitting those soldiers is going to be entertaining. They have no idea what they're up against."

Wild Wind chuckled. "You're right about that."

Shadow motioned for them to follow him and they continued through the cellar to a hidden staircase. They climbed it and stopped at a door. Shadow pressed a knothole and the door slid open a crack. Shadow slid it all the way open and entered the closet in Marvin's office. Stepping into it, he looked through a hidden peephole and saw that the office was empty.

"This goes into Marvin's office. Only come up this way if there's an emergency of some sort. I don't want the children to see you because they wouldn't understand the situation and might inadvertently let something slip if the military comes here to search for you," Shadow said. "Can you find your way back into the lair?"

Roxie said, "Yes. I remember how to do it."

"All right. I'm going to go inform my family about what's happening. Go back. We'll be down with provisions for you. I can assure you that you'll be safe here. As I said, I lived here undetected since I was sixteen. I'll be back shortly," Shadow said.

Wild Wind and Roxie descended the stairs and made their way back into the lair. They looked around it more, still amazed by its existence. Then they settled on the sofa in the small sitting room.

Roxie put her arms around her husband and leaned into him. "Wild Wind, we have to do whatever is necessary to keep you off the reservation. I love you and I need you, especially now."

He tipped her chin up so he could look into her eyes. "What do you mean by that?"

She smiled. "We're going to have a baby."

As he absorbed her words, a huge grin spread across his face. He laughed with joy and hugged her close before kissing her softly. "I'm so happy," he said. "I was wondering when it would happen." His fierce warrior's nature rose to the fore. "You're right. I'll do anything to stay with you and our baby. I won't let them separate us."

They sat on the sofa holding each other, hoping and praying to be delivered from the sudden nightmare that had descended upon them.

Alfredo stood outside their front door, legs planted wide, his muscular arms folded across his chest as he stared Lt. Finnley down.

"You've no cause to enter our home," he said. "You'll have to shoot me to get inside. My son-in-law isn't here."

Finnley narrowed his eyes. "Yes, I know that he married your daughter. It doesn't matter. He's not a citizen and he hasn't been adopted. He doesn't work in agriculture, either."

Alfredo snorted. "You don't know what you're talkin' about. He works for me and he's a vet's apprentice. He treats livestock and helps us with our crops and cattle. I'd say that counts as working in agriculture. He's married to a citizen and I'm in the process of adopting him. Now, if you keep up this harassment, I'll see that you're court-martialed."

Finnley let out a sarcastic snort.

Alfredo stepped closer. "You don't think I know people? I do, and I've also got deep pockets, so I'd have no trouble goin' to court over this."

The fire in Alfredo's blue eyes made Finnley back up slightly. "You do what you have to do and I'll do what I have to do. I'll be posting a guard here for when he comes back."

"You don't have any right to be on my property," Alfredo said. "Get out of here and don't come back."

"Sir, we're the military and we don't need your permission to be on your property," Finnley said.

"You oughta be ashamed of yourself. How do you sleep at night knowing that you're hurting innocent people and breaking up families?" Alfredo said. "You'll take that boy over my dead body. You've stirred up a hornets' nest, sir."

He stopped talking when he saw Marvin Earnest ride up to the house. The handsome blond-haired, blue-eyed man dismounted gracefully and mounted the stairs, shouldering his way through the four men standing on the Terranovas' veranda.

"Excuse me, gentlemen," he said in a disdainful tone. "I have a prior meeting with Mr. Terranova." Marvin's eyes locked on Alfredo's, letting him know that it was imperative that they speak.

Alfredo said, "That's right. You go post your guard and play at bein' soldiers. I have more important things to do than standing here talkin' to you. I have a business to run. C'mon, Mr. Earnest."

Marvin smiled coldly at the soldiers. "Have a nice day, gentlemen," he said before following Alfredo inside their house. Once the door was shut and locked, Marvin said, "Where can we speak privately?"

"C'mon. We'll go to the Lion's Den."

Marvin smiled. "And what, pray tell, is that?"

Alfredo chuckled as they walked through the house. "It's our conference room and office. That's what we call it."

"Very clever," Marvin said. "I've never been in your house before."

"No. Don't get used to it, either."

Marvin and the Italian family had been enemies for a long time and didn't socialize.

Entering the Lion's Den, Alfredo closed the door. "Now, what do you want?"

"We are hiding Wild Wind and I'd like to do the same for Arrow. I'm also going to start adoption proceedings for Wild Wind. Lucky will adopt him and Arrow, too, if Arrow is agreeable. It's just too bad that the Supreme Court changed the ruling on Indians being citizens if they married a white person. That would solve the whole matter."

"Where are you hidin' Wild Wind?" Alfredo asked. "Why would you do that?"

Marvin smiled. "He's a friend—a new concept for me, but I'm learning. Since he's a friend, I'll do whatever I can to help him. Isn't that how friendship works?"

"Yeah. Where is this hiding place? How do we know it's safe?"

"Alfredo, I can assure you that no one will ever find them. It's best that you don't know. That way they can't force it out of you," Marvin said.

The patriarch didn't know what to think. On one hand, he didn't trust Marvin, but on the other, if there was a chance of keeping Arrow safe until the situation could be sorted out, he was willing to chance it.

As Alfredo looked into Marvin's eyes, he saw that there was something different about his nemesis. "Gino went to Dickensville to send a telegram telling Arrow know to stay away."

"Perfect. Shadow will leave tonight to go pick them up. He can be back with them tomorrow night," Marvin said.

"They're gonna be watching the roads in and out of town," Alfredo said. "That won't work."

Marvin chuckled. "Who said anything about using roads? Shadow's been traveling in and out of town for years without using the roads. Don't worry. He'll get Vanna and Arrow home safely. They'll be safe and together with Wild Wind and Roxie."

Alfredo didn't like the idea of Vanna being in Marvin's care. However, he could see no advantage for Marvin to harm his girl. "Ok, but if anything happens to her, I'm gonna rip your heart out and shove it down your throat."

"I would feel the same way if it were my Eva," Marvin said. "You have my solemn vow that we'll take good care of her."

Alfredo said, "All right."

"Now, when I leave, we're going to fight. We don't want them to think we're colluding. We must play the part of enemies," Marvin said.

"Who's gonna be playin' a part?" Alfredo said. "Don't think we're gonna be bosom buddies because of this."

"I wouldn't presume any such thing," Marvin said.

"Good. Get out," Alfredo said.

They walked back through the house to the front door. Alfredo followed Marvin outside.

"I'm sorry we couldn't do business, Mr. Terranova," Marvin said in an icy voice.

Alfredo grunted. "You wouldn't know a good deal if one hit you upside the head, which is what I'd like to do."

"I think you're getting senile. I offered you a more than fair price, but it seems as though your brain is too addled to realize it," Marvin said, descending the porch steps.

Two of the soldiers had remained behind.

"Just get out of here!" Alfredo shouted. "Don't come back!"

As he mounted, Marvin said, "That suits me just fine." He sent Alfredo a malevolent glare and then rode away.

Chapter Six

Late that night, Nick sat out by the fire pit that Arrow and Wild Wind had made that past fall. Arrow had led them in a dance to appeal to the Great Spirit to help make Alfredo well after suffering a heart attack. Nick was of the opinion that God and the Great Spirit were the same entity and that He had, in fact, heard their heartfelt pleas. Alfredo had recovered well and had shown no sign of a relapse.

Nick was working on getting drunk in an effort to quiet his mind. Between the upheaval they were experiencing due to the military, the strange woman who'd trespassed and stayed in their home, and his usual demons, he was experiencing an emotional overload. No one knew that most nights he drank himself to sleep. He prayed continually for the strength to give up the bottle, but there were times when it was the only way he could get any peace when he wasn't cooking.

Opening up a restaurant with Sylvia was a godsend in itself because the long hours spent cooking and managing it kept his demons at bay. Cooking was his salvation, giving him the peace he sought late at night when sleep wouldn't come. And even when it did, nightmares in which he watched his wife and son drown plagued him. When he was plastered, it knocked him out and he didn't dream.

Losing Ming Li was bad enough, but losing Jake at the same time had rendered Nick beyond grief stricken. He'd been debilitated by the anguish their deaths had caused him. It had taken a long time for him to start living again, and he'd lost his faith in God for a time. Anger and sorrow had consumed him and it was all he could do to get out of bed each day.

His family had also grieved for Ming Li and Jake. Both of them had been dearly loved by the Terranovas and their sudden loss had devastated them, too. They'd also been deeply worried over Nick, who had lost all of his zest for life. Before the tragedy, Nick had been outgoing and quick to laugh. Afterward he'd been withdrawn, reticent, and barely smiled.

Sylvia had pulled him out of his crushing depression by asking him to help her cook. He'd always cooked, but as soon as he'd stepped into the kitchen and gotten involved with cooking a meal, he'd felt a little better. He'd been cooking ever since, experimenting with recipes and getting lost in preparing meals for their family.

But once all of the cooking and cleaning up was done, he was right back where he'd been. He knew his family was right. He needed to not think about it all the time, but they didn't understand. Nick tried not to wallow and most of the time he was successful. Except at night.

As he took another swig from his bottle of scotch, he thought about Arrow and Vanna. Gino hadn't been able to send a telegram to them because the military was monitoring the telegrams for just such a message. If Gino would have sent them a warning, he would've been caught aiding and abetting someone the army considered a fugitive.

So he'd come home and they'd all been praying that Shadow could get to them before the military located Arrow. Nick thought that it was a strange twist of fate that had them relying on their enemy to deliver their loved ones safely home.

He was so lost in his musings that he didn't notice Maura walking out to the fire. It seemed to Nick as though she'd appeared out of nowhere and he started a little. She settled on the grass a short distance from him, casting furtive looks at him. What the heck were they going to do with her? She had no one, nowhere to go, and no money. In every sense of the word, she was an orphan.

"Can't sleep?" Nick asked, signing the question as well.

"No," she whispered. Maura knew a few English words now, "no" being one of them.

"Me neither," Nick said. "Nothing new there. I wish I didn't have to open the restaurant tomorrow. I would've—" He broke off because there was still a guard posted on their property and he'd almost blurted out that Shadow was going for Arrow and Vanna. "There's just too much going on. I don't know if I'll be able to concentrate."

Maura didn't understand what he was saying because he'd stopped signing, but she could tell he was upset. He looked the way she felt a lot of times. There was no way to count how many times she'd wished that she'd had someone to comfort her. Moving closer to him, she resettled herself and put her hand over his where it rested on his knee.

Nick felt her touch and looked down at her small, pale hand against his much larger, tanned one. Hers were not the soft hands of a lady of leisure. He could see that they were strong and feel that they were slightly calloused. His mother's were the same way from all the work she did in the kitchen and in taking care of their home.

He looked over at Maura and saw her glance at him and then at her hand. She didn't know if he'd be angry that she'd touched him. He smiled at her so she understood that he wasn't upset with her. Nick knew he shouldn't, but his judgment was compromised at that moment, so he turned his hand over and held hers.

Then she smiled back at him and he was suddenly very glad that he'd returned her small gesture. It was nice to see her smile instead of being nervous and scared. He squeezed her hand a little and then went to take another drink only to discover that the bottle was empty. It was probably just as well since his vision was starting to blur.

"Time for bed, Maura," he said, getting to his feet.

She stood with him and noticed that he was slightly unsteady as he started dousing the fire. She helped put it out and walked with him to the house. He stumbled a little bit and she caught him, keeping him from falling over. This was no little feat since he far outweighed her, but she was strong and had quick reflexes.

Nick stood still, taking deep breaths to clear his brain. The last thing he needed was to do something to tip his family off that he was drunk. He didn't want to make noise by stumbling up the stairs or breaking something. When he felt more in control, he opened his eyes and patted Maura's shoulder to let her know that he was all right now.

She let him go and followed him into the house. Nick locked the door and went up the stairs with Maura close behind him. In the hallway, he stopped at her door.

"Goodnight, Maura," he said, signing it to her even though it was dark in the hallway.

"Goodnight, Nick," she whispered back to him, catching the meaning of the words.

He smiled and went on to his room. Maura went into hers, undressing and putting on the nightgown Lulu had given her. Crawling into bed, she drew the covers up thinking about what a strange day it had been. The military had arrived looking for Indians and making it impossible for Nick's new brother-in-law to come home. She felt badly for Arrow even though she'd never met him.

She'd just rolled over when she heard a noise she immediately recognized as someone getting sick to their stomach. Getting out of bed, she went into the hallway. It came from the bathroom. Her natural inclination was to help whomever it was. Softly knocking on the door, she heard someone groan in response.

Opening the door, she poked her head inside and saw Nick kneeling in front of the commode, retching. She knew how to prepare a drink that would help, but she had no idea if they had the right ingredients. Nick sat back on his haunches, breathing in deeply to fight off another wave of nausea.

Someone pressed a cool cloth to his forehead and it helped. Looking up, he saw Maura standing by him. He took the cloth from her and held it against his hot face for a few moments. He flushed the toilet and rose shakily to his feet. As one of the wealthier families in the area, they'd had the money to dig a well deep enough to allow them to put in flush toilets, an extravagance that most people in the region weren't lucky enough to have.

Nick was glad that they did because it made it easier to keep his secret. Otherwise, whenever he got as drunk as he was that night, it would have been hard to dump a chamber pot to avoid detection. Looking at Maura, he figured that his secret was no longer safe since she might say something.

Leaving the bathroom, Nick silently beckoned Maura to come with him downstairs. He wanted to take some bicarbonate of soda, but he didn't know how to tell her what it was since she didn't read or write. He had her come with him so she could steady him if he got off kilter.

In the kitchen, he lit the smaller lamp and got out a packet of the bicarbonate, pumped a little water into a glass, and put some of the medicine in it. It fizzed and Maura watched it with fascination. Sitting the glass on the counter while it bubbled, he told Maura that it would settle a sick stomach.

"What does it taste like?" she signed.

He smiled at her curiosity. "Not very good. Do you want to taste it?"

She nodded and he handed her the glass. Maura took a sip and, although she liked the way the bubbles felt against her tongue, she had to agree that it didn't have a pleasant taste. She'd tasted worse things, though.

"It is not as bad as some things," she signed.

Nick took the glass and drank down half of the medicine, grimacing as he did. He let out a muffled burp and then drank the rest. He rinsed out the glass and set it in the sink. His stomach felt better and he thought he could sleep now.

"Thank you, Maura," he said. "I appreciate you not letting me fall on my face and for the moral support."

"You are welcome."

He blew out the lamp and they went back upstairs, Maura keeping him steady as they did. It was too dark in the hallway to sign, so he patted her shoulder and went on to his room after whispering, "Goodnight."

She recognized the words that meant she should go to bed, but she was worried about him. She'd seen enough drunk men to know that the alcohol didn't leave the body right away. He might get sick again and need more medicine. There had been shame in his expression in the kitchen and something told her that he didn't want anyone to know he'd been drinking.

His movements were slower than usual, allowing her to follow him into his room before he could close the door.

"What are you doing?" he asked when she closed it.

"Shh," she said.

He frowned. "Was I loud?" he asked in an exaggerated whisper.

"Shh," she repeated.

"Ok." Normally, Nick would have marched her right back out of his room and told her sternly to go to bed, but the expensive scotch had left his brain sluggish. Combined with his slightly nauseated stomach and a brewing hangover, he didn't have the energy to question her presence in his room.

His mouth tasted foul and he felt his stomach roll again. Going over to his bed, he sat down and pulled open a drawer in his nightstand. He got out a bag of peppermint candy and popped a piece into his mouth. Then he held out the bag to Maura, urging her to take a piece. She did, sniffed it, and put it into her mouth. The explosion of sweetness and mint made her smile.

Nick crunched his piece instead of sucking on it since it released the flavor quicker. He swallowed and put another piece in his mouth to eat more slowly. Maura sat down on the bed. She saw Nick's eyes close and he swayed a little, almost falling asleep sitting up.

"Nick," she whispered.

"Hmm?"

"Goodnight," she replied, saying the word carefully.

"Goodnight," he mumbled, but didn't move.

She giggled softly. "Nick, goodnight."

He opened his eyes. "Ok."

Shaking her head, she got up and took his hand, tugging a little. Nick complied and stood up. Maura pulled the bed covers down and motioned for him to lay down.

"Goodnight," she said.

Nick sat down. "Ok." Again his eyes started closing.

Maura shook her head again and started undoing his shirt buttons. Like a child, Nick let her remove his shirt. She still thought of Nick as her new master and as such it was her job to take care of him. She made him stand up again and she undid his belt and let his pants drop to the floor. He still wore his long underwear.

That woke Nick up. "Hey!" he said.

"Shh," she admonished him.

"Was I loud?" he asked. "Sorry. What are you doing?"

Patting the bed, she said, "Goodnight."

Nick frowned. "Why do I feel like we already went through this?"

Patiently, Maura sat down on the bed, pulling him down. When he sat, she stood and pushed him back onto the bed.

"Oh, I get it now," he said, chuckling as he lay there.

"Shh."

Nick thought this was funny and started laughing. Maura crawled onto the bed to put a hand over his mouth, trying to quiet him. She hadn't been able to reach him from where she'd stood. Nick removed her hand, but she put it back over his mouth since he was still laughing.

He took it away again. "I'm sorry, but it's funny."

"Nick, shh!"

"Ok, ok," he whispered. He sat up suddenly and their heads collided.

"Ow!" both of them said.

"I'm so sorry," Nick said, rubbing her forehead. "Are you all right?"

She guessed that he was asking after her welfare so she said, "Yes."

He kissed her forehead and she giggled because no man had ever done such a thing to her. Nick liked the sound of her giggle so he kissed her forehead again and she did it again.

During the day, Nick was a very principled, honest, and forthright man. However, Nick was very aware of his weaknesses, which was why he never went to a bar when he drank at night—his personality changed when he had booze in his system.

One night about six months after he'd lost his family, he'd gone to the Burgundy House.

Unable to control his temper, Nick had ended up in a fight and had wounded his opponent badly. The same night as the fight, he'd gone home with one of the saloon girls. His loneliness, grief, and drunken state had impaired his judgment and his normal strong control had melted away. Sal had been with him that night and had rescued him in the morning, getting him home before their parents were aware that he hadn't come home.

Horrified by his transgressions, Nick had never put himself in that situation again, knowing that he was susceptible to making bad choices. Instead, he drank at home alone, where he couldn't get into trouble. He hated his reliance on alcohol and he struggled against its pull. There were times when he was able to stay away from it for a couple of days. Then he'd have a soul shaking nightmare and be right back on the bottle.

Looking at Maura with his guard down, Nick saw what a beautiful young woman she was. When he'd kissed her forehead, it was soft and the scent of the jasmine soap that Sylvia had given her to use smelled heavenly. The moonlight illuminated her face, emphasizing her large, dark eyes. Her pink lips beckoned to him and before he could stop himself, he kissed her.

Maura had seen the desire in his eyes. She was well acquainted with what it looked like. Men had desired her from the time she'd been sixteen and she'd been trained to submit. Because she still saw herself as Nick's property, she didn't resist him. It was his right to take her.

The difference in the way other men had kissed her and Nick's kiss was like night and day. Instead of the hard, punishing, and sometimes sloppy kisses that had been forced upon her, Nick's kiss was soft and sensual. Maura enjoyed it as well as the gentle way he slipped his hand around her neck and cupped her head.

She'd been taught what pleased a man and she wanted very much to please Nick. He was handsome and kind and she wanted to make sure he'd never want to trade her. Resting her hands on his muscular chest, she leaned closer to him, deepening the kiss. Nick's libido roared to life. Gathering her close, he slid his fingers into her soft, flame-colored hair.

56

Maura had only felt desire with one other man: a Comanche boy who'd taken a shine to her. He'd treated her with kindness and had made her feel special. He'd talked about buying her and marrying her, but he'd been killed during a skirmish with a warring tribe. She'd been heartbroken over his death and had missed him greatly.

Nick created desire inside her and his kisses excited her even more than WhiteBull's had. His skin was warm against her palms and he held her firmly yet didn't crush her. His hands caressed her back and her blood warmed at his touch. Maura lightly rubbed his neck and ran her hands up into his hair.

His embrace tightened as he growled his approval. When Maura wrapped her arms around his neck and responded to him, his control completely snapped. He needed to feel something good—something other than grief and anger. He could tell that Maura wanted him, too.

He made quick work of her pretty nightgown and shift before getting rid of his underwear. Passion flowed between them and they embraced again. A powerful, fiery connection was forged as desire gripped them and pulled them into its all-consuming flames.

Chapter Seven

"Sal, please go see what's keeping Nick," Sylvia requested the next morning. "We have a supply shipment coming in this morning and I don't want to be late getting to the restaurant to meet the delivery man."

"Sure, Mama," he said, kissing her cheek good morning.

Humming, he jogged up the front stairs and went down the hall to Nick's two-room suite. Most of the estate bedrooms had been designed this way, Nick's included. He knocked and waited, but no one answered. "Nicky! Are you up?" he called through the door. No sound of movement reached his ears. Turning the doorknob he found that it was open.

He entered Nick's sitting room, but it was empty. "Nick?" Walking through the room and into Nick's bedroom, he stopped cold at the shocking sight of Nick and Maura lying in the bed together. They were still entwined among the rumpled, twisted covers.

"Oh, my God. I don't believe it," Sal said. His brain couldn't reconcile what he was seeing.

He and Nick used to fight all the time, usually about Sal's former womanizing, hard-drinking ways. Ever since Sal had met Lulu, that behavior had stopped. He'd fallen in love with Lulu and had never wanted to go back to living that sort of life. Nick had always attempted to rein Sal in, trying to make him see the error of his ways. Although Nick had meant it with brotherly love and concern, it had only served to drive a wedge between them.

They'd since ironed out their differences and were now enjoying the friendship they'd shared growing up before Nick had joined the seminary. Nick had always been scrupulous, holding himself to a higher standard of conduct. He'd exhibited respect, kindness, and love for his fellow man. He'd also been clear on where he stood on sexual relations.

Therefore, Sal finding out that his big brother had slept with a woman whom he'd only known for a couple of days was almost beyond his comprehension. It reminded him of the one time he'd seen Nick lose control, and just like he'd come to Nick's rescue that time, he would do so now.

"Nick," he said, walking over to his brother and shaking him. "Hey, Nick. Wake up."

With a start, Nick's eyes popped open. "Sal?" The throbbing in his head was a familiar sensation in the mornings.

"Yeah. You gotta get up and get Maura out of here." Sal shook one of Maura's bare feet that stuck out from under the covers. He noticed that she had shapely calves. Although he was completely in love with Lulu and didn't look at other women in a lustful way anymore, he could still appreciate a beautiful woman when he saw one.

Maura certainly fell into that category and he couldn't fault Nick for desiring her. However, he was astonished that Nick would have given in to that particular urge—that was until he caught a whiff of Nick.

He sniffed. "Are you drunk?"

Nick didn't answer him because he was too busy looking at Maura, trying to remember what had happened. Bits and pieces came back to him. As she stirred and opened her eyes, she smiled at him. Guilt and shame crashed down on him over how he'd used her to feel good and escape some of his torment.

Sal moved, startling Maura. She hadn't noticed him yet since she'd been looking at Nick.

"Get moving, Nick. Mama's lookin' for you. You have those supplies comin' today," Sal said. "Good morning, Maura," he said, smiling at her. He couldn't help being slightly amused by the situation, but he realized that it was very serious. He left then to go back downstairs and keep Sylvia occupied until Nick came down.

Maura smiled at Nick again and ran a hand over his arm as she propped herself up on an elbow so she could kiss him. When she did, Nick's memory filled with what had transpired between them and shame coursed even stronger through him, making him pull gently away from her.

"What is wrong?" she signed. "Did I displease you somehow?"

The anxious look on her face compounded his guilt. "No, Maura. You did not displease me," he signed, meaning it. "Far from it, but I am ashamed of how I treated you. Last night should not have happened. I was drunk and lonely and I gave in to lust. I am so sorry for what I did, but it will not happen again."

He couldn't have hurt her any more than if he'd cut her with a dagger. Last night had been the single most wonderful experience of her life and knowing that he regretted it stung. She didn't say anything as she untangled herself from the sheets, throwing them away from her. Nick turned away from her to give her privacy and it sparked fury inside Maura. Not covering herself, she stomped around to stand in front of him.

"No one has ever been as kind to me as you have been. No man except one other than you has ever touched me with kindness and tenderness. And no man has ever given me the kind of pleasure that you did last night. I do not regret it and I am not ashamed. Neither should you be. Other men who have used me and hurt me should be ashamed of how they have treated me, but you should not be. Every slave should be lucky enough to have a master like you!"

Her tirade fascinated Nick for many reasons. He'd never had a gorgeous, naked woman give him a tongue-lashing in Indian sign. He was mesmerized by the way the sun turned her auburn hair to fire and how it made her pale skin seem to glow. That he'd made her feel good was great for his ego, but did little to minimize his shame.

"Maura, I am not your master and you are not my slave," he signed. "I do not regret it for the reasons you might think. In my culture, relations between men and women who are not married are highly improper and looked down upon. I regret last night because I was disrespectful to you. I should not have slept with you since we are not married."

Maura had never spoken so forcefully or openly with a man before, but she couldn't stop herself. "Why should you be ashamed of sharing something so beautiful with me? I am not offended. You say that what you did with me last night was disrespectful to me, but it was not. What *is* disrespectful to me is making me feel ashamed because it meant more to me than you will ever know."

Maura found her shift and nightgown and put them on. Then she stomped from the room, slamming the door after her. She ran right into Sal, who had been guarding the door since coming back upstairs. Sal apologized and moved out of her way. As Maura hurried away, Sal heard a soft sob escape her.

"Uh oh," he mumbled and went into Nick's room. "What did you do to her?"

Nick pulled on his pants quickly as he said, "I apologized and told her how ashamed of myself I was for giving into my baser needs while I was intoxicated and in a vulnerable place."

Sal put a hand over his face. "You insulted her, in other words."

"I didn't realize I was insulting her," Nick said. "I was trying to be respectful of her."

"You never, ever tell a woman who hasn't indicated that she regretted the night before that you're sorry about it and that it was a mistake unless you're *trying* to insult her and get rid of her," Sal said.

"What?" Nick said. "I'm too hung over for this right now. What was I supposed to say?"

"You tell her how much you enjoyed yourself and let it go at that for the time being. Then tonight you could have talked to her about it when you had some time to think about it and say it in a way that wouldn't hurt her," Sal said. "How is it that you don't know this?"

Nick stopped fastening his jeans and gave Sal a deadpan look.

Sal made a dismissive motion with his hand. "Yeah, yeah. You were a virgin until you married Ming Li. I keep forgetting about that. I don't know how since you always act so high and mighty. I guess you can't do that now, though, huh?" he remarked with a grin.

Nick gritted his teeth in anger, but not at Sal. The anger was self-directed because it was true. He had no business judging anyone about anything. "No, I can't. I was never trying to be high and mighty. I was trying to be helpful, but it came off all wrong."

Sal let it go. "So did she indicate that she regretted it?"

Nick gave him an irritated glance as he gathered up a shirt, his watch, and his wallet. "No."

"I see. And just how *did* she feel about it?"

A smile played around Nick's mouth, but he wouldn't answer.

"Ha! She liked it, didn't she? Sounds like Nicky has some skills that you can't talk about in church," Sal said.

Nick whipped his alarm clock at Sal, who quickly ducked. Even so, it glanced off his shoulder.

"Damn it, Nick!" Sal said, rubbing it.

A knock sounded on Nick's door. "Nick!" Sylvia shouted. "Hurry up! You're gonna make us late!"

Nick rolled his eyes and pinched the bridge of his nose in frustration. "I'll be right there, Mama!"

Sal went out into the sitting room and opened the door into the hallway. "It's my fault, Mama. I was asking his advice on something. Sorry. He'll be right along. I just have one more little thing to ask him, ok?"

Sylvia sighed. "Fine. The buggy is already hitched. Your other brother, my *good* son, hitched it up while you two were having a conference," she groused, walking away.

Sal went back inside. "Nicky, you better scrub real good and real quick. You smell like booze. If Mama gets a whiff, she's gonna start askin' questions. And you know her once she gets started."

"Yeah, I know. I really messed up, Sal. I don't know what to do.

Actually, I do know what to do, what I *have* to do. I have to marry her."

Sal let out a bark of laughter then sobered when Nick didn't laugh. "You're serious. Are you crazy? You can't marry her. You've only known her a couple of days."

Nick said, "I don't have a choice. I know her a lot better than some men know their prospective wives. It's the right thing to do. What if she gets pregnant because of last night? I won't have a child out of wedlock and I won't touch her again until we are."

"Look, we'll figure this out. Don't do anything crazy," Sal said.

"Oh, you mean like getting drunk outta my mind and sleeping with a woman who's a complete stranger to me and thinks she's my slave?" he asked. "I think that ship has already sailed, Sally. I gotta go. See you tonight."

"I will not hide like some yellow dog!" Arrow said.

Shadow hadn't planned on still being in Billings the next morning, but Arrow was being obstinate about going into hiding. It was pissing him off and he was very close to knocking Arrow out, tying him up, and taking him and Vanna back to Echo that way. Diplomacy wasn't his strong suit, but he was trying.

"Arrow, you wouldn't be hiding out of cowardice, but out of common sense. We simply have to figure out a way around the military. You've just gotten married. Think of Vanna. Doesn't she deserve a say in the matter?"

Vanna took Arrow's hand. "Listen to Mr. Earnest. You know what it's like on the reservations and they might not even put you on a Cheyenne reservation. What if they stuck you in with the Comanche or Apache? They would kill you."

Arrow couldn't argue with that because it was true.

"Please, Arrow, do as Mr. Earnest is suggesting. For me?"

Looking in her eyes, Arrow couldn't refuse her, but he also couldn't completely go against his pride. "Ok, but I will not hide forever."

Shadow's irritation lifted. "You won't have to. Now get packed. We won't leave until sundown so we can minimize the chances of you being noticed. We'll be traveling on horseback since we won't be using roads. There are all sorts of trails leading from Billings back home. The army doesn't know about them."

Arrow grinned. "I'll enjoy sneaking around them."

"I thought that might appeal to you," Shadow said. "Use those saddle bags to pack with. You'll have to leave your suitcases. I'm sorry about that."

Vanna said, "I don't care as long as we can get home safely. I'd ride home naked if I had to."

Shadow laughed. "I'm sure Arrow would enjoy watching that, but you might get cold."

Arrow grinned and Vanna blushed.

"Stay here. Don't go out and don't answer the door for anyone except me," Shadow said, opening the door to find a soldier standing outside the door. "What do you want?" he asked in a surly tone. Behind his back, he made the Indian sign for "hide" as best he could with one hand.

The soldier blinked at his abrupt manner. "I'm looking for Arrow Swift."

"Who? I've never heard of an Arrow Swift."

"He's an Indian," the soldier said.

Shadow glanced at his insignia. "Corporal, do I look like an Indian?"

"Well, no."

"That's right. I'm not. What I *am* is late for a breakfast meeting, so if you'll excuse me...."

"We were told that the Indian is in the honeymoon suite."

"Well, perhaps he checked out or left unexpectedly. I rented this room because I'm going to be entertaining some business colleagues and would like to do so in a private setting. Why am I explaining this to you? Get out of here and leave me alone!"

"I'll need to come in and look around, just to make sure."

Shadow sighed. "Very well. Come right on in."

As the soldier walked past him, Shadow spun him around and

slammed his fist against the corporal's jaw. The young man crumpled to the floor.

"Sorry about that, but you should have left me alone," he said, shutting the door and taking off his dark glasses. "Arrow, come here and punch me a couple of times."

Arrow stepped into the room. "Why?"

"No time to explain. Just do it," Shadow said. "Don't knock me out, but maybe bloody my lip or some—"

Shadow staggered back a little from Arrow's blow to his right cheek. It was followed up by another to the left side of his mouth. Relishing the pain, Shadow laughed as he felt blood run down his chin. "Excellent," he said taking out a hanky. "I'm sure he's not alone. You two have to get out of here while I keep his cohort busy down at the front desk. Go out through the kitchen and go to St. Michael's. I'll meet you there."

Arrow nodded and put on the bowler hat that Lucky had brought for him—he'd told him that it would make him look more assimilated. He and Vanna went down to the first floor by the back stairs, entered the dining room, and then passed through the kitchen at a leisurely pace as though nothing was wrong. Once outside, they kept walking. Arrow pulled his hat down as much as he could and avoided looking directly at people.

Once they felt they were safely away from the hotel, they jogged along until they reached the church, hurrying inside. They went up front, sitting in the pew, praying for Shadow and for God to get them all safely home.

Back at the hotel, Shadow packed what belongings of the newlyweds' he deemed the most important and put the rest in their suitcases. The solider stirred so Shadow hit him again and he sank back to the floor. Quickly, Shadow made sure that he hadn't missed anything. Then he walked to the room across the hallway and knocked on the door. No one answered, so he picked the lock and sat Arrow and Vanna's suitcases inside the door before locking and shutting it again.

Then he gathered up his saddlebags and descended the front stairs. Shadow marched right up to another soldier, grabbed his shoulder, and turned him around.

"I don't know who you think you are, but I don't appreciate your pal coming to my room and accosting me!" he shouted.

"What? *Your* room? He was supposed to go to the honeymoon suite," the man said.

Shadow nodded. "He did. I rented it because I was going to entertain some business associates there this evening. He said he was looking for some Indian or something. As you can see, I'm not an Indian." He pointed to his face. "He wanted to come inside, but when I refused, this is what he did to me. I retaliated, of course. You can find him in my room. Well, it *was* my room, but I'm leaving. I don't have to stand for this."

He threw the room key at the clerk, who ducked, and strode angrily away. Once outside, he mounted his horse and rode away, chuckling to himself the whole time.

"Nick! Watch what you're doing!" Sylvia admonished her son. "You're gonna burn that!"

Nick quickly turned his attention back to the chicken he was browning. He saved it from scorching, but barely. "Sorry," he mumbled.

Sylvia's expression was one of concern. "Are you all right? You're not yourself today."

"Yeah, I'm ok. Just worried about Vanna and Arrow, you know?" he responded. It was only half a lie, he thought. The family was trying to keep things as normal as possible, but it was difficult.

"Yes, I know. They were supposed to be back," she said quietly, lest they be overheard. "I hope nothing happened."

Nick said, "Me, too. We'll probably hear something soon. Until then, I'll try to keep my mind on what I'm doin'." He finished browning the chicken and went on to the next step of preparing the cacciatore.

"My mind keeps wandering, too. Don't feel bad. The thought of anything happening to my baby has me on edge," she said. "I can't understand why they have to come here bothering Wild Wind and our Arrow. They're only two Indians, for crying out loud."

Nick said, "I thought about that, too. They did want Billy, too, but they can't touch him, thank God."

"You're right. What are we going to do with Maura?" Sylvia asked.

Nick jerked a little at the mention of the beautiful redhead. "Uh, I don't know. That's a strange situation. I'll see if Evan has any reports about a woman matching her description being missing."

"Good idea. Then we might know a little more about what we're up against," Sylvia said.

"I'm not gonna let anyone hurt her again," Nick said. "That much I know."

"Well, she's safe with us for now until we figure things out," Sylvia said.

Not safe enough, Nick thought. *Dear Lord, please help me find the strength to resist all of these temptations. I can't keep on drinking like I am, but I can't sleep without it. Maybe I should go see Erin. She could give me something to help me sleep. Then I wouldn't have to drink to get me to that point. I'd keep my head better. I'll do that this afternoon.* His mind made up, he felt a little better and was able to focus on the task at hand.

Chapter Eight

When Nick arrived home that night, two soldiers were stationed at the entrance to their ranch. He was tired and irritable.

Stopping his horse, he said, "You're pathetic, sending out a bunch of soldiers to round up two Indians who aren't hurting anyone. They're married to white women and they're assimilated into the community. You're all idiots."

"I can't believe that you let one of your women marry an Indian," one of them challenged him.

"He's a decent, hardworking, smart guy. Better than you, apparently," Nick said. "Thanks to you, they'll probably never come home again." He glared at them for a moment and then went on to the ranch and put his horse away for the night.

Going inside, he went into the parlor where his parents sat. He flopped down on the sofa.

Sylvia chuckled. "If you're that tired that means business was good."

"Be glad you leave at two," Nick said, smiling. "We need a bigger place. There were more people waiting to be seated and we had to turn them away so we could close on time."

"I'm glad to hear it," Alfredo said. "Keep going like you are and maybe next year you'll be able to expand the place. You'll have the cash flow by then."

"I'm glad, too, Pop. Mama and I have wanted to do this for a while. Thanks for all your help in getting it off the ground," Nick said.

Alfredo said, "You're welcome."

"Where is everyone?" he asked.

"Sal, Gino, and Lulu went to Spike's and Maura is out by the fire," Sylvia said. "The poor thing is so lost. We invited her to stay here with us, but she said she wanted to sit out there. So she made a fire and she's been out there ever since. She's probably bored."

Nick said, "I'll go check on her."

After he left, Alfredo said, "It's always nice to see the way Nick cares about people. I'm not sure what we're gonna do with the poor girl."

Sylvia nodded. "He's always had a big heart. We'll figure something out. I'm more worried about Arrow and Vanna."

"Me, too," Alfredo said, his jaw clenching as he fought against tears. He was close to his boys, but Vanna held a special place in his heart. He'd also come to love Arrow as a son and he didn't want to lose him. "Earnest better come through or I'll make him pay."

Sylvia took his hand. "We'll keep praying and have faith, Al. God will see them safely home."

He patted her hand. "You're right, but then what? How long can they stay hidden? Even if the army leaves, someone's gonna just turn them in again."

Sylvia said, "One thing at a time. Once we get them home, we can figure things out from there."

Thinking of the girl out by the fire, he said, "We sure have a lot to figure out right now."

"Yes, but we'll do it together, just like we always do," Sylvia said.

Alfredo smiled at her and said, "Let's go to bed. We'll have a nice nightcap and get some sleep."

Sylvia laughed. "I know what your idea of a nightcap is and it doesn't involve alcohol."

Grinning, he said, "I never hear you complain. We can add some wine if you want."

She arched an eyebrow at him. "You get the wine and I'll turn down the bed."

"Now you're talkin'," Alfredo said.

Maura saw Nick approaching the fire and her stomach clenched with anxiety. She shouldn't have spoken sharply to him that morning. What if he kicked her out? Where would she go? She had no way to take care of herself. As he sat down next to her, his dark eyes meeting hers, she gave him a hesitant smile.

He returned it and then sighed. In sign, he said, "I am sorry I made you feel ashamed about last night. I did not mean to. You were right; it was beautiful. At least what I remember of it. There are things I need to explain to you so you understand why I am ashamed of my behavior. I am not ashamed of *you*. You do not know the way our culture thinks about relationships so you would not understand."

"You do not need to explain," Maura said. "If you just tell me what you want me to do, I will do it that way."

"Maura, you are not a slave any longer. I am not your master. You have no master anymore. Do you understand me?" His signing was emphatic and his voice was firm as he said the words that were foreign to her.

She nodded and looked into the fire. "I understand."

"I do not think you do, but I will try to help you understand," Nick said. He clenched his jaw for a moment before beginning his story.

Maura listened attentively, her heart moved by the grief in his eyes and voice. She'd never had a spouse to lose or had a baby, but she understood pain and sorrow. She shed tears as she thought about the agonizing loss he'd experienced and she also felt terrible that Ming Li and Jake had perished.

Nick said, "I have been lost for a long time now and I am not sure how to find my way back. I was training to be what in Indian culture is called a spiritual medicine man. I was going to be a priest."

Maura said, "Priests visited us a few times. They wore black clothing and white collars."

He smiled. "Yes. But then I met Ming Li and fell in love with her. I had to make a choice to either go through with becoming a priest or being with Ming Li."

"Why could you not do both?" Maura asked.

"Priests are not allowed to be married or have romantic relationships with women," Nick said. "The reason for this is that if they have a family, their loyalties will be divided. If a priest does not have a wife and family, he will be able to fully devote his life to the Lord, the Great Spirit. It was a sacrifice I was willing to make because I felt called to give my life to God. But that all changed when I met my wife. I did a lot of praying, trying to figure out what God wanted me to do."

Maura asked, "What did He say to you?"

"He did not tell me in words, but He kept putting Ming Li in my path, so to speak. I came to understand that I was meant to be with her," Nick said. "I think that is why I am so angry with Him over their deaths. If I was supposed to be with her, why would He take them from me? Why did He not save them? We are not to question, but to accept that He has a plan and a reason for everything. I used to take that on faith and counsel others to do the same.

"But when they died, I could not accept that a good and righteous God would wish them to perish. To what end? And this is where I find myself stuck: between wanting to believe again and the anger and grief in my heart. I am ashamed about last night because I used you to make myself feel better for a little while. Men and women are not supposed to have relations outside of marriage. Many do, but I believe that sex between unmarried people is wrong. I do not love you and you are not my wife. I disrespected you because I was weak and gave into my physical and emotional needs without thinking about your welfare. I am sorry."

Maura sat for several minutes as she collected her thoughts. "From the time I was a young girl, men have used me. I have cooked, cleaned, made their clothes, and did whatever I was told. I was taught to submit to them and shown how to please them in all ways. Because I was only a slave, I was not held in high regard. Men in Comanche culture are allowed more than one wife and they can also have relations with their slaves.

"You speak of my welfare and feel that you did not look out for it. That is not true. You were kind and gentle and made me feel things I never have before," she said. "Perhaps in your culture what we did is considered wrong, but it was not in my mind and you have nothing to be ashamed about. Relations have never been pleasurable for me, but they were last night. So even though you are sorry, I am not."

Nick's protectiveness towards women caused rage to flow hotly through his veins as he understood what Maura had been through. He could only imagine the degradation, pain, and cruelty she must have suffered.

Daring to look into his eyes, Maura signed, "You may not believe me, but you gave me as much comfort as you took. I do not call that shameful."

In her gaze, Nick saw trepidation, conviction, and a little glimmer of happiness. He gave up arguing, knowing that nothing he said would change her perspective on the situation. Maybe he should look at it that way, but his upbringing wouldn't let him. He wasn't like Sal, who had broken almost every Commandment there was and hadn't felt much guilt about it. His own moral compass used to always point true north, but over the past couple of years it had gone south in a lot of ways.

Maura asked, "Why do you hold on to so much guilt? What have you done to make you feel that way?"

Nick looked away from her, his brows furrowing as he struggled against the emotions her questions brought to the surface. He signed, "I am a fraud and a liar. Every day I get up, go to work, act happy, and play the role of dutiful son and good brother. I help with our ranch and I help other people. But at night, after everyone else goes to sleep, I drink. The way I did last night. I drink so I can forget and sleep. Even then, it does not always keep away the nightmares. It takes more and more whiskey to do the job.

"I get drunk at home because if I go to a saloon I will get into fights and sleep with women. There are no single women here at home or people to fight with, so both temptations are gone. I am not strong enough to resist them if they are present, as you found out last night. No one except Sal knows about us and he will not tell. You are the only person who knows about my drinking problem."

"I will not say anything," she said.

"Thank you. I have tried to stop, and sometimes I can for a few days, but I cannot stay away from it. I get shaky and irritable and I cannot eat. All of these things would be noticed by my family. We are very close, as you can see," Nick said.

"Why have you not told them?"

Nick's smile held no mirth. "I do not want to disappoint them. I was going to be a priest, someone who is held to the highest moral standards. Now, I am a liar, fraud, and a drunk."

Maura said, "But you do not have to be. You are not like me."

"What do you mean?"

"You have people who love you. They would help you, but they cannot if they do not know that you need it," Maura said.

"I cannot tell them," Nick said.

Shifting closer, she put a hand on his arm. "If it keeps getting worse, they will know eventually."

Nick nodded. "I know."

"Which thing will disappoint them more? Your problem or not letting them help you?"

He met her gaze. "You are a wise woman. I wish I could stop the problem before it gets any worse. I have another problem, though. What to do about you."

Maura's pulse skipped and her eyes widened in fear. "I will not tell anyone about last night or anything you have told me. I promise. Please do not get rid of me. Do not let them find me. I will do anything. Please."

Nick grasped her arms. "Maura, it's ok," he said aloud. "I'm not going to let anyone hurt you. I'm not getting rid of you. It's all right."

His soothing tone of voice calmed her and she relaxed.

Releasing her, Nick signed, "I did not mean to frighten you. What I meant was that in our culture it is common for a man to marry a woman he has had relations with outside the bonds of marriage. Therefore, I should marry you. You might become pregnant because of last night. I will not have a child out of wedlock."

The idea of being married to a man like Nick filled Maura with such joy, but then her spirits plummeted. "Your family will not want you to marry someone like me. I am not worthy of someone like you."

Nick said, "Maura, your past life was not one of your own choosing. You could not help your circumstances, but that life is behind you now. You are worthy of anyone."

"You would marry me just because of last night?"

"Yes," he said. "It is the right thing to do. Think about it." He rose. "It has been a long day. Goodnight."

"Goodnight," she said aloud.

Maura couldn't sleep. She was worried about Nick. Was he drinking? Most likely. What if he was as drunk as he'd been last night? She felt responsible for him even if she wasn't his slave. Rolling over, she tried to quiet her mind, but it was no use. Getting out of bed, she left her room, going to Nick's door. If she knocked, someone else might hear. She could scratch softly on the door, but if Nick was very drunk, he might not hear it.

Turning the knob, she let herself into his room. The lamp in the sitting room burned low, but gave enough illumination to allow her to see Nick sitting in one of the chairs. She sighed when she saw that he held a bottle of liquor in his hand. Silently, she went to him and put her hand on the bottle neck, tugging a little.

Looking up at her with misery-filled eyes, Nick relinquished the booze. Maura set it on the stand by the lamp, which she blew out. Going back to him, she took his face in her hands before bending over and pressing her lips to his.

Nick grabbed her arms and pushed her back a little. "No, Maura. It's not right. Go to bed."

Maura moved away from him, picked up the bottle of whiskey, and went to the window. She opened it and held the bottle out the window.

Nick knew she was going to dump it. "Hey! Don't do that!"

She overturned it quickly and the liquor poured down onto the bushes below. Nick ground his teeth in anger. Maura was used to facing anger and although it frightened her to see it in Nick's eyes, it didn't scare her as much as it might have had it been another man. When the bottle was empty, she brought it back inside and shut the window.

Sitting the bottle down, she approached him again, reaching out to touch his arm. Looking in his eyes, she trailed her fingers down to his hand. He didn't resist as she raised it and kissed his palm. The light in his eyes changed from anger to desire. Letting go of his hand, Maura undressed while Nick watched. His hands clenched at his sides and he said, "No, Maura. Get dressed and go to bed." He turned away from her and went into his bedroom.

He was shocked when she ran past him and opened his nightstand drawer. Seeing a bottle, she pulled it out, but Nick took it from her.

"Stop it," he ground out between his teeth.

Maura was willing to risk his wrath if she could help him defeat the demon that plagued him. She had a hunch that he had more alcohol hidden. Racing to his dresser, she started opening drawers. Nick went after her, but halted when he realized that in order to stop her, he was going to have to touch her.

Her nakedness was already wreaking havoc on his body, but if he touched her, he would lose the battle that raged inside him. He groaned when she found the fifth of whiskey he'd hidden in the bottom drawer. Like an animal, he paced while she dumped it out the window. When she was done, she set the empty bottle on his dresser and held out her hand for the bottle he held tightly.

His reluctance prompted her to sign, "Which do you want more? Me or the fire water? You cannot have both."

After a few moments, he gave her the whiskey and watched hungrily as she poured its contents out the window. She'd barely gotten the window shut before he was on her, kissing her with an urgency that she matched with her own. Nick wasn't victorious over the lust that burned inside, but he thought that maybe it was the lesser of the two demons.

Maura offered herself to Nick, but she wanted him as much as he did her. She needed his caresses and kisses, needed to feel the joy he'd given her the night before. She'd never known such delight and she craved it.

As he held her that night, Maura knew that she'd never regret giving herself to him. What he saw as sin, she saw as wondrous and sacred. Although they had different opinions on the matter, they derived the same things from the passion they shared: pleasure, comfort, and a lessening of their past agony.

And much later, as he slept soundly in Maura's arms, she held him for a long time, enjoying their closeness. Finally her eyes closed and she slipped into a contented slumber.

Chapter Nine

That same night, Shadow, Arrow, and Vanna arrived at his lair. They were tired and hungry. Vanna wasn't used to riding a horse for such long distances and she'd grown saddle sore. She hadn't complained much, figuring it was a small price to pay for keeping Arrow safe.

The winding route Shadow had taken them on was a longer way to travel to Echo from Billings, but they hadn't encountered other people, which had ensured their safety. As they had traveled, it had given them all a chance to become better acquainted. Although Shadow's sense of humor was different than other people's, they still appreciated the amusement he provided them.

He'd told them how he'd handled the other two soldiers in the lobby of the hotel and they'd laughed about it. The trio greatly enjoyed the fact that they'd been able elude the army. As they stopped at the secret entrance to his lair, Shadow enjoyed Arrow and Vanna's confusion, which turned to amazement when they saw the rock door open.

Their incredulity continued as he took them into the actual living space. Wild Wind and Roxie had heard them come in and hurried to greet them, hugging them and taking their possessions from them.

Roxie said, "I'll go put on some coffee and heat up the shepherd's pie we had for supper."

The new arrivals were happy for her hospitality.

Wild Wind said, "Come with me. A sleeping area has been set up for you."

Arrow followed his brother into the dining room, which had been converted into a bedroom. "I cannot believe this place," he said in Cheyenne. "It is huge and must have taken a long time to build."

Wild Wind put the saddle bags he carried on the bed. "Yes, it did. It is a fascinating story and I am sure they will enjoy telling it to you, too."

Arrow put his bags down. "What has it been like? Have they treated you well?"

"They have been gracious and entertaining. They take turns bringing food down to us and visiting with us. Someone has to stay with the children to make sure that they do not know we are here. There is too much at stake to risk Eva saying something. We are bored, but other than that we have everything we could need," Wild Wind said.

"I am glad to hear it," Arrow said.

Wild Wind said, "I have good news."

"Oh?"

"Roxie is pregnant," he said.

Arrow grinned. "I am very happy for you. Perhaps it is the Great Spirit's way of telling us everything will be all right."

"I hope you are right. I am sorry that your honeymoon was cut short," Wild Wind said.

Arrow smiled. "Do not be troubled about it. At least we are safe and free."

Shadow passed through the dining room then, saying, "I'm going to let Marvin know we're back."

The brothers nodded and then went to the kitchen to join the women and have something to eat.

No sooner had Shadow gotten upstairs and informed his family that they had returned than there was a knock at the door. Marvin pulled the door open to see Lt. Finnley and two soldiers standing on the porch.

"To what do I owe the displeasure?" he asked Finnley with a smirk.

Finnley said, "I need to see your brother."

"Why?"

"He accosted one of my men yesterday morning, that's why. Is he here or is he with your friends?" Finnley said.

"Which friends are you speaking about?" Marvin asked, delighting in irritating Finnley.

Finnley kept a hold on his anger. "Your other Indian friend and his wife. Now, is he here?"

"Yes. Come in, but I warn you: if you do anything to upset our children, I'll make you sorry in ways you can't even imagine," Marvin said coldly.

There was something in Marvin's eyes that gave Finnley pause for a few moments. "We just want to ask him some questions."

"Very well," Marvin said, stepping aside. He had very little anxiety about them questioning Shadow. His twin was as talented a liar as he was, so he was sure that Shadow already had a story handy.

The three soldiers followed Marvin into the large parlor. Four children of various ages played on the floor. Eva, now four, ran over to them.

"Hello. Who are you?" she asked.

Finnley had children of his own and he missed them greatly. Crouching, he said, "I'm Lieutenant Finnley. You can just call me Dirk."

"Ok, Dirk," she said, playing with the brass buttons on his uniform.

He smiled. "Have you seen your Indian friends?"

"Wil' Win' and Awwow?" she asked. "No. I miss 'em."

Knowing that a child Eva's age would be honest, Finnley felt certain that the Indians were not in the house anywhere. The kids were sure to have seen them if they had been. "Ok," he said, standing. Seeing Shadow calmly reposing in a chair with his legs crossed irritated him further. "Deputy, why did you hit Corporal Abrams yesterday morning?"

"Well, I'd rented out the honeymoon suite because I was going to entertain some of our business associates there. When he showed up demanding entrance into the room, I refused. We scuffled since I wouldn't let him past me. There was no need for him to come in. I knocked him out. After that, I didn't think it prudent to keep my meeting because I had the feeling that your men would have kept harassing me and that wouldn't look good in front of my associates. I sent them a telegram letting them know the meeting was canceled."

Finnley smiled. "You rented the same room that Arrow and Vanna happened to have been occupying?"

"Was that their room?" Shadow asked, straight-faced. "I had no idea what hotel they were staying in. The front desk clerk never mentioned anything about it when I registered, so I can only assume that they had already departed by the time I arrived."

"Funny thing is, the clerk we spoke to said he never rented that room to you," Finnley said. "How do you explain that?"

Shadow smiled. "You obviously haven't investigated thoroughly enough. I know a few things about investigating. I am a deputy, after all. Perhaps you could take some lessons from me. The clerk who rented me the suite was a she not a he. Her name was Arnelle—a very pleasant older lady. I remember her because she was so helpful to me. Normally, I don't remember hotel clerks."

Finnley turned to one of his men. "Sergeant Hadley, did you question all the clerks?"

Hadley's face reddened. "No, sir. Just the fella that was on duty that morning."

Shadow said, "Tsk tsk. Just as I feared. Not thorough enough. There was more than just one clerk working."

His sarcasm and Hadley's poor investigating infuriated Finnley. "When did you get home?"

"Not long ago, actually. I stopped in Dickensville last evening and decided to stay overnight there. I did my friend Billy Two Moons a favor by looking in on the artwork he has on display in one of the shops there. He pays the owner of the shop a certain percentage to sell his work. Unfortunately, he only sold one piece." To Bree, he said, "Remind me to let Billy know tomorrow, please?"

Bree nodded, enjoying the game. "I will. If I don't keep on top of you, you'd forget everything."

"Yes, and you keep on top of me so well," he said, grinning at her and kissing the back of her hand.

Marvin snickered and Hadley smiled until Finnley gave him a withering look.

Finnley said, "Abrams doesn't remember hitting you."

"I'm not surprised. I did hit him rather hard, but as you can see, I was perfectly within my rights to defend myself," Shadow said.

Finnley saw the scrapes on Shadow's face and that the right side of Shadow's mouth was a little swollen. He had only one chance at proving that Shadow's story was a fabrication: interviewing the clerk Shadow had named and checking with the shop in Dickensville where Shadow said that he'd stopped.

"Do you mind if we have a look around?"

Marvin said, "Be our guest, but do not break or ruin anything or I'll have my lawyers bring a suit against you and believe me, you do not want to be on their bad side."

Finnley nodded and he and his men split up. It took them close to twenty minutes to thoroughly search the big house, but they turned up nothing. There was no sign of any guests, and they'd even searched the attic.

"Where's the basement?" Finnley asked.

Marvin rose. "I'll show you, but there are a lot of spiders down there. We don't use it much except for some canning." He kept his cool, smug façade up, even though he was slightly nervous.

He unlocked the door and lit a lantern, leading the men down the stairs on the opposite end of the basement from the other set of stairs that led up to his office. That staircase was hidden by a section of stone wall that had been designed to conceal its existence. Finnley saw that the basement was exactly as Marvin had described.

Marvin frowned. "As you can see, there isn't anyone here. Now, I would like to get our children to bed and go to bed myself. We have a busy day ahead of us as usual and I'd like to get some sleep. I've been a good sport long enough."

Having no reason to stay any longer, Finnley and his men took their leave. Marvin watched them ride away before shutting the front door and laughing. Bree, Ronni, and Shadow joined him as he entered the parlor.

"This is so fun," he said, careful to not mention that they were scheming in front of Eva. "I haven't had this kind of enjoyment in a while."

Shadow grinned. "Me neither."

Marvin said, "I'll have to go to see Alfredo right away in the morning to let them know."

Ronni said, "They'll all be so relieved. I would be if it were me."

"Now we just have to figure out how we're going to get rid of our unwanted pests," Marvin said.

Bree said, "Between everyone, I'm sure we can figure something out."

It wasn't long until they gathered up all of their little ones and headed to bed.

Arliss knelt at the altar in the dark church, praying for guidance. He'd been there for quite some time, but he wasn't any closer to making a decision. The problem was that it wasn't only his decision to make, but he didn't want to approach Andi about it. He'd put her through enough last fall when he'd faked his death in order to escape his old life as an agent.

Although he'd done it so that they could be together, it had devastated her. Her grief had been compounded because she had lost three people at the same time instead of just one. She was the only one outside of his parents and grandmother who truly comprehended the concept of there being three people inside of his body.

Resting back on his haunches, Arliss looked at the large cross on the wall behind the lectern and asked, "Why won't You answer me? What should I do?"

He heard footsteps in the back of the church and knew that it was Andi. He looked at her and she said, "I'm sorry. I didn't mean to interrupt. You weren't home, so I figured you had gone out to Lucky's or to Spike's."

"It's all right, darlin'. You know we're always glad to see you," he said, rising. "C'mon and sit down with me. There's something we need to talk about."

Andi didn't get inside his mind, but she could feel his anxiety as they settled on a pew.

"I'm wrestlin' with something and I've been praying, but I'm not coming up with an answer."

"All right. Go ahead," she said.

"It's about all this stuff with Wild Wind and Arrow," he said. "I don't know where they're hiding out and that's a good thing. The less people who know, the better. The problem is that they can't hide forever. These soldiers will eventually leave, but if those boys come out of hiding, they'll just get turned in again. We need a permanent solution."

Andi said, "I've been thinking the same thing. A lot of people have. I take it you have an idea about a permanent solution."

Blowing out a breath, he nodded. "Yeah, but you're not gonna like it. We don't like it, either, but it would be the only way." He stared into the eyes he loved so much. "Andi, we didn't work for Pinkertons. That was just a cover. The truth is that the people we've worked for are much more important than that.

"There are a lot of favors I could call in, but if I do that, people are gonna know that we're alive and you know that there are people who might come after us. It's why we faked our death in the first place. If I don't reach out to these people, two of my friends are gonna either wind up dead or back on a reservation. If I do contact them, I might bring danger here to everyone. I'm between a rock and hard place and I don't know which way to turn."

Andi knew what she wanted him to do, but it was for purely selfish reasons. After thinking she'd lost her men and being bereft, she'd just begun to come around when he'd come back from the grave. He'd promised to never go away again and she knew he would keep that promise. So far no one had tracked him down, so the ruse had worked. She'd told Arliss that she couldn't go through losing them again and she'd meant it.

But this wasn't just about herself. The pastor side of her demanded that she put others ahead of herself, but the part that was just a woman in love wanted Arliss to keep his mouth shut and stay safe.

"Are you asking me for permission?"

"Sort of. We think this is something we should decide together since it affects all of us," Arliss said. "We haven't forgotten our promise to you, and we'll keep it and never leave you again. We're supposed to do all we can to help others, but in this case, it's hard to know what will help the most."

Andi looked down. "Is this why you haven't proposed yet?"

"Yes. If I reach out to these contacts, are you willin' to take the risk on someone comin' after us? Can you live with that possibility?" he asked. "If you can't, I won't do it."

"If you don't, the outlook for Arrow and Wild Wind is bleak," Andi said. She reached out to brush a lock of sandy-brown hair from his forehead. When she touched him, something flowed through her, something that came from outside of them.

Arliss saw an intense expression on her face that signified that something powerful was taking place. He waited for her to speak.

Andi gave him a serene smile. "Arliss, you once said to me that God sent me back here so that I could do great things. Do you remember that?"

He smiled. "I sure do and I meant it."

"It's not just me who's supposed to do great things. It's you and I together," she said. "If we can help, we should. God will take care of the rest."

Taking her in his arms, Arliss said, "It's no wonder we love you so much. You have the biggest heart in the world, Andi Thatcher." He kissed her cheek. "Now, we need to figure out a creative approach to this. Something that will guarantee their safety from the military forever."

"Well, we have a bunch of creative friends. Maybe we should get together with them and discuss it," she said.

"If we do that, our friends in hiding should be there," Arliss said.

"I agree. I'll reach out to Marvin and see if we can set something up. It won't be suspicious for me to do that since we sit on town council together," Andi said.

"All right. We'll talk to Lucky and company," Arliss said. The weight he'd felt pressing down on him lifted and he knew that God had answered his prayers. "Let's set something up for Saturday night."

"That sounds good," she said.

"Ok. Now that that's settled, let's go play cards. I'll let you beat me this time," he said.

As they got up, Andi said, "There won't be any *letting* me win. I'll win fair and square, so be prepared to lose, Mr. Jackson."

"I look forward to it," he said, taking her hand and lacing his fingers through hers.

Hand in hand, they walked from the church, teasing each other, reassured about the future.

Chapter Ten

The following morning, Nick woke up to find that Maura had already gone. Although the guilt over being physical with her again was there, it wasn't as heavy as it had been before. His brain had been fuzzy the night before, but he remembered what had occurred between them. He smiled as he thought about the way Maura had run around naked while she'd dumped his stash of alcohol.

Thinking about the liquor made him thirsty for it and he looked over at his closet where a bottle of vodka sat behind some boxes on a shelf. The temptation to have just a little before breakfast was almost overwhelming, but he fought it. To keep from giving in to the urge, he got up, threw on his robe, and took his clothes over to the bathroom.

After washing and dressing, he went down to the kitchen. Usually he was down before Sylvia, getting the stove going and beginning to prepare breakfast. However, the stove was already hot and a bowl of freshly washed eggs sat on the counter. His mother didn't usually gather the eggs, so he wondered who had.

As he got out a couple of frying pans, Maura came in the kitchen door that led outside, carrying a milk pail.

She grinned at him as she set it on the counter. "Good morning," she signed.

"Good morning," he signed while saying the words. "Say it." He repeated it.

Maura said the phrase a few times and Nick praised her. She'd braided her hair and she looked pretty in the green gingham dress that Lulu had given her. He needed to buy her some clothing of her own.

She slid her arms around his waist. "Good morning," she said again, looking up at him.

A wave of longing swept through him as he gazed into her dark eyes. His eyes moved lower to her mouth. Cupping her face, he kissed her softly. "Good morning," he said, smiling. "Thank you for doing the milking and getting the eggs."

"I want to help. You work so hard. I should earn my way," she said.

"I appreciate it," he said, getting out a cutting board and an onion.

Maura watched in fascination as he cut up the onion with rapid, dexterous movements. She was good at cutting up food, but not like Nick. She'd never seen someone chop so quickly before. Sylvia entered the kitchen and greeted Nick in Italian. The family spoke it quite a lot, enjoying keeping the language alive since no one else in Echo spoke it. Maura liked the sound of it, but she hadn't tried to master any of it yet.

Nick kissed Sylvia's cheek. "Good morning, Mama."

"Good morning, Nicky. What are you making?" she asked, switching back to English.

"Omelets. I wish we had some fresh peppers, but I'll use onions, cheese, and ham since we don't," he said.

"Your father will eat anything with ham in it, so you can't go wrong," Sylvia said. "Good morning, Maura."

"Good morning, Sylvia," Maura said, enunciating carefully.

Sylvia smiled. "It's wonderful to hear you speak. I'm not all that good at Indian sign."

Nick said, "Keep practicing."

Maura stepped back as mother and son began cooking in earnest. She was happy to sit on a stool in a corner and watch them work. As they did, the rest of the family came and went from the kitchen. Gino usually set the table, but when Maura saw him taking the plates, she followed him and requested that he show her how.

Gino was happy to and Maura caught on quickly. She couldn't keep just sitting around all day. If she learned how they did things, she could make herself useful. Once the table was set, she went back to the kitchen and sat on the stool again. She didn't understand everything Nick and Sylvia said to each other, but she liked the way they argued good-naturedly over the food preparation.

She watched his expressive, handsome face and the way he moved his hands. He also hummed and sang softly, and she was entranced by his beautiful baritone voice. Sal would come into the kitchen and sometimes they sang harmony with each other, which was entertaining. It was easy to see how much they all loved each other from the affectionate way they interacted.

She wasn't left out. They all talked to her in sign and words and she began putting some of the English into context. Once they were all seated, Alfredo said the blessing and they began eating.

When someone rang the front doorbell, Gino got up to answer it. Marvin stood on the porch.

"Good morning," he said pleasantly. "May I have a word with you all?"

"Yeah. C'mon in," Gino said.

Everyone stopped eating when they saw Marvin follow Gino into the dining room.

He smiled at them. "I'm sorry to intrude on your meal, but I'm very happy to report that your loved ones are safe and sound in the hiding place." He took an envelope out of his suit pocket. "This is from Vanna."

He handed it to Sylvia who opened it immediately. Her eyes filled with tears as she read it and then passed it on.

Sal asked, "What are we gonna do about all of this? They can't stay hidden forever."

"You're correct," Marvin said. "We're working on a solution, but for now they're out of danger."

Sylvia said, "I want to see them. We all do."

Marvin said, "We'll set up a way to make that happen and very soon. We need to be very cautious about it. Finnley and his men came and searched our ranch last night. I'm sure we're being watched. Shadow was able to get them out of Billings without being found, but only barely. He's covered his tracks very well, like always, but going forward, we mustn't do anything to arouse suspicion that they're in the area."

Alfredo said, "You're right. It's hard, but we have to be patient."

"I'll let you know as soon as we can arrange for you to see them. In the meantime, Shadow will come over tonight to get the things that Vanna requested in her letter. He'll be able to sneak around without the guards out here being any the wiser. Put them outside the back door around ten and he'll take them to her," Marvin said.

Sal looked suspiciously at him. "What are you gettin' out of doing this? Is this some trick?"

Marvin smiled. "No. It's no trick. I'm friends with Wild Wind and Roxie. I don't know Arrow all that well, but I'm trying to extend some friendship to him and Vanna. Perhaps even to you. The other thing I'm getting out of it is the fun of scheming against the military. Scheming is one of the things I do best."

Nick grunted. "Yeah. We know."

Marvin chuckled. "Well, I'll let you finish your meal, but I'll be in touch soon."

"Thank you," Alfredo said. "I'll walk you out."

The Terranovas' relief was great, but their anxiety over the situation was only partially lessened. At that moment, they had no way to help find a solution. They had no friends in the military or any other organization who could assist them. Alfredo's comments to Finnley about that had been pure bluster, but Finnley had no way to know that.

As they finished breakfast, Alfredo remarked how ironic it was that they were now depending on their enemy for the protection of their loved ones.

Gino said, "I guess this is one of the mysterious ways God works, huh, Nicky?"

Nick nodded. "Yeah. It seems like He's working in a lot of mysterious ways lately." *Such as a beautiful redhead showing up here who still thinks I'm her master and who seems to want to help me.*

"Amen to that," Sylvia said.

Maura helped them clean up and then asked if she could go to the restaurant with Nick and Sylvia. Nick told her that she'd be bored since they'd be working, but Maura assured him that she wouldn't. So the three of them set out for Echo. She hadn't been away from the ranch since she'd arrived there in a state of panic, so she took the opportunity to look around.

Gazing back at the ranch, she thought that it was beautiful. The huge red brick structure stood in the foreground with the barns, bunkhouses, a windmill, and silos behind it. Cattle roamed the pastures that extended beyond the horizon and horses grazed in another pasture.

Since he would be coming home much later than Sylvia, Nick rode his horse beside the buggy that Sylvia drove so he had transportation once his mother went home. Nick was careful to include Maura in the conversation but not to stare at her. Images of the previous night plagued him and he knew that he had to curtail what was happening between him and Maura.

Maura had never been to Echo before. The people who'd had her hadn't made it that far before she'd escaped. She was sure that they would have searched the town for her, though. Hopefully they were gone. Although she'd mostly lived in Indian villages, she had been to various towns, so she wasn't unfamiliar with what one looked like.

Her hosts spoke to quite a few people, and she was introduced to some of them. They drove around the back of a row of store fronts and pulled up to the back of the third one. Nick made both of the horses more comfortable since they would be there for the day. When they went inside,

Allie was already there, getting the stoves heating and putting large pots of water on to boil.

Nick wasn't happy about it. "Hello, Allie. How are you?"

"I'm good, boss," the pretty blonde said, smiling.

He smiled briefly at her, but said, "Where's Tyler? He's supposed to be doing all of this."

"I don't know. He wasn't here when I arrived and he hasn't shown up yet."

Nick clamped down on his anger. "I'm gonna have to talk to him again. This is ridiculous."

Knowing how Nick expected punctuality and dependability, Allie didn't blame him for being upset. She refrained from saying anything, however.

Sylvia said, "Go ahead with your other work, Allie, sweetie. I'll help Nick with these other things."

"All right, Mama T.," Allie said.

Nick introduced Allie to Maura, but was nonplussed since he didn't know Maura's last name. He ended up just saying her first name and not giving an explanation or further details. He told Allie that Maura was a friend of the family.

"It's nice to meet you, Maura," Allie said.

Maura carefully repeated the phrase back to her and Allie went out into the dining room. Looking around the kitchen, Maura saw that it was as spotless as the Terranovas' kitchen at home. The white walls and green curtains made the space light and airy. The floors gleamed from their nightly scrubbing and the windows sparkled.

While Sylvia was the boss of the kitchen at home, Nick ruled at the restaurant. Maura was aware of a change in Sylvia's demeanor. Instead of the person in charge, she became a co-chef, content to hand over the reins to Nick and concentrate on what she loved most, the actual cooking.

When she was making meals at home, she didn't have to direct a lot of people since she normally cooked alone, outside of Nick, of course. Even though the kitchen at the house was usually a busy place, her family members knew what to do and how things were done. However, at the restaurant, there were new people to instruct and correct if necessary and Sylvia was a little too tenderhearted about it. While she was tough with her family, she found it hard to be so with other people.

Nick did not. He demanded a lot from their employees, but no more so than he was willing to give of himself. He usually wasn't nasty—unless pushed to be—but he was firm about what he wanted done and how he wanted it accomplished. Sylvia knew that much of their success was due to his excellent management skills and his ability to multi-task. She didn't know how he knew what was happening in the dining room when he was cooking, but he did.

Sylvia could tell that Nick was very angry from the sudden tension in his shoulders and she pitied Tyler whenever the boy showed up. She was irritated about it, too, but she knew that it was best dealt with by Nick, who wouldn't let Tyler give him any excuses.

Maura wasn't sure what to do with herself, so she did what she'd done at home: retreated to a corner and sat on a stool. This way she could observe without being in the way. And there was a lot to observe. One of the local farmers, Rocky George arrived with a load of fresh chickens for them and Nick chatted with him a few minutes while they unloaded them.

Tyler Scoggins showed up, sauntering through the kitchen door. Catching sight of Maura, he said, "Hello there. Where'd you come from, beautiful?"

Maura said, "Hello."

"Hey!" Nick shouted from over by the stoves. "Where've you been? You were supposed to be here by nine getting everything ready. It's not Allie's job to do that and you know it. She has her own work to do."

Tyler scowled and put on an apron. "Sorry. I overslept," he said, his blue eyes holding resentment in them.

Nick came over to him. "Do you wanna keep your job?"

"Yeah."

"Then start being here on time and be ready to work. I don't pay you to goof off and leave everyone else to pick up the slack for you. Don't be late again or you're fired. Got it?" Nick asked.

Tyler nodded. "Got it."

Nick regarded him silently for a moment. "Good. Now go over to Ross' and get our usual order from him. He'll have it ready so don't be longer than fifteen minutes. If you're not back here by then, don't bother comin' back. I don't have time for games, Tyler."

"Ok, ok," Tyler said, going out the door.

Nick let out a frustrated sound and looked at Maura. She was so quiet he'd almost forgotten she was there until Tyler had spoken to her. He smiled at her. "Are you bored?" he signed.

"No. I like watching everything," she said, glad that he wasn't angry with her. "I am fine. Go back to work and do not worry about me."

"All right," he said. "Let us know if you want anything."

She nodded and he got back to the task at hand.

Watching Nick in his element as he cooked and ran the kitchen was the best entertainment Maura had ever witnessed. He and Sylvia argued and collaborated on dishes, he yelled at Tyler when the young man moved too slow for Nick's taste, and kidded around with whoever wandered through the kitchen.

It was funny to watch Nick tell one of his friends to take customers' food out to the tables if Allie was swamped. Nick called them his "guest wait staff". People had become accustomed to this and even considered it an honor to be chosen. Some had learned the numbering pattern of the tables. Billy Two Moons was Nick's guest waiter that day.

The handsome brave had come over to see if Nick wanted more lamb for the next day and Nick had put him to work.

He'd just come back into the kitchen from serving a table of three and said, "I have news."

"Yeah? What's that?" Nick asked.

"There's another little Two Moons on the way," he said, grinning.

Nick and Sylvia congratulated him.

"Our little girl should arrive in September sometime," Billy said.

Sylvia chuckled. "So you're a magician and know what it's going to be, huh?"

Billy laughed. "Well, I'm prayin' awful hard for a girl, so hopefully those prayers are answered. Put in a good word for me, ok?"

"You got it," Nick said. "Now take this out to table four."

Billy saluted him, picked up the loaded tray, and went into the dining room. He came back into the kitchen with the empty tray, upon which he'd stacked some dirty dishes from one of the tables he'd been passing. He put the tray on the table by the sink where Tyler was washing dishes.

He noticed Maura and smiled at her. She smiled back and signed, "Hello." She was intrigued by the sight of an Indian. He was the first one she'd seen since she'd been traded.

He came over to her and said, "I'm Billy Two Moons," as he held out a hand to her.

She took it and Billy shook hers. "Maura," she said.

"Good to meet you, Maura. Did Nick hire you?" Billy asked, letting her hand go.

In sign, she said, "I do not speak much English. I was raised by the Comanche."

Billy was surprised. "Comanche? You are white."

"I was captured when I was little and they kept me," she said.

Billy knew that some tribes didn't treat their captives kindly. "I see. How did you get here?"

"They sold me to some fur traders from the far north. I escaped from them and Nick's family took me in. I am his now," she said.

Billy arched an eyebrow at her. "Nick is courting you?" he asked, hoping he'd understood her correctly.

"He does not like me to say so, but I am his slave now," she signed.

Both of Billy's eyebrows rose and he looked at Nick. "We do not have slaves in this culture. I think that you are mistaken. Nick is a good man. His family is very good, too."

"But he captured me," she said. "This is very confusing."

"Perhaps I can help clear things up for you. Tell me what happened."

Maura told him her story, omitting the part about her and Nick becoming lovers and his drinking problem. "Because he captured me, I am his," she finished.

Billy pulled over another stool and sat on it. "You are no longer a slave, Maura," he signed. "We do not have slaves anymore. You are free to do as you like. I can understand why you would be confused about this since you were in captivity so long, but you do not belong to anyone."

Maura's gaze was trained on Nick as he worked. "But I have no one or anything except him and his family. They are kind and generous. I do not want to leave them."

Billy was sympathetic to her plight. "I am so sorry for everything you have endured. You are safe with them. I would not worry about leaving them just yet. You need to learn more English and more about how to live in this culture before you go out on your own. I will be happy to help you in any way I can."

She smiled. "Thank you. What tribe are you from?"

"I was adopted by white people when I was a baby and raised in this culture. I found out a few years ago that I am Cheyenne, Lakota, Nez Perce, and I have some white blood. That's why my hair is reddish-brown," he replied. "My son has my dark hair, but my wife, Nina's, green eyes. She was also a captive, but was raised by the Kiowa and then traded to the Cheyenne. I met her when I went to the reservation where she was living.

"My friend, Wild Wind, escaped with me and my other friend, Lucky … well, that is a long story for another time, but just know that you are not alone."

"Thank you."

"You are welcome," Billy said. He patted her shoulder and left out the back door.

It gave Maura a warm feeling inside to have made a friend and it gave her hope that things might work out for her.

Chapter Eleven

After Mama T.'s closed, Maura helped Allie fold napkins and set the tables in preparation for the next day. She'd also washed some dishes when Keith had gotten busy hauling up food from the basement that Nick needed. He'd relieved Tyler around five o'clock. Keith knew Indian sign since he was good friends with Lucky and Wild Wind and he conversed easily with Maura.

She liked the big young man and she'd been happy to help, enjoying the feeling of camaraderie with everyone else. It also made her feel good that she was contributing to the business in a small way.

Sylvia had asked her if she'd wanted to go home with her, but she'd declined, indicating that she could help if needed. Just like Nick put his friends to work, he wasn't averse to Maura doing simple work. He'd shown her how he wanted things chopped up, which way he wanted the meats cut, and where things were located.

The way he worked was much the way he made love: passionate, intense, and yet fun. Once Tyler had gone for the day she saw Nick's attitude soften a little since he didn't have to keep on Keith about what needed to be done. Much like he did at home, Nick hummed, sang, and joked around with whomever was around.

Allie didn't mind Maura's help since it would allow her to get done early. Her and Adam's wedding was only two weeks away and it would give her a little extra time to do some things. She knew that Maura didn't understand much of what she said, but the other woman didn't seem to mind listening to her as she prattled on about her fiancé and their upcoming nuptials.

Maura had had a couple friends in her tribe and she felt that she and Allie could develop a good friendship. It was much the same with Lulu. Although Sal's wife didn't know much Indian sign since she hadn't caught on to it very well, she was still friendly with Maura. It was nice to have women to talk to again.

Nick sat up front by the register, counting the intake of revenue from the day. He smiled at the amount of profits they'd made. They'd done so well that he decided to give everyone a little extra in their pay that week, except for Tyler. He hated being hard, but the boy wasn't performing well at all.

When Tyler had first shown signs of laziness, Nick had asked more about his home life, if he was tired, or had any other difficulties that might contribute to his lackluster work performance. His family wasn't well off, but they were making ends meet. There was no one severely ill in the family that required care, no recent deaths, and Tyler himself had no condition that would account for his mindset.

Therefore, Nick could only conclude that Tyler simply wanted to get paid for doing as little as possible. Accordingly, he didn't deserve a bonus. His family might be well-off now, but it hadn't always been that way. From the time he'd been old enough, Nick had worked the family business, doing his part to grow it into the successful enterprise it was now. He expected no less of his employees.

He watched Allie and Maura working and chatting and smiled. Allie was a force to be reckoned with and ran the dining room, along with Jessie, with a friendly, yet iron, fist. She knew the patrons very well and what their favorite dishes were. She and her mother were fast, attentive servers who were able to anticipate customer needs.

97

When he and Sylvia had decided to open a restaurant, they'd offered Allie the job of managing the dining room, knowing that she'd be perfect for it. They hadn't been wrong, which was why they'd already given Allie two raises. Keith had also made himself indispensable and if he hadn't already been dedicated to Leah Quinn's business, Nick would have tried to convince Keith to work for him full-time.

He'd offered full-time to Jessie, but since she'd recently had a baby, she didn't want to be away from home any more than necessary. She and Thad also had three other younger children and she didn't want to lose time with them, either. Four part-time shifts per week was all that she was willing to work.

Once he was done with the sales receipts and had made up the deposit for the next day, Nick put the money into the floor safe and went to see if Keith needed any help. However, Keith was already finished and getting ready to leave.

"All set, boss," he said as soon as Nick entered the kitchen. "The floor is clean enough that if you spilled a plate of spaghetti on it, I'd eat it right there."

Nick laughed. "I appreciate the good job, but we're not gonna try it."

Keith put his apron in the dirty clothes bin and said, "If that's everything, I'm going home to my beautiful wife and the rest of our crazy family."

"Say hello to them all and tell Molly that I really liked that last ad she ran for us," Nick said.

"I will. Allie! Are you ready?" Keith shouted.

"Yes! I'll be right there!"

Nick said, "You guys have been around my family too much."

Keith said, "We're like that, too. T.J. is so used to it that he doesn't wake up anymore."

Nick smiled as he thought about Thad and Jessie's baby. The little fellow had Thad's brown eyes, but Jessie's brown hair and smile. The one-year-old was a busy boy and the apple of his father's eye. Thad was sixty now and it was the first time he was a father to an infant. He was enjoying the experience to the fullest, too. However, he also loved their other kids, and always made sure they never felt slighted.

Keith said, "Um, I can't help but notice that Tyler isn't pulling his weight. Stuff shouldn't be so backed up when I get here."

Nick's jaw clenched. "I know. Nothing I say is getting through to him."

"I figured. He's always been lazy," Keith said. "That's not gonna change. I think you should hire Maura. She was keeping up pretty good with things and she seems like a quick learner."

Oh, boy. "She doesn't know English, so I'm not sure how well she'd do until she learned more. It would be hard for her to deal with the customers." Nick wanted to put some distance between them and that wouldn't be accomplished if Maura was working with him every day.

"She can keep up with the dishes and help you cook once Mama T. goes home. That's more than Tyler's been doing," Keith said. "She'll pick up the language before long."

"I'll think about it," Nick said. There was no way he could explain to Keith how complicated the situation was, but he had no one but himself to blame for it all.

Allie and Maura came into the kitchen and Keith and Allie left. Nick made sure that all of the lamps in the front were out and did the same in the kitchen. As he and Maura stepped outside, he realized that she was going to have to ride double with him.

He saddled his horse and swung up, holding out his hand to Maura. She took it and he swung her up behind him. Her arms encircled his waist and he felt her lean her head against his back. He didn't start out his horse right away, instead sighing at how nice it felt to just sit like that.

After a few minutes, Nick got underway, his thoughts turbulent. He didn't understand what was happening here. There had been women he'd caught looking appreciatively at him since Ming Li's death, but he'd never been interested outside of that one woman. That was only because he'd been drunk, though.

Chelsea was a desirable, eligible woman who had made her interest in him only too clear and yet she didn't move him at all. But Maura had appeared only three days ago and he'd slept with her twice. Of course, he'd been drunk, but still … Judging by the craving for her he was feeling at the moment, it didn't matter whether he was drunk, he'd still want her.

I've fallen so far that I don't even recognize myself most days. I used to know right from wrong—well, I still know it, I just don't seem to have the strength to keep to the right path. I used to think that with God's help I could weather anything, that I could face any foe and win.

I know that's not true now. I never had anything truly horrible happen to me before I lost my family and I didn't know how to handle it. I still don't. The weakness isn't yours, Lord, it's mine. Help me find the strength to stop my self-destructive behavior and to do the right thing by Maura.

While Nick prayed for deliverance, Maura's thoughts were very different. She was the happiest she'd ever been and in her happiness, she hugged Nick a little tighter. Nick and Billy had told her that she wasn't a slave and maybe she really wasn't. Nick had certainly never made her feel like one, but she felt devotion to him anyway.

Her allegiance to Nick was one of her choosing instead of one borne out of fear. She thanked the Great Spirit for delivering her from her hellish existence and for giving her to Nick. His suffering was different than hers, but no less painful. She had been a slave to people, at the mercy of their whims and moods, but he was a slave to the bottle, grief, and guilt.

Whose misery was worse? There was no way to measure it, but Maura felt that hers was ending while Nick's was ongoing. He'd said his being with her was disrespectful to her, but it didn't feel that way to her. He didn't want to use her and she was touched by his thoughtfulness, but it didn't feel like he was using her. Somehow she had to make him understand that the way he treated her made her feel special, as though her feelings mattered.

Arriving home, Nick sent Maura inside and put his horse away. His body clamored for alcohol and he thought about the bottle of vodka in his closet. The burning thirst inside intensified tenfold since he hadn't had as much booze the night before as his body was used to. He'd made it through the day, but it had been hard.

Going inside, he heard laughter coming from the dining room and found his family playing cards there. His stomach knotted because he knew they were going to want him to sit in for at least a few hands.

Alfredo said, "There's the other one. Your mama said that things were busy again today. C'mon and sit down. There's a nice plate of cheese and crackers and we just opened some of that wine that Lulu's folks sent us."

Nick's mind screamed *noooo!*, but his body screamed *yes!* If he didn't drink any wine, it would be noticed. Maybe if he just had a little, it would take the edge off and he could prevent getting plastered later on.

He smiled and sat down. "All right. What are we playin'?" he asked, popping a piece of cheese in his mouth.

"Gin," Gino said, dealing him in. "Sally's winning."

Nick said, "Not anymore."

Sal raised an eyebrow. "Oh, yeah?"

"Yeah."

"We'll see about that," Sal said.

Nick lost at everything: cards, his battle with the bottle, and in his resolve to stay away from Maura. He'd kept from getting sloshed during the card game, but as soon as he'd come upstairs, he'd cracked the vodka open, downing almost half of it before Maura had shown up and taken it away from him. She'd gotten rid of it, but between the three glasses of wine he'd drunk and the vodka, the damage was done.

Maura had gotten him undressed and into bed before crawling in with him. He'd been so intoxicated that he'd just gone to sleep with her lying against him. And that's how he came to wake up close to dawn with a sour stomach and her next to him. Slowly, so he didn't wake her, he pulled open his nightstand drawer and got a piece of peppermint candy.

Easing back in bed, he sucked on it and watched Maura sleep. As his gaze roamed over her face, he knew he needed to broach the subject of marriage to her again. How would he explain that to his family? What reason could he give them? That they'd fallen in love? No. That wouldn't wash, not when he'd avoided women so much.

He didn't want them to think less of Maura, so it would have to be something plausible. Protection. He would do it to protect her, which wasn't a lie. Marrying her would protect her reputation in case she did become pregnant and it would also protect her from whomever had kept her as a slave. If they came looking for her, which was a possibility, she would be under his protection and that of his family.

Lightly running the back of his knuckles over her delicate cheekbone, he couldn't imagine anyone wanting to hurt her, but he knew that sort of men existed. A wave of anger rolled over him as he thought about her suffering so. He was startled to hear a soft knock on his suite door. Slipping out of bed, he put on a robe and left his bedroom, closing the door softly behind him.

Opening the outer door, he found Sal in the hallway and let him in.

"Are you alone?" Sal whispered.

"No."

Sal caught the mingled scents of vodka and peppermint on Nick's breath. "Were you drinking again last night after we all went to bed?"

Nick shut his eyes. "Yes."

Sal was deeply troubled. Drinking and sleeping around were not things he associated with Nick. Something was wrong. "Nicky, what's goin' on with you? Don't lie to me, just talk to me. I'm not gonna say anything. It'll just be between the two of us, ok?"

He wanted to lie to Sal, to tell him that he'd just been having trouble sleeping and that he'd be fine, but he couldn't force the lies past his lips. When he opened his eyes, tears glistened in them. "I'm an alcoholic, Sal, and I can't stay away from Maura now."

Again, Sal couldn't connect what he was hearing with the man he'd thought his big brother was. Nick's former seminarian life had seemed to still be a part of him in a lot of ways even after he'd married Ming Li. Even after he'd come home a broken man from Japan, Nick hadn't shown these tendencies.

The only aberration from Nick's strict beliefs had been the night at the Burgundy House. Nick had never gone back with him and any time he'd ever accompanied Sal to Helena, he'd never gone out to a saloon with Sal. He'd always stayed in their hotel room. He knew that Nick drank wine here and there, but their whole family did, except for Vanna.

"You're not an alcoholic, Nick. You're just having a little too much here and there. I know all about that," Sal said. "Just cut back. As far as Maura goes, I can understand. She's beautiful and it's been a long time since you were with someone."

Nick said, "Sal, there are days when I can't wait to get home and open a bottle and it's nothing for me to kill almost a fifth of whiskey by myself on a daily basis. If I don't drink for a couple of days, I go into withdrawal. It's not a question of will, it's a question of what my body wants. That's an alcoholic."

The honesty and shame in Nick's expression convinced Sal. His brother wasn't stupid, and what he was describing certainly fit with alcoholic behavior. Sal had cut back a lot on his drinking, mainly because he loved Lulu and had no need to go out drinking anymore. But even when he'd still been carousing, he'd never craved alcohol that way. He'd never had any kind of withdrawal symptoms.

"How long has it been going on?" he asked.

"It started not long after I came home from Japan," Nick said, sitting down in a chair. "It's been a gradual thing. Sort of snuck up on me, I guess you'd say."

Sal sat down with him. "It was a way to cope with it all, huh? I understand that. When did it start getting out of hand?"

"I'm not exactly sure, but I knew after that night at the Burgundy House that there was a problem. That's why I've never gone with you to a bar again."

Sal nodded. "I gotta admit, you really surprised me that night, but I just figured you needed to let off some steam. I never judged you for it. You'd been through hell and I thought that you deserved a night to just let go."

"I let go, all right," Nick remarked. "I've never let go like that again—until the night after Maura arrived. I was drinking out by the fire and it was a good thing she came out there because I was really drunk. She helped get me in the house and took care of me when I got sick. I explained to her about the drinking." He smiled. "She dumped my stash the other night. She just didn't know about the vodka I still had in here. She dumped that last night."

Sal chuckled. "So she's appointed herself your guardian. You should marry her just for that." Sobering, he said, "Nick, the rest of us need to know. We have wine with dinner almost every night, and the wine cellar and other booze, too. You're not strong enough to stay away from it and it's too easy for you to get it here."

"I know, but I don't want everyone else to have to give it up because of me. It's not fair to you."

"No, what's not fair is you not sayin' anything. I feel bad because I've been contributing to the problem all this time. We all have, but we didn't know it. Everyone else is gonna feel the same way," Sal said.

"They don't need this right now. With everything going on with the military and Noodle and Arrow being in hiding, this will just add more strain and I'm worried about Pop. I don't want him havin' another hard attack."

"He's fine," Sal said. "He's gonna be more upset if you wait much longer to tell them."

"You don't understand, Sal. You don't know what it's like to be me, how everyone holds me to this standard because I was gonna be a priest. They're gonna be so disappointed in me. I'm sure you are."

"You're right; I *am* disappointed, but only because you didn't reach out to me. You didn't talk to me about anything. I knew you had to be suffering, but you wouldn't talk about it. You were constantly after me about my transgressions, but you wouldn't let me help you," Sal said. "I might be your little brother, but I'm not a kid anymore."

Nick nodded. "I know. I didn't want to admit my weaknesses. I thought I could get a handle on it. The only reason I kept on you was because I was worried that you would turn into an alcoholic and I didn't want that for you. I really was trying to protect you, but I couldn't tell you the real reason why I was so pushy about it. I'm your big brother. You're supposed to be able to look up to me, not be disappointed in me."

Sal read between the lines and he realized that his family had been doing an unknown disservice to Nick. It was meant in a complimentary way, but they'd been putting pressure on Nick to be better than other people. Nick had partly brought it on himself, but their family had taken it the rest of the way.

They'd relied on him for spiritual and moral guidance as though he really was a priest. He wasn't. He hadn't finished his training and he wasn't experienced in the vocation. They wanted him to say the blessing most of the time and were always asking him to pray for them. Had they prayed for Nick? He was sure his parents had, but Sal wasn't much for praying. He wasn't sure if Gino prayed much.

They had all tried to be there for Nick, but he'd always seemed to have things in control. It was a lesson to Sal about looks being deceiving and in not paying close enough attention to a loved one. He felt terrible.

"I'm not disappointed in you because you have a problem, Nicky. It takes courage to admit you even have one. I just wish that you'd felt comfortable enough to tell us," Sal said. "I'm disappointed in myself for not being there for you and for just assuming that you were doing better than you are, then what you have been all this time."

"It's all right. I worked hard to hide it, so don't blame yourself." Nick rubbed his eyes. "I don't know how to tell everyone else."

"The same way you just told me. I'll help you," Sal said. "You better do it sooner than later, though."

"I'll call a family meeting after dinner on Sunday. Just don't let me drink wine during the meal."

"Ok."

"In the meantime, what do I do about Maura?"

Sal scratched the side of his head. "How does she feel about being with you?"

"She doesn't feel ashamed or like I'm using her. She's been through her own sort of hell. From the time the Comanche captured her, she was just a slave to them. No one adopted her. She's been abused, misused, and has hardly ever known kindness.

"She told me that only one other man besides me ever touched her with kindness. She says that what's happening between us is beautiful, not shameful."

Sal said, "Far be it from me to preach to you about anything Godly, but maybe He brought you together so you could heal each other. I think the drinking is your worst problem. Deal with that for the time being."

"I gotta marry her, but I can't wait for her to learn English and go through Catechism classes. That'll take a couple of months. She could get pregnant at any time. I know how this sounds, but I can't control myself around her. I feel so ashamed about it."

"I understand why you feel that way, but you need to cut yourself some slack, Nick. You're only human. Would her getting pregnant be such a bad thing?"

Before Maura had come along, he hadn't entertained the notion of becoming seriously involved with anyone, let alone having a child. However, as he and Sal talked, he found that the idea greatly appealed to him.

"No. Not really. I can't tell you how much I miss Jake, how much I want to hold him and see his smile," Nick said.

Sal blinked away his sudden tears. "Me, too, Nicky. Me, too."

"He could never be replaced," Nick said. "But I would love to have another baby."

"Maybe this is what's meant to be. Maybe you can't fight it because you're not supposed to."

"You might be right. I don't know what to think."

Sal said, "You'll just have to explain it all to the folks and you'll just have a wedding here. You already know that Andi does a great wedding. Lulu didn't convert until after we were married and that was her idea. I never expected her to do it. Maura could do the same thing if she's willing."

Nick regarded Sal for a few moments. "I owe you a big apology, Sally."

"For what?"

"I didn't know you were so smart. I underestimated you."

Sal's grin matched Nick's. "Apology accepted, but just don't do it again. I'll give you some other advice. Get Maura out of here before the parents get up. And get this wedding planned pronto. That way you won't have to keep sneaking around like Lulu and I did."

Nick laughed. "Everyone knew you were doing that. You two didn't hide it very well."

Sal covered his face with his hands. "You knew? Why didn't anyone say anything?"

Shrugging, Nick said, "It really wasn't my business and I think Mama and Pop figured there wasn't much to be done about it."

"Well, I don't regret it, and I have a hunch you won't, either," Sal said. "I'll go now so you can get Maura up and out of here."

Nick stood when Sal did, pulling him into an embrace. "Thanks for everything. You're a good brother and from now on, I won't underestimate you. Your support means a lot to me."

Sal clapped his back. "You're welcome. What are brothers for if not to lend support?"

Nick kissed the side of his head and let him go. "You're right."

"I'll see you at breakfast," Sal said.

"Ok."

After Sal left, Nick went back into his bedroom. The sight of Maura in his bed did something to him inside. He remembered watching Ming Li the same way. Both women were so different in appearance and so beautiful. He used to love seeing Ming Li's coal black hair spread over her pillow. Now it was Maura's auburn tresses that adorned a pillow. The wavy locks looked like a beautiful, copper river flowing along the bed.

Going over to her side of the bed, Nick gently shook her. "Maura, time to get up."

She opened her eyes a little and gave him a sleepy smile.

"Good morning," he said.

"Good morning," she said, looking him over.

Playfully, she reached out and undid the tie of his robe. Nimbly, she stood up on the bed and kissed him while pushing the robe away from his shoulders.

Nick groaned and pulled away from her. "I cannot do this right now," he signed. "I have to go help make breakfast like I always do."

"You cannot be late just this once?" she coaxed before kissing his shoulder.

"Just this once," he said, shuddering a little as she kissed him again.

Maura kissed him, her hunger for him building. She squealed a little when he tipped her over onto the bed. Laughing softly, he took off his robe and lay down with her, giving in to the passion she ignited in him.

Chapter Twelve

A while later, Nick explained the concept of brushing teeth to Maura. She understood it, she had just never used a toothbrush before. Usually she just chewed the end of a twig and used the frayed end to clean her teeth. She'd also never used toothpaste before.

Nick showed her the new tubes that Colgate had just started to make. They were easier and cleaner to use than the jars the paste used to come in.

"You just squeeze some on the toothbrush and scrub your teeth with it. Like this," he said, demonstrating with the clean toothbrush he'd given her.

He handed it to her and she sniffed the paste. She could smell the mint in it and then touched the tip of her tongue to it to taste it. It wasn't bad.

They stood in the bathroom with the door open. Gino walked by, backed up, and smiled.

"What are you doing?"

"Showing Maura how to brush her teeth," Nick replied.

Gino chuckled. "I'm sure it's strange for her to use a toothbrush instead of a stick. Toothpaste, too."

Nick signed, "I'll leave you to it," to Maura. "I better get downstairs."

She nodded and began brushing her teeth as he left the bathroom. It was another thing in what she knew would be a long list of new things to learn.

Arriving at the restaurant, Nick was relieved to see Tyler's horse tied out back. When he went inside, he was even more pleased to see that Tyler had the stoves going and water boiling. He'd hauled potatoes and flour up from the basement and everything was arranged as it should be.

Maybe my attitude with him yesterday did some good after all, he thought.

Tyler came into the kitchen from the dining room and Nick smiled at him. "Looks like you've been busy. Good work."

Tyler smiled a little. "Thanks. I'll go get the meat order."

"Ok," Nick said.

Once Tyler had gone, Sylvia said, "Is that the same Tyler? I don't recognize him."

"Me neither. Let's hope this one stays," Nick said. "All right, Mama. Get that sauce goin'."

Sylvia gave him a stern look. "Don't think you're gonna boss me around. I know my job. Now get out of my way and let me do it."

And so the usual bickering began.

Lulu missed Vanna. Since coming to Echo, she'd grown close to her sister-in-law and loved working with her in their joint venture, Bella Donna. They had opened the boutique/beauty salon in February and business was going well. She operated the boutique side while Vanna cut and styled hair.

Vanna also advised ladies on their makeup and suggested new techniques to hide imperfections. Some of the women were hesitant about using it, but Vanna explained to them that makeup had been around since ancient times and that much of the upper classes and nobility used it— even men.

The ladies were afraid of being branded a harlot like the soiled doves in the saloons if they used lip rouge and the like. Vanna showed them how just a little bit can improve a person's appearance and still look natural.

Her desire to help people feel good about themselves stemmed from her own low self-esteem over her plumper build. However, since meeting Arrow, who preferred women with a fuller figure, she'd blossomed when she'd seen how much he desired and loved her.

These thoughts made Lulu smile as she opened the shop door and led Maura inside. Nick had asked her to help Maura pick out some clothes so that she didn't have to keep borrowing hers. She had some clothes in the store that she knew would fit Maura. She thought that it would be better to start with the simpler dresses since Maura didn't seem the type to sit around all day in fancy dresses that weren't conducive to work. She also thought that a few skirts and blouses would be a good choice, along with underclothing and sleepwear.

Maura followed Lulu through the shop as she assisted her in choosing apparel. She liked all of the pretty dresses, skirts, and blouses. Lulu was very helpful and they had fun deciding which outfits worked best for her body type and coloring. She decided that Maura also needed dresses for social events.

She chose two: an emerald blue and a sea foam green dress. Both would look wonderful on Maura. She had Maura try on the blue dress and was thrilled that it fit the redhead perfectly. Staring in the mirror, Maura liked the way she looked and wondered what Nick would think. It was so important to her that she please him, not just so he would keep her, but because she cared about what he thought of her as a person.

She almost said as much to Lulu, but then remembered that no one except Sal knew about her and Nick. So she kept those thoughts to herself as she changed back into her other dress. Lulu packaged up all of her new things and said that she'd take them home with her when she closed the shop that day.

Maura knew where Mama T.'s was from Bella Donna, so she set out for it, walking quickly and keeping to herself as she made her way along the dirt street. She was just turning the corner when a hand slipped under her arm and yanked her to a stop.

"There you are!"

Maura's worst nightmare, Red Timmons, stood glaring down at her with rage in his blue eyes. She pulled against his grip, but he was too strong.

"Oh, no," he said in Comanche. "You are not getting away from me again. I will teach you to run away."

Maura had no doubt just what sort of lesson he intended to teach her. She thought of Nick and his family and how much she wanted to be with Nick. He and Billy had told her that there was no more slavery and she believed them. Resentment and anger gave her the courage to raise her chin and meet his gaze.

In her native tongue, she said, "I am not your slave. Slavery is not allowed in this culture. Take your hand off me and leave me alone."

Red's nostrils flared as his anger grew stronger. "I paid for you and you are mine. I will also teach you to not talk back to me."

"I do not belong to you or anyone. Let me go, or else," she said.

He let out a short laugh. "Or else what?"

She might not be a physical match for him, but she wasn't stupid. Filling her lungs, she let out the loudest scream she could and struggled in earnest, drawing attention to them.

"Shut up!" Red shouted. "Shut your mouth!"

Maura kept screaming and fighting him. He pulled back his hand and cracked her across the face. Pain and dizziness made Maura fall to her knees. A swift kick to her side followed the first blow.

"Make one more move and I'll drop you where you stand, mister," said an icy voice that stopped the foot Red had poised for a second kick.

"She's my wife," Red said. "She ran away."

The man came around to Red's front and he saw that the man wore a sheriff's badge. He held a gun on Red.

Evan said, "I don't care who she is or what she did. We don't allow abuse around here."

A crowd had started to gather around them. Lulu had heard the commotion and she came running to Maura as Shadow, who had been with Evan, picked her up. Maura cried out at the pain being moved caused her even though Shadow was as gentle as possible.

"Maura! What happened?" Lulu asked Evan.

"This piece of scum here says that she's his wife and that she ran away from him. I guess he figured that gave him the right to beat her. He figured wrong," Evan said.

Fury turned Lulu's green eyes to glittering emerald. "She's not his wife! He bought her from the Comanche and he was keeping her as a slave! She ran away and came to our place to hide. He has no claim to her."

Red sneered at her. "She's lyin'."

"I am not!" Lulu said. "I was there when we found her."

Evan put a pair of handcuffs on Red. "Well, I guess we can add slavery charges to your assault ones. Now, move." He shoved Red in the direction of the sheriff's office.

Shadow said, "I'll take her to the clinic."

"Ok," Evan said.

Lulu said, "Maura, it'll be all right now. I'll just close up the shop and be right along, Shadow."

He nodded, his face tight as he smiled coldly at Red. "I'll see you soon, you cowardly piece of crap. You better hope that the good sheriff keeps me on my leash. I don't take kindly to men who hit women." He moved off down the street with Maura.

Evan said, "Forget him. I got first dibs on your pathetic hind end."

Shadow heard him and laughed.

Lulu had barely gotten her story out to Nick before he dropped the plate of food he'd been preparing down on the counter and hurried from the kitchen. He ran through the dining room and out the front door, making a right and sprinting for the clinic. Entering, he stood in the waiting room for a moment before sitting down.

He didn't know what room Maura was in and he figured it was best to let Erin work without interruption. Leaning forward in his chair, he leaned his elbows on his knees, bowed his head, and prayed. His prayer was interrupted by the sounds of hooves on the wooden floor. Looking up, he saw Erin and Win's burro, Sugar, walking into the waiting room.

During the day, she often kept Win company in his side of the medical building, but she sometimes sneaked over to Erin's practice to visit with the patients. Trotting by her side was a little jack that was about a month old. Sugar's son was a comical sight with his spindly little legs and big ears. He'd inherited his dam's outgoing personality and was, as Thad liked to say, hell on hooves.

The little fellow followed Sugar over to Nick, sniffing him over as Sugar nudged Nick's arm to be petted. Even though it wasn't cold out, she still wore a lightweight, pink sweater that Evan had made for her. The burro was very proud of her sweaters and loved wearing them. Nick laughed when he noticed what Sugar's son wore. The little leather vest sported a deputy's badge on the left shoulder.

Nick scratched Sugar behind her ears and the foal put his little front hooves up on Nick's knee, butting in for his share of the attention. Win came looking for his wayward burros.

"Sugar! You're not supposed to be over here," he said.

Nick smiled at the Chinaman. "That's what you get for teaching her how to open doors."

Win said, "Very funny, Nick. How are you?"

"Uh, well, not great at the moment. My friend Maura was brought here. She was attacked by a man," he said.

"Oh, she belongs to you. I heard about what happened from Shadow. He crossed through my side before heading over to the jail. He was really angry, so I calmed him down a little," Win said.

"Me, too. Lulu said that he claimed Maura is his wife, but she's not," Nick said.

Win sat down by Nick. "I know. One of the reasons Shadow was so ticked off is because the guy kept her as a slave. He can't stand the idea of someone being held against their will."

The foal trotted around the waiting room, came back to them, and promptly turned around and kicked Win's shin.

"Ow, Basco! Knock that off," Win said. "You wouldn't think that would hurt much, but it does. He's like Sugar: small but mighty."

"Basco?" Nick asked.

Win laughed. "Otto named him Tabasco, but Mia can't say that. It comes out as 'basco', so that's what we call him. Otto decided that we should make it a spice-related name."

"He does have a kick to him," Nick said.

Win groaned at the bad pun and Nick laughed. One of the exam doors opened and Erin came into the waiting room.

"Hi, Nick," she said.

He stood. "How is she?"

"Her cheek is swollen, but that'll heal quickly. Her left hipbone is badly bruised, although I don't think it's broken. She's able to put weight on it, but it's painful to walk. His boot connected with it when he kicked her."

Nick's face turned bright red as rage flowed through his veins. He paced around the waiting room a little until he brought his temper under control again.

"Will she be ok?" Nick asked, his voice rough with emotion.

Erin nodded. "With some rest and cold compresses, she should feel better in about a week. It might still be tender, but she'll be able to walk better."

"Ok," he said with a relieved expression. "Can I take her home?"

"Yes. I'll give you some laudanum for the pain," Erin said.

Nick followed her into the exam room and his anger returned when he saw Maura's swollen face and the fear in her brown eyes. They filled at the sight of him and she signed, "I am not his wife. I promise. I am not. Please do not give me back to him."

Nick carefully embraced her. "It's ok. You're not going back to him," he said, stroking her hair. "It's ok, Maura." He kissed her forehead and made her look at him. He signed, "You will not go back to him. I promise. I am going to take you home and take care of you and I will make sure you are safe from now on."

As Win and Erin watched, it was evident that Nick and Maura weren't just friends. The tender way he touched her and spoke to her said that she meant much more to him than that.

"I am going to go get our buggy so I can take you home. I will be right back," he said.

Maura nodded, putting on a brave face. "All right."

He smiled a little and left the exam room with Erin and Win.

Chapter Thirteen

"Are you sure about this?" Sal asked Nick as they sat on a couple of hay bales in one of their barns late that afternoon.

Nick ran a hand through his hair. "No, but what choice do I have? I can't drink because I need to help take care of Maura. I can't do that if I'm passed out drunk. I can't stay away from it if it's served at dinner. If I don't drink any, it'll raise suspicion. The time has come to tell everyone else."

"Ok," Sal said. "I'll be there to support you."

"Thanks. You have no idea how bad I want a drink right now," Nick said, his leg bouncing up and down. "It's the way someone gets when they haven't eaten for a couple of days. I hope I can eat without my hands shaking." He held them out in front of him.

Sal saw the way he trembled and he now truly understood that Nick was right; he was an alcoholic. "Jeez, Nick."

"Yeah," Nick agreed. "Let's go get this over with."

"What are you gonna tell them about why you want to marry Maura? I don't want to say the wrong thing," Sal said.

Nick squared his shoulders. "The truth. I'm done with lying."

Sal admired Nick's fortitude and honesty. "Ok. I'm with you all the way."

After lunchtime, Sylvia had closed Mama T.'s, putting a sign in the window stating that there had been a family emergency. When Sal and Nick went inside, she was just coming down from upstairs after checking on Maura.

"She's sleeping," she told Nick.

"That's good. She needs the rest," Nick said. "Mama, I'm calling a family meeting before dinner."

Sylvia gave him a quizzical look, but he wasn't giving anything away. "All right. What's wrong?"

"I'll tell everyone at the same time," Nick said. "It'll be simpler. Where's Pop?"

"He went down to the wine cellar," Sylvia said.

Nick almost groaned.

Sal said, "I'll go get him."

"Thanks. I'll go get Gino and Lulu and we'll meet in the dining room," Nick said.

Once the family was assembled at the dining room table, they waited expectantly for Nick to speak.

Gathering his nerve, he said, "I'm going to ask that you don't interrupt me until I'm done. What I'm about to tell you is shocking, but I'm going to be completely serious and honest with you about it all. I'm also not above asking for compassion and understanding."

All of them exchanged confused looks except Sal, who just trained his attention on Nick. Hiding his shaking hands under the table, Nick began his story. He went back through the ship's sinking, telling them about the nightmares and when his heavy drinking began. He told them about his night of debauchery and how the drinking had gotten steadily worse until he was addicted to the alcohol.

His face was flushed with shame the entire time he spoke. He ended with what had transpired between him and Maura and that he was going to do the right thing and marry her. "That's all of it."

The silence that met his ears seemed to roar with disappointment and anger as he waited for their reactions.

Alfredo cleared his throat, opened his mouth to speak, and shut it again. His mind spun with many different emotions and he didn't know where to start. No one else said anything and he knew they were waiting for him to set the tone since he was the head of the family. He saw the pain and self-loathing in Nick's eyes and he felt the compassion in his heart that Nick had asked for.

At length, he said, "I am so mad at you, Nicola, I'd like to take a switch to you!"

"Pop, I'm so sor—"

"Shut up," Alfredo said. "I'm angry, hurt, and disappointed in you, but not because you have a problem. I'm your father, Nick. I've always told you kids that there's nothin' you can't talk to me about, haven't I?"

"Yes."

"You should have come to me or your mother. Have we ever failed to help you?" Alfredo asked.

"No."

"That's right and we never will. We'd have helped you with this, too. If we'd have known we could've kept it from gettin' so bad," Alfredo said.

"I couldn't, Pop. You don't understand what it's like bein' me," Nick said.

"What does that mean?" Sylvia asked.

Sal jumped in. "It means that we've always expected him to be perfect since he was gonna be a priest and it hasn't been fair to him. He's not a priest, but we've sort of treated him like he is. Even after what happened with Ming Li and Jake, we thought that he was strong enough to get through it. I'm ashamed to say that I wasn't as supportive as I coulda been."

Nick said, "Don't try to make excuses for me, Sal."

"I ain't. It's the truth. I was so caught up in my own life that I didn't pay enough attention to you. I'm sorry," Sal said.

"Now you know why I was always on your back about all of your drinkin'," Nick said. "I was worried that you'd turn into what I'd become and I love you too much to let that happen."

He'd put his hands up on the table as he'd spoken and Sylvia saw the way they shook. "Nick, are you all right? You're trembling."

"Nerves and withdrawal," Nick said. "I'm used to having a little wine at the restaurant over dinnertime."

Gino said, "I'm mad at you for the same reason Pop is. You shoulda told us, Nicky. I mean, here we've sat, night after night, drinkin' wine with dinner and when we play cards or whatever. I feel lousy knowin' it only made things worse."

Sylvia said, "We won't be having wine with dinner anymore and we'll keep the wine cellar locked. Is there alcohol in your room? Don't lie to me, Nicola."

"No. Maura dumped it all a few nights ago. I promise," he said.

She nodded stiffly. "I guess we'll be planning another wedding, and we'd better make it soon. It's my fault. I should have insisted that she go stay at the boarding house. I just never figured that Gino or you would have done something like that—especially you, Nick."

"I know, Mama," Nick said.

Lulu said, "Nick, do you think a marriage between you and Maura will work?"

"I've been thinking about that," Nick said. "I believe it will."

"Why?" Lulu asked.

Nick said, "She's kind and sweet. She's strong, too. She's been through her own terrible ordeal, but she has a good disposition and a good sense of humor. And she's beautiful."

Lulu asked, "Do you think you would have been attracted to her without the alcohol?"

Nick thought about the way he'd desired Maura that morning while he'd been sober. "Yeah, I do."

Alfredo asked, "Have you talked about it with her?"

Nick nodded. "Yeah. A little bit. It's hard for her because she feels so unworthy of love since only a few people have ever shown her kindness. She's been a slave her whole life and doesn't really understand the concept of being free. She's been treated with some of the worst degradations and yet she still has hope in her heart. She's an amazing woman in many ways."

Sylvia's eyes widened as she listened to Nick. "Are you saying that she's been …?"

Nick nodded. "Since she was a teenager."

Her eyes grew moist and she pressed fingers to her trembling lips, shaking her head a little. Alfredo took her other hand and put an arm around her. "I know, Syl. I know." At the questioning looks from the others, he said, "One of Sylvia's best friends was assaulted that way by a man who'd started courting her. It happened a couple of times and she hung herself because she felt so ashamed."

Lulu gasped. "That's horrible! And that it's been going on so long for Maura is simply unspeakable." An intense look crossed her face. "Nick, you propose to Maura as soon as she's better and I'll start designing a dress for her tonight. She needs your protection. All of our protection. I'll be damned if anyone will come after her again. I'll tell Sheriff Taft that, too. Whatever it takes. I'll have Sal teach me how to shoot a gun and—"

"Whoa, slow down, *bella donna*," Sal said, soothingly.

Sylvia said, "No, she's right, Sal. We're a family and we'll get through this like a family should. Nicky, we'll help you in any way we can. You marry that girl and you get your head on straight. No alcohol at work. You let Keith or Allie take it out to the customers. Or me. You don't touch one bottle, do you hear me?"

"Yes, Mama."

"I had an uncle who was an alcoholic," she said. "You're gonna have a rough road for the next few days while you dry out. You fight it and we'll help you. I don't care what happens, don't you drink one drop. You make sure to come get one of us if you don't trust yourself. *Capirsi*?"

"*Si*, Mama," Nick said.

She nodded. "Good. Now, I'll go make a plate for you to take up to Maura."

Saturday night arrived and the parlor of Shadow's lair was filled almost to capacity. As he looked around at all the people, he thought it was amazing that the place that had been built because of the heinous way his parents had treated him was now a sanctuary and a secure meeting place.

He felt Bree's hand on his and looked at her.

She smiled at him. "It's nice that it's being used for something good, isn't it?"

His wife never failed to surprise him with her intuitiveness. Squeezing her hand, he said, "Are you sure you're not a mind reader? I was thinking much the same thing."

"Well, you know what they say about great minds thinking alike," Bree said.

He chuckled. "I wonder what Arliss and company want to talk to us about?"

"I guess we're about to find out," she said.

Across the room, Arliss cleared his throat and said, "Ok, folks. We'll get started now." He fidgeted and looked at Andi, who gave him a reassuring smile. "We're gonna do something that we only do with a couple of people in our life. We don't need the phrases to change who's talking and for this meeting it'll just be easier if R.J. and Blake can speak when they want to. Doing it used to embarrass us when we were kids, so that's why we came up with the keys."

Marvin leaned forward eagerly, as did Win. Arliss' father, Dennis Elders, had told them that Arliss and his brothers could do it, but they hadn't witnessed it yet.

R.J. said, "Anything that is said at this meeting must be treated with the utmost secrecy. We are entrusting you with very sensitive information. For the sake of our friends, Wild Wind and Arrow, we mustn't divulge this information, no matter what may happen. If you can agree to this, please hold up your right hand and repeat after me."

The group was so fascinated by the swift transformation from Arliss to R.J. that they didn't respond right away.

He smiled, enjoying their amazement. "Now, now, let's not stare. You'll make Arliss self-conscious. Raise your hands boys and girls."

Everyone did as asked.

"Repeat after me: I solemnly swear to uphold the secrecy of this meeting and to uphold my allegiance to the cause for which we are fighting," R.J. said.

The room was filled with voices repeating the oath.

"Thank you," R.J. said. "I know that you all understand that this situation is rather dire. We're pinned down by the enemy and, yes, that is how we must view the army at the moment. Even if we wait them out, someone will report our friends should they come out of hiding. We need a permanent solution."

Billy said, "Yeah, but what? We can try to guess who turned them in, but there's nothing we can do to stop them from doing it again."

Arliss said, "Exactly. We can reach out to some people we know, but that means that some of my enemies will know that we're not dead. Last year, one of them came looking for me, and if we do this, more people who mean me harm might come to Echo. So we're not the only ones it involves. It affects all of you, too."

Usually Evan stayed on the fringe of these sorts of situations to maintain plausible deniability so that he didn't get in trouble. This wasn't due to any cowardice on his part; it was a protection measure for Echo so that they didn't lose the best sheriff they'd ever had. Evan played what in modern times would be considered the good cop to Shadow and Thad's bad cop routines.

All three parties enjoyed playing their parts and it was an effective strategy for keeping the peace. While crimes still occurred, it wasn't as prevalent and the townspeople felt more secure. They wanted it to stay that way. However, Evan felt that he needed to be at least a little involved in whatever was occurring so that he could assist as much as possible.

He asked, "Who is it that you would reach out to?"

R.J. said, "Preston Landry."

Marvin visibly jerked. "Secretary of War Preston Landry?"

"Yes," R.J. said. "The very same."

Alfredo had been allowed to come so he could see Vanna and so his family would be in the loop. "Who are you that you know someone so important?"

R.J. smiled. "That would be a very long and complicated story, I'm afraid. Let's just say that we've done a lot of work for some very high level people."

Wild Wind asked, "Why would he help us?"

Arliss said, "He's sympathetic to Indian affairs and we know that if we could come up with a plan that he would approve of, he could get the army off our backs and you would be protected."

Wild Wind asked, "What sort of plan?"

Blake came to the fore. "You and Arrow would be part of an experimental program that would help Indians assimilate into white culture without the requirements of the Dawes Act. Wild Wind, you almost meet the criteria, but you're not working within the confines of any reservation. The land you own doesn't count, in their eyes. Arrow, you don't own any land at all, so you don't meet *any* of the requirements. We need to get you two recognized as citizens and recommending this type of program would do that."

Wild Wind seethed over the injustice of it all. He'd worked hard to help build their sheep farming operation. It was an insult that the government didn't think that all of his work measured up. Arrow was of much the same mind, but he realized that his situation was even more tenuous than his brother's.

"Would that make other Indians eligible to do the same thing?" he asked.

R.J. said, "Yes, but since this would be a pilot program, it would most likely be limited to only a certain amount of Indians. If successful, it would possibly open the door for other Indians who would be agreeable to it."

Wild Wind stood up. "I have already proven myself! Why should I have to do such a thing when I have done nothing wrong?" His eyes blazed with anger.

Blake pushed back. "You're right. It's not fair. You shouldn't have to, but, in the government's eyes, both you and Arrow are fugitives. You both belong in Oklahoma, not in Montana. You escaped from a reservation. That makes you criminals and the army is famous for making examples out of those who defy them. What we want to do is put them in their place, put them on a leash, and take away their power where you and Arrow are concerned."

Wild Wind tried to calm down, but the whole situation was beyond infuriating. "I am sick of white people telling us what to do, where to go, and how to do things! They treat us no better than dogs they are trying to train! I am done with hiding! Let them come after me. I have proven myself against many white men before and I can do it again!"

With angry strides, he left the room, Roxie following him.

"You can't leave, Wild Wind! What about me and the baby?" she asked. "What about Arrow? If they find you, they'll torture you until you tell them where he is. I know how hard this is, but please don't do anything rash. Let Arliss help us."

"You have no idea what it's like to be hunted down and bound like an animal. What it's like to be pushed and prodded along like cattle and then put on a reservation that might as well just be a pasture. You don't know what it's like to lose your whole way of life. I've made a life here with a wife I love and now a baby on the way and I can't enjoy it all because the army says I'm not a citizen!

"I was peaceful, respectful, and contributed to the town, but that wasn't good enough just because my skin is red. So be it. I can't stay down here anymore, Roxie. I can't keep hiding like a yellow dog or a rabbit. I'm going insane!"

She hugged him around the middle, trying to comfort him with her embrace, but he was overwrought and not very sensible at the moment.

Lucky joined them. "Listen to me, brother," he said in Cheyenne. "You are a warrior at heart, but, like all good warriors, you must adjust to the situation. You are not hiding like a coward, you are just taking a different sort of approach to the battle. We often rely on allies to help win battles. This is no different. You must let Arliss do what he can so that you can be victorious. If not for yourself, do this for your wife and child."

Wild Wind's jaw clenched as he looked into Lucky's kind, gray eyes. "I need to be alone. Tell Arliss that I'll do whatever he says."

He moved away, heading for the bedroom he and Roxie were using. Roxie hugged herself as sobs rose from her chest. Lucky took her in his arms.

"It'll be all right, lass," he said. "He just needs a little time to calm down."

Roxie said, "He's at the breaking point, Lucky. I don't know how much more he can take, and I don't blame him."

"I know it's hard, but we have to do whatever we can to keep him as calm as possible," Lucky said. "Yer not alone, Roxie. Come on back to the meetin'."

Roxie nodded and let him take her back into the parlor.

Arliss had halted things, but when Roxie came back in, he resumed the meeting. "Roxie, is he all right?"

"No," she said, shakily. "He needs this resolved as soon as possible. I'm so worried about him. He said he'll go along with what you want him to do."

Arrow said, "So will I. I'll enjoy beating the army at their game. We will wage a different kind of war."

Vanna was proud of her husband for his viewpoint.

Arliss said, "All we gotta do is vote about us reaching out now. All those willing to take the risk say 'aye'."

Every person said "aye", willing to put their safety on the line to stand in solidarity with their friends against the enemy.

Arliss nodded. "All right. Looks like we'll be sending a telegram tomorrow. Meeting adjourned. We'll leave in staggers and go in different directions."

The meeting broke up, but Roxie, Arrow, and Vanna stayed behind along with Alfredo, who wanted to visit with them a little. He wanted to tell Arrow and Vanna about Nick and the situation with Maura.

The others took their leave in ten minute intervals, all of them filled with hopeful anticipation that they could succeed at their plan.

Chapter Fourteen

A couple of days later, Preston Landry sat in his office with his assistant, Gunther, going over notes for a meeting that was scheduled for the next day when one of his aids knocked on his door.

He sighed, irritated with the interruption. "Come in."

The aid entered his office and handed him a telegram. "It's marked urgent, sir," he said.

As Preston read the succinct telegram, his eyebrows rose high on his forehead.

COME SEE ME. STOP.

Those three words set his heart pounding with happiness. He smiled and said to the aid, "Find out where this originated on the double." To Gunther he said, "Clear my schedule for the next couple of days."

"What? Sir, you have that meeting with—"

Preston frowned. "This is more important than any meetings I have this week. Do whatever it takes to clear my schedule or you can find another job. Have I made myself clear, Gunther?"

The aid quickly left the office while Gunther nodded and began gathering up the notes he'd been making.

"Very clear, sir," he said. "I'll take care of it."

"See that you do," Preston said, leaning back in his desk chair. "Arliss, you son of a gun. Just wait until I get a hold of you. I'm going to skin you alive," he said with a chuckle of fondness for his friend.

"He'll come to Dickensville next week," Arliss said to Andi the next evening as they sat in his carriage house. He arrived back that afternoon from the next town over from Echo. He'd stayed overnight in one of the hotels so he could be reached quickly with the reply from Landry.

Andi's stomach felt a little queasy at the knowledge that someone outside of Echo now knew that her men were alive. "I'm glad he'll be here so soon so that this can be done quickly. I think Wild Wind feels better since he help iron out the details of this program."

"He and Arrow should since it's all about them," he said. "I would have liked to have seen Preston's face when he got that telegram. I'm sure that it was a big shock to him."

"I'm sure it was, too." Her worried expression caused a pang of guilt in his chest.

"Darlin', it's gonna be ok. Preston knows not to tell anyone who he's meeting. He'll have people with him, but you know my plan about that. It'll be all right," he said.

"I know. I still can't help worrying," she replied. "I'm not panicking or anything, though."

"No need to," R.J. said, coming forth. "Now, you have plans for tomorrow night, so keep your dance card free."

She smiled at him. "What are we doing?"

"That, my dear, you'll have to wait to find out," he said.

Andi said, "Well, I do like surprises as long as they're of the nice variety."

"This will be of that variety, I assure you," he said. "How about a walk?"

"All right. That would be nice," she said.

R.J. rose and held out his hand to her. She gave it to him and let out a cry as he jerked her out of her seat and wound his arms around her waist, bringing her into contact with his hard chest. Her breathing quickened as she saw the fire in his eyes right before he claimed her lips in a slow, searing kiss that left her senses reeling.

Drawing back slightly, he gazed into her pretty brown eyes and asked, "Do you have any idea what you do to us?"

She nodded as she regained her equilibrium. "Yes, I do. You know what happens when you kiss me like that."

He laughed. "I somehow keep forgetting that you can't keep your wall up completely when I do. Sorry, love."

She ran her hands over his shoulders and said, "It's all right. It's nice that you desire me like that."

"Yes, well, be that as it may, we try to keep a lid on that, but it sneaks out every so often. Let's go on that walk, shall we?" he asked.

"We shall," she said, giggling when he playfully pulled her out the door.

Per Arliss' instructions, Preston registered at the Four Corners, a lower class hotel in Dickenson. He'd left his entourage behind in another part of town, knowing how to slip away from them. He could imagine how angry they were with him, but he didn't care. He owed Arliss a great deal and he understood that if word got out that he was alive, it would put his friend in jeopardy. Preston wasn't going to do that if at all possible.

Going to room four, he opened the door and was immediately grabbed from behind. A gun barrel was jammed into his back and a hand clamped over his mouth.

"Did you come alone?" asked a rough voice in his ear.

He nodded.

"You better have or the consequences will be dire for you. I always enjoy dealing out dire consequences."

He was released and spun around. Preston didn't know the man. The dark glasses he wore made his countenance unnerving even though he was very handsome.

"Arliss, I do believe it's safe," he said.

Arliss came out of the closet while two other men stepped out of the small, private washroom. Preston saw that they were Indians.

Smiling broadly, Arliss said, "It's good to see you, Preston."

Preston smiled back. "Likewise, Arliss. I've been mourning you. I could kill you for faking your death, but since you've already been dead, I'll refrain from murdering you."

The two men embraced as they laughed.

Arliss said, "Preston, meet two very good friends of mine, Wild Wind and Arrow."

Preston shook hands with them without hesitation, grasping arms in the Indian fashion. "Good to meet you, gentlemen."

Wild Wind nodded, his expression stony. Arrow was a little more hospitable, smiling in return.

"Come on over and sit down," Arliss said.

A table had been set up with a couple of chairs around it. It was situated near the bed where a couple of people could sit. Preston took one of the chairs while Arliss took the other one and the brothers sat on the bed. Shadow guarded the door.

Preston got down to business. "Now, why have you called me here?"

"I don't live in Dickensville. I've been living in a little town south of here called Echo Canyon. The military is after my friends here. They're Cheyenne and they escaped from a reservation in Oklahoma. It's a long story, so you're gonna be here a while," Arliss said.

Preston said, "In that case, I hope you have some refreshments."

Arliss smiled and went to the closet. He came back with a couple of bottles of scotch and some sandwiches. "It's the good stuff. I remembered what you like."

Preston chuckled. "Very good. Crack that bottle open and let's get on with it, shall we?"

The men took turns telling him everything from the way Wild Wind had escaped and the reason behind it. Arrow related his own escape experience and they told him about the attack on Wild Wind before ending with the military's arrival in Echo.

Then they laid out the experimental program they had come up with that would allow Wild Wind and Arrow to become citizens and perhaps be a pathway for other Indians. Preston listened attentively, his keen mind going over their proposal.

When they'd finished, he sat silently for a little while before he spoke. "I'm rejecting your plan."

Blake spoke up. "Why? It's a good plan."

Wild Wind snorted. "I'm not surprised."

"Now, just hold on, son," Preston said. "I didn't say I wouldn't help. I agree that the program would be a good one. If it were up to me, I'd implement it right away, but I know that I can't sell it to the powers that be. However, what I *can* sell is setting up a small, private boarding school similar to the one at Ft. Shaw."

The brothers bristled.

Arrow said, "You mean a school where our boys are forced to keep their hair short, all of them always have to wear white man's clothing, and give up their traditions? Those schools make our children undergo military training and the students are paraded around in front of the people in your culture like show horses. You are no better than the rest of the bureaucrats and military officers."

Preston smiled. He liked their fiery attitudes and he couldn't blame them for thinking the way they did. "Please just hear me out."

Arliss said, "Fellas, Preston really does care. Let's just listen."

Wild Wind and Arrow grudgingly acquiesced.

"Fort Shaw is doing very well, but they're overrun with students and we could use the new facility as an overflow school. I can get that approved. You said that most people are fine with you and Arrow being around, correct?"

Wild Wind nodded. "Yes. I have many good friends and my wife is white. Her family does not mind our marriage and my brother and sister-in-law were my friends before I married Roxie. I am co-owner of a sheep farm and I contribute to the community. I've never caused trouble. The only requirement I don't meet is operating my farm on reservation land. I think that's a ridiculous stipulation since I meet all the others."

"I agree," Preston said. "Now, you and Arrow are very well spoken, intelligent, compliant men who have obviously assimilated well into mainstream society. Starting right this minute, I will offer you my protection. I'll go to Echo with you and talk to this Finnley. I'll tell him to cease and desist in his pursuit of you on one condition: you and Arrow sit on the board of this new school. Who better to help other Indians assimilate than Indians who have already done it?"

Arrow arched an eyebrow. "You would let us help teach them?"

Preston nodded. "Yes, I would. Fort Shaw has three Indians working as teaching assistants at their school and it seems to help the students. Now, a qualified administrator would have to be appointed, but you could help choose them. Your town would also receive federal funding to aid in the construction of the school and to offset any drains on their resources, so there's advantages for your town council approving such a venture. You could start out the trial with a small number, say eight or ten."

Wild Wind said, "Will they be allowed to wear their native clothing, stop the practice of cutting their hair, and let them keep some of their traditions?"

Preston asked, "Do the townspeople object to you wearing your own clothing?"

Arliss said, "I haven't heard one word against it and most people are friendly with them. There's just this one group who have it in for them. They don't deserve what's being done to them."

Preston said, "I can see that this is very important to you, Arliss. I know you wouldn't have called me here if it wasn't. I do have a quid pro quo, however."

Arliss leaned back in his chair. "I had a feeling. What is it?"

"I may have need of you in the future. If I do this for you, you'll owe me," he said.

Thinking about the promise he'd made to Andi, he frowned. His gaze settled on his friends and he heard Andi's voice telling him to do this and that God would take care of the rest.

"All right," R.J. said. "We want all of this in writing, though. It's not that we don't trust you, but we know how other people have a tendency to butt in and throw a wrench in the works."

"Of course. Gentlemen, I'm going to enjoy working on this with you," Preston said, holding out a hand to them.

This time, both men smiled at him as they grasped arms.

Preston said, "Well, take me to Echo and let's get started. No sense in my going back to Washington before we get all of this worked out."

The men left quickly, eager to get to work on their new project.

Chapter Fifteen

As they entered Echo, Arrow and Wild Wind proudly rode their horses right down Main Street, relieved that they no longer needed to hide. It wasn't long until they encountered a couple of military men.

Preston alighted from the carriage in which he rode with his security detail.

"Hello, gentlemen," he said to the soldiers. "Do you know who I am?"

One of them nodded, looking at Daniel with wide eyes. "Yes, Mr. Landry. You're the secretary of war. I'm Corporal Hadley."

"Very good, Corporal. These two men are under my protection and are no longer to be hunted. They're free and I am making them citizens entitled to all of the liberties that any other citizen enjoys. Now, I need to see your superior, Lieutenant Finnley. We're going to the town hall. Have him meet me there forthwith," Preston said.

Hadley saluted him and the other soldier followed his example. "Yes, sir," Hadley said.

Both soldiers rode away as people started coming over to greet the two Indians, welcoming them home. News of their return had already begun spreading, and they were soon surrounded by well-wishers.

Preston took all of this in and he became even more convinced that a boarding school in Echo could work based on the warm reception Wild Wind and Arrow were receiving. He smiled at people as Arliss introduced him around. Eventually, they moved to the town hall and Arliss ran over to the church to get his lady and start rounding up the town council to start planning a town meeting for the following night.

The town hall auditorium was full to bursting with people. Voices were raised, some shouting as the two opposing sides faced off. The proposal of the Indian boarding school had stirred up a hornets' nest, but Preston thought it was a good thing. Better to get it all out in the open and deal with it right off. He let it go on for a little while before he nodded to Jerry that he'd had enough.

Jerry put a thumb and forefinger in his mouth and let out a long, blasting whistle. The crowd quieted down and Preston stood up, moving towards the audience.

"I understand that some of you have doubts about the school, but unless I hear some sort of valid argument against it, it's going to happen. Does someone have sound reasoning for not building it and implementing the process?"

One man stood up. "We just don't want a bunch of filthy Indians around here. God only knows what they'll do. That one there is a murderer!" He pointed at Wild Wind, who stood erect and unflinching at the hurled insults.

Preston said, "To be fair, a large group of men attacked him, a lone man, in his own home when he wasn't causing any harm to anyone. Neither Wild Wind nor Arrow appear filthy to me. They're both intelligent, law-abiding men who have adopted many of your ways.

"Mr. Swift has recently converted to Catholicism and he's married to a United States citizen and is accepted by her family. Again, I'm not hearing sound reasons as to why there shouldn't be a school built here. All I hear is hate and misconceptions."

"I don't have a problem with these two since they're peaceful, but what guarantee do we have that others who come here would behave the same way?" a lady asked.

Preston said, "A very good point. Wild Wind and Arrow, along with the town council, would screen the potential students, choosing only those who would be the most suitable. That way, it would lessen the chances of any difficulties arising. Also, they would be children, not adults, so the chances of violence would be considerably lessened."

"That sounds reasonable," she said; several other people made noises of agreement.

Preston said, "Also, Echo would receive federal funding to help with the financial burden of operating the school. As I understand it, Echo could use the influx of cash."

People nodded and murmured affirmative words.

"Where are you gonna put it?" a different man asked. "I don't want it out around my place."

Lucky stood up and said, "Excuse me, Mr. Landry, my name is Lucky Quinn and I'm one of Wild Wind's business partners. I have a suggestion about a location."

"Go ahead," Daniel said.

"I lived with Wild Wind and Arrow's tribe for three years before we were captured. So I understand both cultures. I'd like to donate some of the land out on Wild Wind's farm to put the school on. That way he'd be close to them and he could teach them about sheep farmin' and other aspects of agriculture. I'd also like to be involved in teachin' them," Lucky said.

Preston nodded approvingly. "That's a very generous offer, Mr. Quinn. I believe we'll take you up on that, assuming that would meet with Wild Wind's approval?"

Wild Wind smiled at Lucky. "Thank you, my friend."

Marvin stood up next. "Our land is adjacent to Wild Wind's and we're prepared to also donate land to the cause. Between us, we could figure out the acreage needed for the venture and perhaps split the land donation."

"Another great idea," Preston said. "So there's your solution to a site."

Andi said, "I'll be happy to indoctrinate them into the Christian religion since I know that's a requirement."

"And I won't mind helping whomever their new teacher set up a classroom," Adam Harris stated. "They'll need books and supplies, too, but we could take up a collection."

Nick, Sal, and Gino had come to support Arrow. Nick raised his hand. "I'd be happy to donate a sizable amount of money to help with school supplies."

Sal and Gino said that they would also chip in. Preston chuckled to himself as the townsfolk continued to come up with solutions. He could tell that they were becoming excited about the idea of helping with the school. Other groups that had started other Indian schools had acted much the same way, but he knew that this school would be different for allowing the students a little more freedom to be true to themselves. In Preston's opinion, assimilation didn't mean that they should have to completely lose their identity. Unfortunately, his opinion on the matter wasn't popular in his professional circles.

The man who'd objected shouted, "How many of them are you fixin' to send here?"

"We'll start out with only a few until we see how it goes," Preston replied. "I think eight is a good number."

"That's eight too many as far as I'm concerned," the dissenter said. Several other men and a couple of women agreed with him.

Preston's face turned pink as his temper rose. "That's too bad. These are children and they deserve an opportunity at a better life. I'm also going to appoint two army men to be stationed here in Echo so that they can guarantee the safety of these children."

Evan said, "My department won't put up with any harmful actions against them, either. So let that be a warning to you. Anyone who harms one of those kids will be dealt with quickly."

"Uh, Mr. Landry, sir?"

Preston saw that Corporal Hadley was the speaker. "Yes?"

"If I'm not being too forward, I'd like to volunteer to stay here in Echo," he said.

"Why would you want to do that?" Preston asked.

Hadley replied, "Because I'm one-quarter Lakota and I'd like to be involved in something like this. It would be a way to honor my heritage and show that Indians aren't the savages people think they are."

Finnley's shocked expression amused Preston. Apparently Hadley's superior had no idea that his corporal had Indian blood in him.

"Permission granted," Preston said. "I'll take care of the transfer paperwork as soon as I arrive back in Washington."

Hadley bowed a little to him. "Thank you, sir."

Jerry said, "Well, to make this official, we'll take a vote. Since there are so many people here tonight, we'll do it this way: all those who approve the building of the school, stand on the left side of the room and those who oppose it, stand on the right. We'll take a head count."

People moved to the requested areas and then stood quietly while they were counted by Evan and Shadow. Once they'd counted, Evan said, "I counted fifty-seven for the school."

Shadow said, "Twenty-four against it."

Jerry said, "Let the record show that the proposal to build an Indian boarding school was passed by a fifty-seven to twenty-four vote."

The group against it started raising a ruckus.

"The whole town isn't here! That's not fair!"

Evan said, "We sent riders out yesterday and today to let them know about the meeting, so if they didn't come, that's their problem."

Preston said, "While you're all here, I'd like to invite those who would like to help out with the school to come to another meeting here tomorrow night at six p.m. to put together a schoolboard and get the ball rolling. Thank you for coming. Goodnight, everyone."

Arrow sat out at the fire with Vanna that night, just staring into the flames as a myriad of thoughts filled his mind. Their movement and crackling sounds relaxed him and allowed his mind to drift. He'd been keyed up after the meeting and just being still with Vanna at his side helped him unwind. He felt her hand settle on his knee and looked at her.

"Do you regret changing so much?" she asked.

He lay down on his back and pulled her down to lay against him. Looking up at the stars, he said, "When I first came here, I hated all people who were from your culture whether it was white, black, or anything else. If they were not Cheyenne or one of our allies, I hated them. That hate was what made me drive Wild Wind and Roxie apart. I hated her because she was white, because of the color of her skin and all of the oppression that represented for me.

"But when I saw how much she suffered without him, I learned that her love for him was stronger than the differences between our two cultures. I started questioning everything I'd thought about your culture, especially when she forgave me. It made me see that like life, people and situations can't be put into neat little boxes where things are always black or white.

"When we found out that Father had died, I didn't know what to do with all of the shame and grief I felt. Our mother had passed shortly before he died and it was another hard blow for me. You saved me from my despair," Arrow said.

"Me? What do you mean?"

"I saw you in town and followed you home. In our culture, we're taught to observe things and animals we don't understand so that we can learn their ways and why they do the things they do. That's what I did with all of you. I watched and learned that although you did things that were strange to me, you seemed to be good people. You especially," he replied.

Vanna smiled. "Was I your prey?"

He laughed. "Yes. I hunted you almost every day, watching you, learning about you. If I didn't see you for a day, I became impatient for the next day to come so I could see you. And that's when I knew I loved you and that I was willing to do anything to make you mine."

She hugged him and giggled. "But you were too shy to tell me, which I still think is very sweet."

"Hush, woman. Men are not supposed to be sweet," he said with mock fierceness, making her giggle again. How he adored her laugh. "I don't think it would have been too much longer until I said something, but that bear made it happen quicker. I'm glad it did. I wasn't afraid to face your father and brothers, but facing your possible rejection terrified me. If you had rejected me and I still loved you, I would have been doomed to loneliness."

"You would have found someone, Arrow. You're too handsome not to have," she said.

"No, I wouldn't have because I wouldn't have been interested in anyone else. It wouldn't have mattered if another woman had found me attractive. It was what's in my heart for you, Vanna. I know that I would never have wanted anyone else," he said. "That's why I was so relieved when you were attracted to me. It meant I had a chance to capture your heart."

"You certainly did that."

He smiled. "All of the things I had to do—cut my hair, learn English, become Catholic, and wear your kind of clothing—none of that mattered because I'll always be Cheyenne inside. None of it can change my true person, but it has made me more open-minded. There's nothing wrong with learning about different cultures and trying to find common ground so that there can be harmony.

"That's what Father was trying to teach me, but I wouldn't listen. I thought he was a soft, old man who had forgotten what our people stood for. I just wish it hadn't taken his death to make me see that he was stronger than many people knew and that I was the weak one. I don't regret one single thing I had to do, Vanna. All of it made me a better person because I understand you better and you understand me better now, too. Those aren't things that should be resented."

Vanna said, "I'm married to a very smart man."

"I'm not sure that I am, but I'm working hard to not be close-minded or let my heart be guided by hatred anymore. What good did it do me? What good did it do the people I was closest to? None. Many in your culture don't understand how Indians think. They don't like it because we're quiet a lot. They think we're stupid because we often don't talk for long periods of time. They just don't realize that there's a lot said in silences and that our minds are most likely figuring out a solution to something or composing a song or just remembering a loved one who passed over into the next life.

"Just because we're quiet doesn't mean that we accept what's forced on us. There are times when we're just waiting for the right opening to make a move. Many of your people associate kindness towards others as weakness. It's just the opposite. It takes more effort and discipline to be kind towards someone, especially someone you don't like, than to act out of cruelty. If both cultures could learn that sort of discipline, it would save a lot of suffering for everyone."

Vanna nodded. "I agree, and I do understand you better because of all you've explained to me. I've learned so much about your culture and it's so beautiful. As far as being quiet goes, though, you married into the wrong family for that."

"I know," he said, laughing. "I don't mind, though. I never have to guess where I stand with any of you or what you're thinking. I like hearing you all pick on each other and argue. You're very funny."

She pinched him. "And you just sit there and egg us on. You're evil."

He grabbed her hand and bit her palm just hard enough to hurt. She squealed and tickled him and soon they were wrestling, laughing, and teasing each other.

"Excuse me."

They broke apart upon hearing Sylvia's voice.

"Am I interrupting something?" she asked.

Arrow said, "Yes. I was teaching your daughter that she shouldn't pinch braves."

"And I was teaching him that he shouldn't bite his wife."

Sylvia chuckled. The young couple certainly acted their ages sometimes and were almost childlike in the games they played. "Behave or I'll separate you."

They smiled and sat up, brushing grass and leaves from their clothing as Sylvia sat down on a large log that had been placed there for that purpose. "Are you settling in all right, Arrow?"

He nodded. "Yes, Mama. I'm glad that I no longer have to leave at night. This is helpful in making you some Italian Indian grandchildren."

Sylvia burst into laughter while Vanna covered her blushing face with one hand and slapped his arm with the other.

"See how she disrespects me?" he asked his mother-in-law.

Vanna said, "I thought Cheyenne men didn't talk to their mothers-in-law."

"Ok. Vanna tell your mother that I love living here since I can be with you—"

Vanna pushed him over and clapped her hands over his mouth while he laughed against them. Sylvia shook her head at them, enjoying their exuberance. She'd missed their playful behavior and it was wonderful to have them back home where they belonged.

It was a funny thing how quickly she'd started thinking of Arrow as another son, and she'd been deeply worried about him. She knew that the whole family would have been devastated had he been forced to go to a reservation. Watching Vanna smile and laugh as Arrow tickled her, Sylvia's eyes grew moist over the thought that she might not have ever seen him again.

Arrow and Vanna stopped their tussling and sat up again, still laughing a little. Vanna picked leaves from Arrow's hair. "I'll be glad when your hair is long like it used to be."

"Me, too," Sylvia said. "You're a handsome young man no matter what, but I do prefer you with your hair long."

Arrow smiled. "Pop should grow his hair long. He could be an Italian Indian."

Sylvia laughed at the picture that made. "No, I think Al is much more attractive just as he is."

"No wonder my ears were burnin'," Alfredo said as he came over and sat on the log with Sylvia. "What are we talkin' about?"

Sylvia caught the twinkle in Arrow's eyes. "Don't you start," she said, chuckling.

"*Si*, Mama," he said.

Alfredo grinned, thinking how funny it sounded when Arrow said something in Italian. He knew it had to sound just as funny when one of them tried to say something in Cheyenne.

"Start what?" Alfredo asked.

"Nothing," Vanna said.

"What do you mean? She just told him not to start. Start what? He must've been doin' something. What was it?"

Arrow got up under the pretense of brushing off his pants. "Talking about making Italian Indians. I am very excited about it."

Vanna scrambled to her feet as he danced away. She chased him back to the house while Alfredo and Sylvia laughed, thinking how wonderful it was that things were getting back to normal.

Chapter Sixteen

Maura was wakened by arms slipping slowly around her waist from behind. Once she recognized Nick's embrace, she relaxed, letting him gather her close. Putting her hands over his, she sighed in contentment. Her hip was healing and she didn't have much pain any longer. Sylvia had stayed with her the first three days after she'd been hurt, but she'd steadily improved and could stay by herself after that. Since then, Nick had come to her every night, not to make love, but to just be close to her.

His demon was strong and didn't want to relinquish its grip. Nighttime was still the worst to endure and for those three nights, Gino had kept him company so he didn't succumb to the charms of the alcohol that called to him. There was no way for him to get any at home, but on the second night, he'd almost sneaked away to go to Spike's.

Gino hadn't let him, though, and while the devil that possessed Nick was angry, his rational side was grateful to his brother. After the third day, Nick had told Gino that he'd be all right, knowing that Gino needed to get some sleep. However, once everyone had gone to bed, Nick hadn't been able to sleep. After pacing in his room for over an hour, he'd gone to Maura's room, crawling in bed with her.

Their closeness was comforting to both of them. For Maura, Nick's arms wrapped around her meant that the nightmares would leave her be. For Nick, holding her kept him from giving in to the powerful, burning thirst inside.

Rolling to face him, she smiled at him in the moonlight. "Hi."

"Hi. How are you?" he asked.

She felt him tremble slightly against her. "Good. You not."

"I'm better now that I'm with you," Nick said.

Maura ran her fingertips through the hair at his temple and he closed his eyes, savoring the touch that had come to feel like a benediction to him. Opening his eyes, he gazed into hers, wondering yet again at how a person who had been treated so cruelly all her life could have so much compassion for others the way Maura did. It would always amaze him. She was infinitely stronger than he.

There was something else in her eyes tonight, however. Hunger, raw and compelling, shone in them and he felt the awakening of his own for her. He was worried about her injury, however, and didn't start anything that couldn't be finished. Maura kissed him softly, her hand caressing his jaw, as she shifted even closer.

When he ended the kiss and would have moved away, she grasped his bicep and held him in place, her eyes pleading with him. "Please?"

His gaze shifted down towards her hip. "But—"

She shook her head a little. "Please? Take bad dreams. Please?"

Hadn't she done that for him on more than one occasion, whether by making love with him or just by holding him? How could he refuse her the same consideration? Looking into her dark eyes, Nick knew that it was much more than that, though. His desire for her was powerful, but stronger yet was the knowledge that there was little he would refuse her. Not out of gratitude, but out of love.

This beautiful woman who was so orphan-like had come into his life and had claimed his heart for her own. Her sweet, gentle ways had broken through his unending cycle of grief and anger and he was able to feel something much more positive now. He'd never imagined himself loving another woman again. Nick had thought that he might come to care for another woman and marry her for the purpose of having children and for companionship. But love had never figured into the equation.

Thoughts of alcohol fled his mind with the joyous revelation of his budding love for Maura. He took her in his arms, giving her the comfort she needed, but as passion flowed between them, he gave her something much more: his heart.

At the beginning of May, as Wild Wind finished the morning milking of the goats, he hummed a war song. He smiled as he poured the milk into the collection barrel and prepared to clean the pens.

At first, he'd been extremely bitter over the idea of another Indian boarding school being built, but once the school board had been formed, of which he'd been voted president, and the plans had begun, he'd grown excited about it.

Preston had kept his word and had used his clout to secure approval for the school. He'd had to agree to certain stipulations, just like all of the other schools did, but he'd been able to bully some of the administrators into allowing the Echo Canyon Indian School to have more leeway in how it was run.

There would be annual inspections and they would be required to submit monthly expense reports to show that they were appropriately applying the government funds paid to them. The combined land donations had been approved and they would start out with ten children.

Wild Wind and Arrow had requested that Fort Shaw send them their ten worst students, intent on showing that they could turn them around by relaxing some of the stringent rules that the Fort Shaw school used. They also wanted to show that with more Indian teachers and others who were knowledgeable about Indian culture involved that they would be more successful than other schools in helping the children adapt. Six boys and four girls had been chosen.

With the establishment of the school, several new jobs had been created. The school would have a full-time cook, a housekeeper, teacher, and a house mother. The carpenters, masons, and other builders in the area would benefit from the increase in work even though it would be temporary. Temple's store would gain more business since some of the school's food would be purchased from them along with some of their ready-made clothing and other goods.

A wondrous thing had happened to Edna Taft, who had suffered from rheumatoid arthritis for almost a decade. The painful, inflammatory disease had limited her activity and caused her to fatigue easily.

Andi sometimes had an overwhelming need to pray for people. She called these her "special prayers" and often when she prayed this way over someone, that person's situation improved. Over a year ago, she'd done this for Edna concerning her arthritis. Since then, Edna's pain and stiffness had begun easing and she'd become more mobile and her energy levels had risen.

Win had sought to improve her condition even more through weekly acupuncture treatments and massages. The result of all of this was that she'd come along so well that she'd regained much of her independence and didn't need to be carried anywhere anymore.

Every so often, when she was feeling particularly spry, she was able to dance a little when she went to Spike's. A sassy woman who appreciated handsome men, she was in her glory when all of her male friends fought over who got to dance with her.

With the improvement of her condition, she'd begun thinking about doing some part-time work of some sort. As soon as the jobs for the school had been posted, she'd approached Wild Wind about hiring her as a part-time house mother to help out during the day so that the live-in house mother would have back up during the busiest time.

He'd thought it was a great idea and the school board had approved it, too. Wild Wind could hardly wait to see the way she interacted with the students, knowing that she would bring a lot of humor and fun to their lives the way she did all of her grandchildren's.

It wasn't only the adults in the community who were excited about the school. Lucky and Leah's seven-year-old son, Otto, who was half-Cheyenne, was looking forward to having some other Indian kids around; there was a boy and a girl who were around his age. Thad and Jessie's kids, J.J., Liz, and Porter were anxious to meet the kids and make them feel welcome.

These were the things Wild Wind thought about as he worked in the barn. He could now see the Great Spirit's hand in all of this. He knew that he'd been meant to come with Lucky so that he could assimilate. Even the attack on him had been meant to happen so that it would eventually lead to the military coming after him and Arrow. Had they not, Arliss wouldn't have contacted Preston and the school would not be coming into existence.

All of this was happening so that he could help shape the future of children and ease their adapting to this new way of life while letting them keep some of their original identity. He owed Arliss and his brothers a great debt that he would try to repay at every opportunity.

The schoolchildren would also learn farming and plant their own garden and he planned to take them out hunting so they could bring in some of their own meat and so that the girls could be taught how to tan hides and make traditional clothing since they would be allowed to wear it. Nina, Leah, and Josie would be instrumental in this. Lucky, Nina, and Billy sat on the board, too, since they were also part of Indian culture.

A Mr. Lance Burkhart had been selected as the administrator who would come oversee the day-to-day running of the school as well as the financial operations. He'd been chosen because he was a sympathizer who spoke Cheyenne and Apache, which would be invaluable since the students were a mix of the two tribes. This would allow the kids to also keep their original language skills.

He was a tall, silver-haired, gray-eyed man in his early sixties. He'd lived with the Apache for a couple of years when he was younger and he knew their culture the way that Lucky did the Cheyenne. The board had discerned that he had a good heart and that he loved children.

Corporal Cade Hadley was getting to know the people of Echo and he was willing to help in the building of the school. His knowledge of Lakota culture would also come in handy whenever Lakota children were in attendance. Even though the Cheyenne and Lakota cultures shared some similarities, there were differences, and he would be able to help any Lakota children feel more at home.

The corporal was an outgoing twenty-four-year-old man with dark brown hair and blue eyes, but if one looked closely, his Indian heritage was evident in his chiseled features and slightly darker skin tone. He'd taken to hunting with Wild Wind, Lucky, Billy, and Arrow in the mornings. There were others who sometimes joined in, but they were the main group who went every day.

Another army man had been forced into the post with Cade. Captain Zebadiah Rawlins was forty-three and a typical military man with a stern, dark-eyed gaze and graying black hair. He'd gotten on the wrong side of Preston a couple of times and the war secretary had gotten his revenge by appointing him the second military officer in Echo.

He wasn't interested in making friends, his focus being on making the citizens of Echo understand that he wouldn't tolerate any foolishness and that he wouldn't hesitate to call in help from Butte if necessary. He and Evan had started butting heads almost immediately. Zeb felt that his military status outranked Evan and the sheriff told him that it was *his* town and that Zeb could go to hell if he didn't like the way he did things.

Zeb wasn't a fan of Arliss', either. He thought that Preston was insane for effectively putting a man suffering from a mental disorder in charge of the two military men. He hated it when Arliss' brothers made an appearance, but there wasn't much he could do but follow orders and bear it the best he could. The good thing was that Arliss wasn't going to be constantly looking over their shoulders. He didn't plan on interfering as long as the two soldiers were doing their jobs.

The Cheyenne brave finished his morning work and left for town to take care of some errands. As he rode, he relished the warm breeze that blew and the sun that shone on him, thankful that he could do so once again.

Chapter Seventeen

Maura worked out in the huge garden at the Terranova estate, planting vegetables and weeding the soil. The family had planned out the garden with the intent of supplying Mama T.'s with fresh produce for the summer and canning as much as possible for the winter months. They had built a greenhouse where they'd started a wide variety of plants, including eggplant, cauliflower, broccoli, and several kinds of tomatoes and peppers. They also grew herbal plants.

That day she was planting carrots, turnips, potatoes, string beans, and peas. She didn't work alone; Alfredo loved gardening and working in the soil was a joy for him. As he watched Maura work, he recognized a kindred spirit in that respect. She wasn't afraid to get her hands dirty and she weeded quickly and picked out rocks as she went.

She wore jeans and a blouse that she'd bought at Temple's and she'd put her hair in twin braids. The effect was natural and beautiful. Alfredo couldn't blame his son for being attracted to her, but he knew Nick well and understood that the attraction went deeper than the physical. If that was all that mattered to Nick, he'd have tried to seduce a lot of women, and he was handsome and charming enough to be successful at it.

But Nick wasn't made like that, which his shame over the one night he'd drunkenly succumbed to those urges proved. While it had been shocking to learn that Nick had done that, Alfredo understood that Nick's sort of grief could make almost anyone susceptible to those sort of temptations. He still remembered when they'd gotten the telegram about the ship sinking and the awful news about Ming Li and Jake's death.

The whole family had been heartsick and their grief had been compounded by Nick's breakdown. Not only had they suffered tremendous loss, but now their other loved one was paralyzed by it all. The expense for Alfredo to go get Nick and for the two of them to come home had put a strain on their finances, but Alfredo's burning need to bring their son safely home had overruled all else.

The whole time he'd been gone, his family had agonized over his and Nick's safety, praying that they both arrived home without incident. Fortunately both trips had been uneventful and the sailing smooth.

As Alfredo finished weeding the current row he was working on, he straightened, images of his broken son coming to him as he remembered how terrified Nick was to get on the ship to come back home. He'd never told anyone, but it had taken dosing Nick with laudanum to get him on board. Alfredo would have knocked Nick out in order get his boy on that ship if that's what it would have taken.

While Alfredo was perhaps of a cooler Italian temperament, when it concerned his wife and children, there was nothing he wouldn't do for them and no one he wouldn't fight against to assure their safety and well-being. It had greatly pained him when he and Sylvia had threatened to kick Sal out in order to get him to wake up to how destructive his behavior had been.

However, it had been necessary and something wonderful had come of it, just as they'd hoped and prayed. They'd endured Sal's anger and spiteful behavior, knowing that it would eventually cool and it had. They'd just had to ride out the storm their son had created. And all the while they were dealing with one son, another was going through his own private hell without any outward sign of his suffering.

When Maura was done with her planting, she started weeding a different part of the garden and Alfredo's gaze followed her. He had a hunch that his son had fallen in love with her. There was a certain light in Nick's eyes that morning, the kind that used to shine in them when he looked at Ming Li. He smiled to himself, hoping that was the case. Nick's happiness was so important to him and Sylvia and if Nick was in love with Maura, it meant that his heart was healing enough for it to happen.

"Maura," Alfredo called out. "Break time. Let's get something to drink."

She left her weeding and came to walk by his side to the house.

He put a hand on her shoulder. "Good work today. I think we've had enough for now though. You're starting to burn."

She smiled up at him. "I do good?"

"Yeah, you did good."

"Pop like me?" she asked.

The hope in her eyes filled his heart with sympathy. Like Arrow had, she called him and Sylvia by their familial names. "Yeah, I like you a lot," he said, putting an arm around her as they walked and giving her a friendly squeeze.

Maura leaned her head against his shoulder, enjoying the fatherly gesture. She'd never had a mother or father, so she appreciated Sylvia and Alfredo more than she could have said.

"I like Pop," she said.

"I'm glad," he said, chuckling. "It would stink if I liked you, but you didn't like me."

She smiled, picking up on his meaning. Once inside, she prepared a snack for them since she was familiar with the kitchen now. Alfredo and she sat at the kitchen table to eat their tea and coffeecake and chitchat. He was glad to have some time alone with Maura so he could get to know her better.

Between her increased understanding of English and Indian sign, they were able to carry on a conversation. Alfredo saw that Maura had a sly sense of humor and that she was intelligent. The longer they talked, the more convinced he became that she was a good match for Nick, which made him happy.

When their snack was over, Maura informed him that she was going to dust. He tried to tell her that Sylvia was very picky about the housework, but Maura turned stubborn and informed him that she knew what she was doing. Then she shooed him back outside and got to work.

Chapter Eighteen

"I'm coming up empty," Nick complained as he sat out by the fire with Arrow that night.

"About what?" Arrow asked, turning the piece of beef he was roasting on a stick over the flames.

Nick watched, his stomach growling at the sight of the juices that dripped from the meat. "How to propose to Maura. I have no father to ask for permission, so I can't honor her Comanche culture by giving him gifts. I could take her to Dickensville for dinner and ask her there, but I'm not sure she'd be comfortable with that. Any bright ideas?"

Arrow took the meat away from the fire and stuck the end of the stick into the soft earth by him to let the meat cool a little before he attempted to eat it.

"Do you play flute?"

Nick chuckled. "No. I don't play any musical instruments."

"But you sing."

"Yeah."

Arrow put another piece of meat over the fire to roast and then said, "You could, um … What's the word I'm looking for. Not sing, but …?"

"Serenade?" Nick suggested.

"Yes. Serenade her instead of playing flute for her. The Comanche do things differently than other tribes and most tribes don't get along with them except for trading purposes. They are the best horseman of all the tribes, though, and I respect them for that. Their courtship practices vary, too, but you're right—in almost every tribe, gifts are a part of courtship. Sometimes if a boy plays a flute near a girl's tipi and if she comes out to listen, he knows that she's interested in him." He gave Nick a mischievous look. "But we already know she's interested in you. In most cultures, you would be considered an eloped couple and it would only remain for the marriage to be formally recognized."

Nick pursed his lips. "Yeah, I know. We shouldn't have been intimate—"

"Perhaps not, but you can't change that now. Stop feeling guilty. You're making it right, which is much more than some men would do." Arrow took the cooked meat off the stick, broke the piece in half, and gave some to Nick.

Nick bit into it and chewed it appreciatively, enjoying the simply cooked meat. "I just can't think of anything that feels *right*. I want it to be special for her. She's never had anyone make her feel special before."

"I understand," Arrow said. "I had trouble deciding how to propose to Vanna. Should I propose the way many in your culture do or the way my culture does it? I tried giving Pop presents, but that didn't work."

Nick laughed. "Arrow, we didn't know what the heck to do with you that day. We didn't want to be disrespectful to you, but at that point, Pop wasn't gonna let you marry Vanna just because you gave us bear meat."

Arrow grinned, taking no offense at Nick's amusement. "I know. It would be like you kneeling and proposing to a Cheyenne maiden with a ring. You would have been laughed out of camp."

Nick chuckled and finished his snack. "I think it was romantic you proposing to Vanna where you met. I can't do that because I met Maura in our upstairs hallway. Not exactly romantic."

"No."

Like a sudden bolt from the blue, inspiration hit Nick. "Ha! I know what I'm gonna do!"

His abrupt announcement startled Arrow and he jerked the stick with the second piece of meat, making it fall into the fire. He grunted in dismay and gave Nick a displeased glance.

"Sorry, buddy. Thanks for the talk," Nick said as he got up and left the fire.

With a sigh, Arrow put another piece on the stick and put it over the fire.

The next morning, the Terranovas had a shock. Arrow's hunting had run late and the family was already sitting down to breakfast when he arrived. He jogged from the patio in through the French doors that led into the dining room dressed in only his breechcloth. It was the first time he'd worn it that year and since he'd met the family in the fall, they'd never seen him in it. He'd shown it to Vanna that morning, but he'd left before the rest of the family had been up.

So the sight of an almost naked Indian striding into their dining room was unnerving to them. Maura didn't bat an eye, however, since she'd seen men dress like that all of her life. It seemed perfectly natural for Arrow to wear such an outfit.

Vanna couldn't take her eyes off her husband as he sat down beside her, bowed his head, and crossed himself. Neither could the rest of them. The three brothers smiled and then snickered while Sylvia chuckled and Alfredo frowned. Arrow raised his head to see everyone staring at him.

"What?" he asked.

Alfredo said, "You're a little under-dressed, aren't you?"

Arrow's brows knitted. "This is what I wear in the summer months."

Gino let out a snort of laughter and Alfredo glared at him.

"Not to the table, you don't."

Grinning, Arrow rose from the table, spreading his arms wide. "I could just go naked."

"You will not!" Alfredo said. "Go put on some clothes."

Arrow laughed and jogged from the room. Alfredo noticed that Sylvia's eyes followed Arrow's muscular form. "Hey! Stop that," he told her.

She laughed and said, "Gino, say the blessing."

Gino made it short because he was barely able to hold back his laughter. Arrow returned presently, wearing leggings under the breechcloth and a buckskin vest.

"Better?" he asked.

"Barely," Alfredo said, noting how much of Arrow's toned chest was still exposed.

Arrow took the platter of pancakes Nick passed to him. "I will get you your own breechcloth to wear. Then you will not be jealous of mine."

"I'm not jealous and I don't want one," Alfredo said. "It's not decent to run around like that, especially around women."

"You're afraid that I'll steal them because I look better in one than you do," Arrow said in a serious tone. "I understand."

Sylvia tried to hide her smile and failed.

"You think that's funny, huh?" Alfredo said to her.

Sal said, "It is, Pop, because he's right. I can't picture you in one. You still have too much belly."

"I lost some of it last year," Alfredo said, offended.

"I know," Sal said. "I'm just sayin' that you don't really have the figure for a breechcloth."

"And you do?" Alfredo asked.

"More than you do," Sal said, patting his trim waist.

Lulu laughed. "I can't picture any of you in a breechcloth."

Arrow said, "Old men in my culture wear them as much as younger men, so it would be all right for you to, Pop."

More laughter followed his statement.

"Are you callin' me an old man?"

Arrow shook his head, but his eyes gleamed with mischief.

Alfredo narrowed his eyes at him. "Yes, you are. Fine. You make me one of those and I'll bet you that by the time August comes that I'll be able to wear it with pride."

"What will we bet?" Arrow asked, rising to the challenge.

"If I win, I get that nice knife you have, but if you win, you get that new whetstone I bought."

"So be it," Arrow said, extending his hand across the table.

Alfredo shook it and the two men exchanged smiles as the bet was sealed.

⌒

Lulu and Vanna helped Maura dress that evening since Nick was taking her out for dinner. They had no idea where he was taking her, but they could only imagine that it was somewhere special. Maura had chosen the blue, satin dress that left her pale shoulders bare and molded perfectly to her trim, toned, curves.

Vanna had pulled her rich, auburn hair back on the sides and curled the rest of it, letting the fiery ringlets cascade all around her shoulders and down her back. Vanna had added a tiny bit of lip and cheek rouge to Maura's face, which only drew more attention to her pretty, delicate features. Lulu had lent her a good set of diamond costume jewelry, the earrings and necklace adding a sparkling quality to her appearance.

"You think Nick like?" she asked nervously.

Vanna nodded and Lulu said, "You're beautiful. He won't be able to resist you."

Maura beamed. "Thank you for help."

"Are you ready?" Lulu asked.

Putting a hand over her stomach, Maura tried to quiet her nerves. She'd learned to eat the way they did and she knew the proper utensils to use. But outside of the diner or Mama T.'s, Maura had never eaten in public and she didn't want to make a fool of herself or embarrass Nick. However, there was no sense delaying, and she was curious to see where they were going.

"Yes, I ready," she said.

Lulu and Vanna accompanied her into the hallway. They were stopped short by the sight of Nick standing on the staircase landing. Maura's breath caught in her chest over how handsome he looked in a beautiful gray suit that showed off his broad shoulders and long legs. He was equally entranced by her and she saw his dark gaze heat with desire as he walked to her and held out his hand to her.

She gave him hers and he bowed, pressing a kiss to her knuckles. "*Siete una splendida visione di bellezza,*" he said and then signed how beautiful he found her.

Maura blushed and smiled shyly. Vanna smiled and looked over at Lulu and did a double-take at the slightly entranced way she was looking at Nick. She elbowed her sister-in-law lightly. Lulu came back to herself and leaned close to Vanna.

"It's just hearing Italian spoken so romantically. It sends shivers down my spine whenever Sal does it," she whispered.

Vanna stifled a laugh. "I haven't done that with Arrow yet."

Lulu whispered, "You should and see what happens."

Vanna nodded as Nick tucked Maura's hand into the crook of his elbow and led her over to the double doors leading to the wide balcony that ran the length of the house.

"Where are you going?" Vanna asked.

Nick smiled and said, "To Nicola's Café."

"What?" She was thoroughly confused, as were Maura and Lulu.

He opened the doors wide and took Maura out onto the balcony. A beautifully set table and two chairs sat on it. Two tall candelabras and two candles on the table provided them with romantic lighting. Nick seated Maura and then sat down himself as Vanna and Lulu peaked out at the lovely setting.

"Excuse me, *bella donna,*" Sal said from close behind Lulu.

She backed up, seeing that he was dressed in a waiter's uniform. "What are you doing?"

He winked at her. "I'm a waiter at Nicola's Café and I better do my job or Signor Terranova is gonna fire me."

"Why do you have wine?" Lulu said, her eyes widening in alarm upon seeing the bottle in his hand.

Sal smiled. "It's just juice. It's ok."

He took it out to the couple and presented it to Nick, just as he would have if he were a real waiter.

"Signor Terranova, I have the finest bottle of juice that you requested.

Would you like me to pour?" he asked in his best Italian accent.

A smile spread across Maura's face as she caught on to the game that was being played.

Nick said, "Yes, that would be wonderful."

Sal uncorked it and poured the faux-wine with flourish.

"Thank you, Sal," Nick said.

Sal gave him a slight bow. "Your antipasto will be along shortly, Signor Terranova."

"Very good," Nick said.

Sal deferentially withdrew, taking Vanna and Lulu with him downstairs to give Nick and Maura privacy even though he wanted to watch, too.

"You look handsome," Maura said and then indicated their table. "This is beautiful."

"Thank you. I'm glad you like it," he responded. "I hope you had a nice day."

"Yes. Pop and I work in garden," she said.

Gino, who also wore a waiter's uniform, brought their antipasto of fried sardines with parsley caper sauce, sitting the silver serving tray on the table, elegantly removing the lid, and setting it to the side. Maura smiled at him and he returned it, bowed, and left them.

Maura took a bite of the sardines and relished their flavor. "These are delicious. Much better than ones I had when I first came here," she signed. "Did you make them?"

Nick grinned. "Yes, I did. Mama saw all of the empty tins in the garbage pail. That's what tipped her off that someone had been in the house."

She giggled and took another bite. It didn't take long for their treat to disappear and, as if on cue, Alfredo arrived with their *primo*, the first course.

"*Il Signor Terranova, è così buono per vedere ancora una volta. Ci auguriamo che il primo.*"

Nick smiled. "I'm sure we will enjoy it. Thank you, Alfredo."

Alfredo winked at Maura and went back through the double doors. She was having such a good time being entertained this way and Nick was enjoying her reactions to it all.

Picking up her fork, she asked, "What is this?"

"Spinach and goat cheese lasagna. This is one of my favorite dishes that Mama makes. No one makes it like she does," he said.

Maura cut a piece and put in her mouth. The earthiness of the goat cheese and the slightly sweet taste of the spinach perfectly melded and Maura had to force herself not to wolf down the rest of the scrumptious dish. Nick smiled at the expression of pleasure on her face.

As they ate, they talked about their day, especially about the garden and how all of the produce would benefit the restaurant. It might not have seemed like the most romantic conversation to others, but to them it was because it involved things they were passionate about. The restaurant was now Nick's life and Maura loved being in the garden, helping things grow, and knowing that the vegetables and herbs would help him and Sylvia make the delicious foods they served.

Their first course was barely eaten before Arrow brought their, *secondo*, the main course. As he unveiled the braised lamb shanks on soft polenta, Maura gasped at the beautiful presentation of the meat on the platter. She knew that Nick had made them. The aroma that wafted on the breeze made her stomach clamor for the entrée.

Arrow said, "Enjoy, *signor* and *signorina*," before departing.

Nick watched him go and when he turned back to Maura, he was amused to see that Maura had already taken a lamb shank and attacked it. This course was eaten in silence because Maura was enjoying it too much to talk. Nick was happy that she liked it so much. He wanted to do nice things for her, knowing that she hadn't had much joy in her life. She deserved happiness and he was going to do his best to give it to her.

Maura looked at the gorgeous man across the table from her and she could hardly believe that she was there with him. He might need her, but she needed him just as much. His kindness, generosity, and goodness drew her to him. She'd never known that men like him existed and to have found someone like him was almost beyond her comprehension.

However, it wasn't just Nick she'd come to adore. His family was wonderful, as well. They could have taken her to the sheriff or given her back to the man who'd bought her, but instead, they'd taken her in as though she was a part of their family. It was one of the reasons that she'd started working so hard in the garden and around the house. She wanted to show them her gratitude and to make herself useful.

She looked up from her plate and saw Nick watching her with a look in his eyes she was coming to know. Lowering her head a little, she met his gaze and smiled a little. His sensual lips curved and she wanted to kiss him. Her gaze was diverted from him by Sylvia's appearance.

She carried another tray and Maura wondered what it could possibly contain. Sylvia sat their *dolce*, dessert, on the table. Served in delicate dessert glasses was espresso chocolate mousse with orange mascarpone whipped cream.

"*Grazie,* Mama. It looks delicious," Nick said.

Maura smiled at her. "*Grazie,* Mama."

"*Di che cosa,*" Sylvia said, which meant, "it was nothing". "*Godetevi.* Enjoy," she said before leaving.

Maura admired the beautiful dessert. "You made it?"

He nodded.

Picking up her spoon, she dipped into the whipped body of the dessert and tasted it. A rich, sweet, chocolate flavor spread over her tongue with a citrus tang at the end of the bite. The way her eyes lit up with appreciation told Nick that he'd hit his mark with the decadent treat.

Maura ate it slowly, savoring it, while Nick did the same. There wasn't any need for words as they enjoyed it together. Putting down her spoon, Maura sighed and sat back, replete.

Maura said, "Thank you very much."

"You're welcome, *dolcezza*," he said.

"What means '*dolcezza?*'"

"Sweetheart."

She smiled, blushing a little. She wasn't used to being called such things and she loved it when he did. "What I call you?"

"*Tesorino* or *caro*," he said. "Either works."

"*Tesorino*," she said. "I like that."

Nick smiled as he rose. "I'll be right back. Just stay here, ok?"

"Ok."

It was only a few moments until Sal came upstairs, beginning to straighten the table and gathering the dishes into a metal tub. He chitchatted with Maura, asking if she'd enjoyed dinner. The strains of violin music began and Maura looked at Sal.

"Come with me, Maura," Sal said, motioning to her.

Her knitted brow showed her confusion, but she did as he asked. He took her inside to the large landing at the top of the staircase and she looked around her in wonder. A few candelabras had been set up there and at the base of the stairs, too. Henley Remington and Arliss stood just out of her line of sight, playing *Oh, Promise Me*.

Nick stood in the foyer and began singing while he gazed intently at her.

> *Oh, promise me that someday you and I*
> *Will take our love together to some sky*
> *Where we may be alone and faith renew,*
> *And find the hollows where those flowers grew,*
> *Those first sweet violets of early spring,*
> *Which come in whispers, thrill us both, and sing*
> *Of love unspeakable that is to be;*
> *Oh, promise me! Oh, promise me!*

As his splendid, resonant baritone voice filled the foyer and stairwell, Maura understood that the song he was singing was one of romance. She didn't know every word, but she knew that he was proclaiming his love for her. His style of singing was passionate and the way he rolled his "r's" was exciting to her.

When he started the second verse, he began slowly climbing the stairs, his dark eyes never leaving hers. She was so focused on him that she didn't notice that his family was creeping closer to watch the serenade.

Oh, promise me that you will take my hand,
The most unworthy in this lonely land,
And let me sit beside you in your eyes,
Seeing the vision of our paradise,
Hearing God's message while the organ rolls
Its mighty music to our very souls,
No love less perfect than a life with thee;
Oh, promise me! Oh, promise me!

Arriving at the top, he sang the last two lines while he held her hands and her eyes filled with happiness and tears. When his voice faded away, he took her back outside, but the violins continued playing. They repeated the song and changed key slightly as Sal took over with his tenor voice, singing the words in Italian.

Holding Maura's gaze, Nick said and signed, "Maura, I never thought I'd meet another woman for whom I would come to care so much. I was so broken and angry, but you're healing me. You've made me remember that even when life seems the bleakest, that there's always hope for the future. You're the strongest person I've ever met because even though such terrible things have happened to you for so long, you're not jaded or mean.

"I admire you so much for that. But much more than that, I've come to love you for many reasons. You've shown me so much kindness, you give me joy when I didn't think I'd ever find any again, and you're so gentle, sweet, and smart. And so very beautiful. I love you and I would be so proud if you would agree to become my wife. Will you marry me?"

Maura felt a little faint with disbelief. Had Nick really just proposed to her? Surely it was her imagination. Shock rendered her mute for several moments and Nick's expression became one of concern.

"You want to marry me?" she asked.

He smiled and her heart beat faster. "Yes. Will you marry me?"

She surprised him by throwing her arms around his neck and burying her face against his chest as she nodded vigorously. He embraced her laughing. "Maura, I need to hear it."

Pulling back, she smiled up at him as happy tears slid over her cheeks. "Yes, I marry you."

Nick took her left hand and raised it so that he could slide a diamond ring on her finger. It simplistic elegance stole her breath as the candlelight shimmered over it. Then he kissed her softly before leaning his forehead against hers and smiling. She smiled back and then he said, "Let's go tell everyone."

Maura eagerly followed him back inside where they all waited expectantly in the foyer.

"She said yes," Nick said loudly with a huge grin.

The house rang with cries of delight and congratulations at the happy news. Nick and Maura descended to the foyer and were hugged and kissed. Glasses of strawberry/raspberry punch were passed around and the couple's new engagement was toasted. Arliss and Henley were happy to provide more music and a little engagement party took place in the parlor.

Nick taught Maura to dance and as they held each other and laughed with their family, love flowed between them and their connection grew stronger. Alfredo and Sylvia watched the young couple and their hearts rejoiced to see their son so happy once again.

Chapter Nineteen

"Well, you look like an angel," Thad said, entering Andi's office where Allie and her bridesmaids were gathered.

Allie grinned. "Thank you. You're looking quite dashing."

Thad ran a hand down his black suit. "I try to look presentable now and again."

She hugged him. "You certainly do look presentable. Thank you for walking me down the aisle."

He returned her embrace. "You're welcome. I'm honored to do it. I'm losing another girl. At least you waited a little longer than that one over there." He nodded his head in Molly's direction.

Molly smiled. "Sorry, Pa. I'm still your girl and I live with you, so don't act so sad."

"Yeah, and you brought that big galute that eats us out of house and home with you."

She laughed. "He buys food, so don't start that again."

He kissed Allie's temple while giving her a squeeze and then released her. "Are you ready?"

She smiled. "Very. I can't wait to marry Adam."

"He's a good man and I can tell he'll be a good husband," Thad said.

"Yes, he will," Allie said, taking his arm. "Shall we?"

"We shall," he said. To Molly and Vanna, he said, "After you, ladies."

They preceded Allie and Thad out of the office and were met by J.J., who wore a white, frilly dress and looked like a little angel herself with her golden curls and big, blue eyes. She was thrilled to be Allie's flower girl.

Although he was a little older than the usual ring bearer, fourteen-year-old Porter had been very touched that Allie had asked him to fill the role. He stood with J.J., looking very handsome in his new suit. The one he'd worn for Molly's wedding didn't fit him anymore since puberty had hit and he'd grown in both height and muscle.

He smiled at the women. "Boy, you all sure are pretty," he said. "I can't wait for Adam to see you, Allie."

"Thank you," she said, giving him a kiss on the cheek.

Bea began playing the *Wedding March* and J.J. tugged on Porter's hand. "Come on. It's time for us to go."

"I know," Porter said.

The siblings began walking down the aisle, J.J. sprinkling her rose petals very nicely while Porter walked proudly with the rings. Vanna went next, smiling at several people as she walked down the aisle in her pale rose, off-the-shoulder dress. Molly followed her and saw Keith watching her as he stood beside Adam as the best man.

Since he helped Adam through his asthma attacks so much, Wild Wind and Adam had become good friends and the brave had been asked to also stand up with Adam. Wild Wind was happy that he was out of hiding so that he could be with his friend on his special day.

Thad patted Allie's hand and led her down the aisle to her groom. She thought he was the most handsome man as she looked him over in his tuxedo. Despite his asthmatic condition, he was a strong young man. Allie knew just how strong he was from the way he held and kissed her. His light brown hair was nicely styled and his brown eyes held a gleam that she knew well as he smiled at her.

Gazing at Allie, Adam knew that he would never forget how lovely she was in her dazzling white dress with a lace overlay on the bodice and a full skirt. He knew what a lucky man he was to have found such a beautiful, wonderful woman like her. She was a dream come true, and he was going to show her every day how much he cherished her.

Reaching the altar, Thad held out a hand to Adam, who shook it.

"Take good care of her, son, or I'll make you sorry," Thad said with a firm look at him.

Adam knew Thad meant it. He solemnly nodded. "I will."

Holding back tears, Thad kissed Allie's cheek and went to sit with Jessie, who held their sleeping son. As he settled next to her, Thad took out a handkerchief and blotted away his tears while Jessie put a hand on his knee. He smiled at her and then focused on the ceremony.

As the service progressed, there were three men who were thinking about a wedding day being in their future. Nick put his arm around Maura, smiling down at her. He was glad that they wouldn't be waiting very long to wed. Maura looked up at him, wishing that they were the ones standing up at the altar exchanging vows. Both were ready to begin their life together.

The other man was Arliss. He and his brothers watched Andi perform the ceremony and he wondered who would perform their wedding. Of course, they had to officially ask her first, but they were fairly certain of her answer since they'd discussed marrying a few times.

Gino felt a stab of jealousy as he watched Adam and Allie tenderly kiss to seal the new marriage. He wondered when it would be his turn to find that sort of happiness. Then he shook off those thoughts and celebrated with everyone else as they clapped for the newlyweds.

Allie and Adam stood for their pictures and then were swept away to the reception, which lasted until early evening. They finally made their getaway, leaving for Dickensville, where they would spend the night before heading on to Los Angeles, California. Both had been saving up the money for the trip and others had also gifted money to them. They had both been interested in the city and wanted to go while Adam had off work for the summer and before they settled down and started a family.

The couple's family and friends sent them off in a flurry of well-wishing as they waved back from their carriage. Thad put an arm around both Jessie and Adam's mother, Charlene. Both women quietly cried wistful, happy tears and Thad was hard pressed not to join them.

Allie might not be his biological daughter, but he'd come to love her like one and he felt the same mix of joy and sadness that parents do when their children grow up and begin their adult lives. Then he led them back inside Spike's for more celebrating.

Beginning on the night of their engagement, Nick had been working on returning to being the man he'd once been. One of the ways he did that was abstaining from intimacy with Maura. He explained his reasoning for it to her, assuring her that it wasn't because he didn't desire her, because he did.

He'd told her that he wanted to do right by her and continuing to partially rely on her as a crutch to overcome his alcoholism wasn't fair to her and it wasn't going to help him stand on his own somewhat. He needed her support, but using lovemaking to avoid his problems wasn't healthy. He'd been doing it long enough and he finally realized that it was time to take things in hand and face his demons instead of running from them.

Although Maura missed him terribly, she was grateful for his consideration of her and she wanted to support him in whatever way she could. She was touched that he wanted the next time they were intimate to be on their wedding night when it was much more meaningful than just the two of them seeking comfort. No one had ever made such a thoughtful gesture on her behalf before.

It wasn't any easier for Nick—not only was he battling missing her, he fought the mental and physical urge to drink. It was good that all of the liquor in the house was locked up because there were a few nights when he was almost unable to control himself. On those nights, he got one of his family members out of bed to help keep him occupied and out of trouble.

They were all proud of Nick for how hard he worked on maintaining his sobriety, and they offered him unconditional love and support. During this time, Nick often went off on late night tirades while one of his loved ones was "babysitting" him, raging at everything from God to the people who made alcohol. Sometimes he made sense and sometimes he didn't, but he got a lot of things off his chest and felt better for it.

He also talked about Ming Li and Jake, something he'd hardly done since the tragedy. It was acutely painful, but also cathartic, and the more he did it, the easier it got. There were times at work when Nick's hands would tremble at the thought that a recipe required wine. He wasn't yet strong enough to be able to handle alcohol without drinking it.

During those times, he asked Sylvia to add the wine and mix it in while he went out into the dining room until she called him. He could have left the alcohol out, but he wasn't willing sacrifice the quality of the dish because of his weakness. Keith, Tyler, and Jessie were very good about keeping the wine away from him.

Nick discovered that Tyler did much better out in the dining room where he could socialize with the patrons. He preferred waiting tables to doing the more mundane kitchen work. He was attentive, charming, and kept things going in Allie's absence. Nick decided to keep him in the dining room even when Allie came back.

Maura loved spending her time in the garden during the day and she and Arrow developed a good friendship. He helped her learn how to read and write, as did the rest of the family. Adam had given Arrow primers and more difficult books and he passed them on to Maura. He also taught her some Cheyenne, but she refused to teach anyone Comanche. Speaking it reminded her of the past too much and she wanted to put that far behind her and only look to the future.

Alfredo and Maura were working in the garden one day when Evan strolled around the corner of the house and waved at them. Maura had been grateful to Evan for saving her from Red and she had grown to like the sheriff. She waved back at him, noticing that a soldier walked next to him.

Alfredo brushed dirt from his hands as he straightened up. "Hello,

Evan. Who's your friend here?" he asked. He was leery about the army now and got straight to the point.

"This is Captain Spencer. Captain, this is Alfredo Terranova and Maura," Evan said. "Maura, he'd like to talk to you."

Maura looked into the soldier's blue eyes. "What about?"

Capt. Spencer said, "Well, ma'am, it's about your husband."

Alfredo's eyebrows drew together. "Husband? She's not married. She's engaged to my son, Nick." He looked at Evan, who wore a concerned frown, which put him on edge.

Maura said, "I do not have a husband."

Capt. Spencer pulled a piece of paper from a pocket and unfolded it. "According to this marriage certificate, you do."

Maura took the certificate and read it. She didn't recognize the first name of Hobart, but she knew that the last name was Timmons, Red's surname. She'd only ever known him as Red. Her hand trembled and she shook her head. "No! I am not his wife! We never had a wedding or anything!" She clutched Alfredo's arm. "Please, I did not marry him. It is not true!"

The certificate dropped to the ground and Capt. Spencer snatched it up before it blew away.

Evan scratched his chin and said, "I'm afraid it's real. Maura, you never had a wedding? Did pastors ever come visit your tribe?"

She shook her head. "Just a couple of priests."

Maura thought back to when Red had first visited her tribe. There had been a priest there one day. Her former master had paraded her around for Red and his friends and Red had pointed at her. Money had exchanged hands and Red had hauled her over to the priest, who had read from his Bible and talked to Red.

Red had made her nod from time to time and then the priest had smiled a little and said something to Red. Then Red had kissed her, which she'd hated. The priest had handed Red a piece of paper, but Maura hadn't paid much attention to it. Her former master had just said she'd been to go with him, that he'd bought her. He'd never mentioned marriage, though.

However, after witnessing a Christian wedding, she now saw that what had occurred that day had been a very hasty, crude wedding. She didn't understand. Red had never referred to her as his wife, even when he'd talked about her to other people. He'd also never called himself her husband.

"I see again?" she asked, holding out her hand for the certificate.

Spencer handed it back to her and her eyes roamed over it. *Kendell. My last name is Kendell? I didn't know anyone even knew my last name. I never heard it mentioned. Why? You were raised as a Comanche slave, that's why. No one cared enough about you to worry about your last name until Red came along. Oh, Great Spirit! What am I going to do?*

Tears fell from her eyes as she gave the certificate back to Spencer. "A priest came when Red bought me from master. I thought that they just talking. He must say a wedding. I did not know." A sob escaped her. "You taking me back to him?"

Spencer replied, "No, ma'am, but I need to ask you some questions about Red and some of his friends. They've been involved in some illegal activity and we're building a case against him."

"I not know how to help you. Red and friends never spoke Comanche. Only to me. Did not know English. Do not know what they said," she explained.

"But maybe you saw something that would be useful to us. Did you ever see him or anyone else with a lot of guns or money?" he asked.

Maura shook her head. "No. I not allowed leave house much. Never did … that in house."

Spencer asked, "What did you do? Surely they must have visited or something."

Maura's face turned tomato-red as she shook her head and looked at the ground. "No. No visit."

"Do you expect me to believe that they never came over to your house? Maybe for dinner or to play cards?" Spencer pressed.

Maura closed her eyes, praying that the Great Spirit would fly her away from that place to save her more embarrassment and pain. "No. They not play cards."

Alfredo said, "She's answered your questions, Captain. I think it's time to leave her alone, now." He put a protective arm around Maura. "She doesn't know anything."

Spencer snorted. "She was his wife."

Maura glared at him, her temper rising. "No! Not wife! Not really. Want to know they did? They make me whore." She poked her chest. "Hit me, make me do … things! Treat me like animal! That what they did! Happy?"

Spencer's face flushed as did the other men's. "I-I'm sorry, ma'am. I didn't know. If that's the case, you have grounds to divorce him. You could get a lawyer and get rid of him."

Maura was too mortified to understand what he was saying. Breaking away from Alfredo, she ran to the house, her chest hurting from her hard sobs.

Alfredo's eyes spat fire at Spencer. "You're just lucky that the sheriff is here or else I'd knock you into next week for embarrassin' her like that. She doesn't know anything, so leave her be or the one who'll need a lawyer is you when I sue you for harassment." He nodded a farewell to Evan and followed Maura.

"What the hell are we gonna do?" Alfredo said to Sylvia after he'd explained what had happened to her after she'd come home from the restaurant that day. "We'll have to delay the wedding until she's divorced." He paced back and forth in the parlor where they'd been talking.

Sylvia said, "Al, you know that she can't get divorced. She was married by a Catholic priest, so she has to apply for an annulment. That's the only way she can marry Nick. No priest would refuse an annulment, but it could take two years to get one."

"I don't believe it. Those poor kids." Alfredo stopped pacing. "Maybe if we paid the tribunal a little extra, they'd push it through faster. If we could get it done in six months, that wouldn't be so bad. But two years?" Lowering his voice, he asked, "What if she's in the family way already? They can't have a child out of wedlock."

Tears gathered in her eyes. "Oh, Alfredo. What a mess this is."

He sat down beside her on the sofa and took her in his arms as his own tears trickled from his eyes.

Chapter Twenty

As he rode home that night, Nick prayed almost the whole way there, thanking God for all of the blessings in his life. He'd gotten a lot of his anger out of his heart and he was now at a point where he could once again look to the Lord for guidance and with gratitude. He knew he would never understand the reason why his wife and child had to die, but he couldn't go back and change what had happened.

He'd suffered so much guilt, thinking that he could have saved them if he'd only gotten on that lifeboat with them. But he'd done the right thing, leaving room for other people and helping to get more people off the ship. He'd been trying to save Ming Li and Jake by putting them in the lifeboat so they could get clear of the ship. The captain of their lifeboat hadn't done it fast enough, which Nick would never understand, either.

Nick knew he would always carry pain in his heart over it, but it was time to stop letting it consume him. He had a lot to be thankful for and he needed to concentrate on that and let go of his bitterness. Thinking of Maura, he smiled in anticipation of seeing her. He missed her during the day and he ached to hold her at night. There had been a few times when he'd almost gone back on his decision to not be intimate, but he'd been able to control his desire.

Arriving home, he noticed that the parlor and dining room windows were illuminated. Maybe his family was playing cards, he thought with anticipation. He was in such a good mood and a card game sounded good to him. Making short work of putting away his horse, he jogged up to the house, entering the parlor where his parents sat.

"*Ciao*, Mama, Pop," he said, smiling. "Are we playing cards?"

Alfredo shifted in his chair and something in his blue eyes put Nick on edge. "I doubt it. Sit down, Nicky. We need to talk to you."

Nick's heartbeat sped up as he perched on a chair. "What it is?"

Alfredo ran his hand through his hair and then started his story. Nick listened, anger, dismay, and sorrow building in heart. By the time Alfredo had finished, he was furious over the situation. He got up to pace back and forth.

"I don't understand! Why is this happening? I finally find someone to be happy with again and now she's out of my reach suddenly! An annulment might take two years or even longer, so we can't get married unless I renounce my faith and I just can't do that. But she might be pregnant and I don't want to have a child out of wedlock. I'm so stupid! So, so, stupid!"

Sylvia said, "We'll pay the tribunal to push it through faster. There's no way they would refuse based on the situation. First off, she didn't understand what was happening and that's one of the rules for a sanctified union. Plus, he abused her and forced her to … serve whoever else. There're even more grounds."

Nick nodded. "Plus, she's never been baptized Catholic or otherwise. I'll wait for the annulment and if we have a baby in the meantime so be it. There's no way to get around that."

Alfredo nodded. "She can't keep living here in the meantime. You know that, Nick."

Nick said, "Well, if she is pregnant, I'm not having her live alone. I want to share in the experience, the way I did with Jake."

Sylvia asked, "Are you gonna be able to control things between you if she stays? What if the annulment does take two years? Are you gonna be able to wait that long?"

"I don't know. I just can't believe this!" Nick said, fuming. "I slept with a married woman and became engaged to a married woman." It was too much for him. Searing anger took hold of him. He picked up a crystal figurine that sat on the table beside his chair and hurled it into the fireplace where it smashed into a million pieces.

"Nicky!" Alfredo said, jumping up. "Stop that!"

"Am I cursed? Is that it? Is this my punishment for something? What did I ever do to deserve this?"

Alfredo took him the shoulders. "You're not bein' punished. It's just something that happened. We'll work through it together."

"How, Pop? God, I want a drink," Nick said. The high stress caused his thirst for alcohol to kick in.

"No, Nick," Alfredo said. "You don't need it. You'll be fine without it."

"Where's Maura? She must be as devastated as me," Nick said.

Sylvia said, "She's locked herself in her room and won't come out. We've all tried, but nothing is getting through to her."

Holding back tears, Nick said, "I'll go see if I can get her to come out."

He ran up the stairs and went to her door, knocking on it. "Maura, it's me. Please unlock the door. We'll work this out."

Maura lay on her bed, staring sightlessly at the wall. "Leave me be! There no way out!"

Nick said, "If you don't open it, I'll just break it down."

Maura closed her eyes in disappointment. She knew that he meant it. Drained emotionally and physically from all of the crying she'd done, she was slow to move. Going to the door, she unlocked it and went back to the bed, lying down again.

"Maura, we'll apply for an annulment and then get married. I know it's a big obstacle, but we'll overcome it," he said.

Alfredo and Sylvia had explained to her about the annulment process and she'd had hope that it would work out until they'd told her how long it might be until it was granted. She knew that Nick would never get married anywhere other than a Catholic church and he wouldn't sleep with her until they were married. She knew that she was considered an adulterer, but she hadn't known she was married. She'd made Nick one, too, and that made her feel so guilty.

"You cannot wait so long," she said, barely looking at him. "I not worthy. I will go."

"Maura, you can't go anywhere and I'll wait forever if I have to. I love you and I want to be with you," he said, sitting down on the bed with her.

When he moved to stroke her hair, she shied away. "No. Don't, please? It hurts too much. I go tomorrow."

"Maura, you don't have any money. Where will you go?" Nick asked.

Maura said, "I find job. Look for place."

"Please, honey. Just hang in there, ok?" he pleaded.

Suddenly angry, she sat up and said, "No! Will not make bad for you! No way out. I must go!"

Nick was horrified to see her slide her engagement ring off. "Maura, don't do that. Please."

She held it out to him. "I not make you wait. Find another wife."

He refused to take the ring. "No. I don't want anyone else. Only you. Put the ring back on, Maura."

"No, Nick. There is no hope. I have none. My whole life wait for you and now cannot have you. Hope … gone," she said despondently, lying back down. The ring laid beside her on the bed.

Nick picked it up and tried to put it back on her finger. "Maura, I'm not gonna let you give up and neither will I. I know things look dark right now, but we're gonna figure this out."

Maura pulled away from him. "No! We are done! Leave me alone! Get out!" she screamed. "No hope! Go away!" She was quickly growing hysterical, the stress of it all making her control slip. She kept screaming at Nick, trying to make him go away and refusing to let him touch her when he wanted to comfort her.

Vanna came into the room. "Nick, leave her be. She won't calm down until you do. I'll take care of her," she said quietly.

Nick shook his head. "I need her to listen to me."

Vanna said, "She can't right now. Please go and I'll take care of her. Just give her some time."

Trying to be reasonable, Nick nodded curtly, put the ring in a decorative dish on the little desk in Maura's room and left. Vanna shut the door and sat down on the bed, hugging Maura and letting her vent all of her emotions.

"I thought you were on the wagon?"

Nick sat at the bar in Spike's staring at the shot of whiskey in front of him. He hadn't touched it yet. He looked up to see Thad sitting down beside him.

"I am, but I'm this close to falling off," he said, holding up his thumb and forefinger so that they were poised very close to one another.

"I thought things were going good. What happened?" Thad asked, quickly scooting the liquor away from Nick.

"Hey! That's mine," he protested. "Give that back."

"Not until after we talk. After that, it's your decision if you drink it, but I hope you don't," Thad said. "Now, come with me." He wanted to move away from the bar because Spike was nosy and had trouble keeping his mouth shut sometimes.

Reluctantly, Nick followed Thad to an out-of-the-way table and sat down.

"Ok. Spill the beans," Thad said, even though he had a good idea what the problem was. He'd been present when Captain Spencer had shown up at the sheriff's office. He knew that Nick needed to talk, though.

"Sure. What the heck?" Nick replied and filled Thad in on the events that had transpired that day. "And so now, I have slept with a married woman, who could be pregnant now. I know she can get both a Catholic annulment and a legal divorce, which we need before we can get married, but she doesn't want to make me wait that long. She's been through so much, Thad. But she came through it all and she's always so positive and strong. Not now. She's given up. Her strength is gone. Her heart and spirit are broken and my heart is broken. She broke our engagement and she wants to move out. She doesn't have any money and there's nowhere for her to go. I'd give her money, but I know she won't accept it."

Thad ruminated on everything Nick had told him. "You know, with Allie moving out, we have an extra room right now. We didn't move Liz over there yet. She could stay with us and we could work on her a little. Make her see that she can't give up. You could come and go as you wanted to and you'd know that she was safe."

Nick's jaw clenched. "I don't want her to go anywhere."

"I know you don't, but she's gonna, so she might as well go where she'll be taken care of."

Nick swallowed hard, working to keep tears at bay. The last thing he wanted to do was cry in front of everyone there. He nodded and quickly left the bar, unable to stop the flow of sadness. He rode away, galloping his horse down the road. Entering the town, he swung his horse over to the church, jumped down and tied it to a hitching post. Hurrying inside, he strode up to the altar and sank down on his knees. Despite being in a Protestant church, he crossed himself.

"Heavenly Father, I don't know why You are putting this trial in front of me. I'm so confused right now. I'm trying to do what You want me to do, but I don't know what that is. Is this Your way of telling me that Maura isn't meant to be my wife? Is it a test of some sort? Help me understand! Thank You for sending Thad to talk to me and stop me from drinking.

"You took Ming Li and Jake from me and I'm making my peace with that. I know You have a plan for everything, even if I can't see it, but what is Your plan concerning Maura? You brought her into my life when I needed her the most, but now it seems like You want to take her out of it. Are You punishing me for not becoming a priest? For choosing Ming Li instead of the priesthood? I don't want to think that, but I can't help it.

"Normally I don't ask for this sort of thing, but can You please give me a sign either way concerning Maura? I need You, Lord! I'm begging You to show me the path I'm meant to take! Please give me the strength to accept whatever it is and to stay away from alcohol. I know I'm asking You for a lot tonight, but please help me find a way for Maura and I to be together. I need her and love her so much. Please."

Nick broke down completely at that point, pouring out his heartache to his Savior, calling on Him for strength, healing, and mercy. He stayed there a long time, even once his tears were spent. The quiet and dimness of the church were comforting to him. He was so wrung out that he lay down the front pew and went to sleep.

Nick didn't remember falling off the pew, but he must have at some point because when he woke up, he was lying face down on the floor. He was stiff from sleeping on the hard surface and rose slowly, sitting down heavily in a pew. Floorboards creaked somewhere behind him and he turned to see Andi coming down the aisle.

She smiled at him. "I was just coming to wake you. I have some coffee in my office if you'd like some."

"I'd love some," he said. "What time is it?"

"Quarter after seven."

He groaned. "My family is gonna be worried when I'm not there," he said, following her into her office.

She took the coffee pot off the little stove in a corner and poured the hot brew into two metal cups. Pushing one over to him, she offered him cream and sugar, which he declined. He took a sip and sighed.

Andi sat down. "I don't mean to pry, but the only people I usually have sleep in the church are either drunk, homeless, both, or in spiritual turmoil. You don't smell like booze and you live in a beautiful home, so, in your case, it must be the latter."

Nick didn't want to get into it all again. He had a full day of work ahead of him and he needed to get his head right so he could do his job. Looking into her kind eyes, he said, "I'm going through something incredibly difficult right now on top of trying to stay on the wagon. Last night, things came to a head and I almost drank. I went to Spike's, intent on getting plastered, but Thad came along and stopped me. I'm glad he did."

Andi nodded. "Me, too. People think it's easy to quit drinking, but it's not. It's something you'll always have to work on. Some people can cut back and be fine, but other people will go right back to it if they have even one sip."

Nick said, "I'm that last statement. I know if I get even the slightest taste of it, I'll be done in. I can tell that about myself. I hope to be stronger about it one day, but that day hasn't come yet."

"It's good that you can recognize that," Andi said. "A lot of people can't and they end up drinking even more than they used to."

"Yeah. Do you mind if I ask you something?"

"No. Go ahead, but I'll bet you're wondering if I ever have doubts about what I do," Andi said.

Nick shook his head. "How do you do that?"

"I just pick up on feelings. It's hard to explain," Andi said. "The answer is yes. I'm sure a lot of other clergy do, too. We *are* human, after all. I love what I do. I never doubt my calling, but I always feel terrible when I can't reach someone. Some clergy concentrate so much on theology, and there's nothing wrong with that, but helping people is what I do best. That can be by giving them money for medicine or just listening to them. Sometimes I can help find them work so they can put food on the table. Being a pastor is much more than just getting up on Sunday and giving a sermon and, while I enjoy being in the pulpit, I love being out helping people in the community even more. That's left over from my time in the Salvation Army."

"You've led an interesting life for someone so young," Nick said.

"I'm not all that young anymore. I'll soon be twenty-four—an old maid by most standards," Andi said.

"Not by mine. I'll be thirty in November."

"What made you want to be a priest?"

Nick smiled. "A lot of people ask me that. I didn't know I wanted to until I was right around your age. I'd always loved church as a boy and I was an altar boy when we lived in New York. We went every Sunday, which annoyed my brothers, especially Sal. Anyway, when we moved here, we were only able to go to church every so often because the only Catholic church was in Billings. We would have come to church here, but the pastor before Sam wasn't fond of Catholics.

"With just starting a new business here, it was hard to find time to get away, so we worshipped at home, which was nice, but I missed our old priest and the whole experience of mass. The school here wasn't all that good and my parents knew that I wanted to go to college for business, so they sent me to live with Father Carini in Billings so I could finish my last two years of school there to prepare me for college.

"That very first week there, when I'd gone to mass with him, I felt like I'd come home. I'm sure you know what I mean. I missed my family like crazy, but I was really happy there. I came home once a month and in the summer and they came there for Christmas and Easter. I went to Chicago University, but it was pretty clear after my second semester that while I loved helping in our family's business, a business degree was going to be useless to me. I was failing fast.

"Mama and Pop were furious since they were putting out so much money for school. I was too distracted because I'd gotten involved with the Catholic church at school and that's where I spent most of my time."

Andi said, "So that's when you decided to become a priest?"

"Nope. I told the parents that it was a waste of time for me to go back to college, but I stayed in Chicago for a few years. My family didn't understand why I didn't want to come home, but I was a grown man, so they didn't stand in my way. My actual calling didn't happen until Father McFarland said to me one night, 'Nicky, you should be a priest.' I just gave him a look, you know? He smiled and said since I spent all of my time at church helping and that I didn't seem interested in girls that I should be a priest."

Andi laughed at that. "It sounds like Father McFarland was a character."

"He was. He was only kidding, but what he'd said was true. Outside of working in a restaurant, I did spend the majority of my time at church or volunteering. It's what made me happiest. Even more so than cooking."

"What about girls?"

"Oh, there was one or two I liked, but they just weren't all that important to me. I mean, like most boys, you have those urges, but I guess mine just weren't as strong or whatever. It wasn't until I went on a mission trip to Japan and met Ming Li that I envisioned myself settling down and having a family. It was a good thing I was only a student then or else I'd have had a hard time staying in the priesthood.

"I fell in love with her the first time I looked into her eyes, I swear. I have no idea why. I'd never met her before, but our eyes met and that was it. I prayed for those feelings to be taken away. Prayed so hard about it, but day after day, somehow or another, she was put in my path. I finally talked about it with the priest I was on the mission with, Father Parsons. After a couple of months of this, he told me that he'd prayed about it, too, and since my feelings hadn't gone away, had only gotten stronger, and it seemed like Ming Li liked me since she was always stealing looks at me and finding ways to talk to me, that I wasn't meant to be a priest."

Andi said, "You're a very nice, handsome man. I can understand why she would be drawn to you."

Nick blushed a little. "Thanks. I thought he was crazy at first, but I couldn't deny it any longer. When Father Parsons said that we would leaving in a few weeks, I knew that I needed to make up my mind: commit to the priesthood or to Ming Li. I guess you know which choice I made."

"Nick, you have nothing to feel guilty about. I believe that Father Parsons was right. Your path was Ming Li—at that time. But we both know that paths can change. Mine did. Arliss isn't the first beau I've ever had. I realize that it's a little different for me since I'm allowed to marry, but still. I had to decide whether to marry at the time or to stay in the Salvation Army. I guess you know which choice *I* made," Andi said.

She'd done it again. Either she really could read thoughts like Nick had heard she could or she was just very good at understanding human nature and reading people. She wasn't a priest, but Nick respected her theological knowledge and her opinion as a clergywoman.

"You're right. Paths change, but I don't understand why that meant Ming Li and Jake had to die," Nick said.

Having just recently dealt with her three-men-in-one's "death", she understood exactly what Nick was saying. The anger, grief, and "whys" had kept her awake on many nights. "Nick, I didn't mean just your path, I meant theirs, too. When I thought Arliss was dead, I felt everything you've gone through. I hadn't lost a child, but I lost three people at once. I don't expect you to understand since you don't know them very well.

"I asked all of the same questions. Why were they brought into my life to love and then taken away? I finally received an answer. Because it wasn't *their* path to be with *me*. However hard it is to accept, and it is incredibly difficult, it wasn't their path to be with you forever. All of the people in our lives have a purpose, you know that. You have a purpose for being in mine and vice versa. They all have something to teach us, no matter how briefly they're with us."

Nick felt the hair rise on the back of his neck and he sat a little straighter. "What was their purpose?"

"To show you what true love felt like and that you weren't meant to live without it. Jake was meant to give you joy and to show you what it's like to be a father, to show you how much you *wanted* to be a father," she said, watching anger build in his eyes.

"But why kill them once I'd been shown?"

"Nick, it wasn't about what you *wanted*. It was about what you were meant to *be*. There's a reason for it, but it might take a while for it to be revealed. It was one of the few things that kept me going once I thought Arliss was gone. I kept holding on to the knowledge that I was meant to do something else with my life, meet someone else, although at the time I knew I would never fall in love again. Or so I thought. But I came to understand that Arliss had had a different path to follow and that God had something else in mind for me."

"But in your case, that wasn't really true because Arliss came back from that hunting trip. It was a false report. So his path *is* with you," Nick said.

"So far," Andi said. "But going through all of that grief, despair, and anger taught me that if they're ever taken from me for good, I must go on and that if I keep myself open to it, I'll find out why. There might be a lot of reasons why, but I'll find them if I keep my eyes open. You shut your eyes, Nick. Your *spiritual* eyes. Your heart was so broken that you kept the blinders on to everything else but your grief for a long time. You didn't keep yourself open and God used alcohol to make you susceptible to Maura, to make you receptive to her because she needed someone who understood great pain to be in the right place at the right time!"

Nick was electrified by Andi's passion and by her perceptiveness. Not only that, but she knew, she *knew*. "How could you know that we ...?"

Andi clapped a hand over her mouth before saying, "I'm sorry. Sometimes when I become excited about something I can't keep up my wall. I'm sorry. But it was meant to be because God knew that otherwise, you would never, ever allow yourself to become involved with her. She's your path and you're hers."

"But how can that be? We have to get an annulment before we can get married," Nick said. "That could take a couple of years. She's already broken our engagement and she has no hope left that we can ever be together."

"You have to be strong enough for both of you, Nick. She's where you were after Ming Li and Jake's deaths. You had your family and friends to help you. She needs all of you, too. But you're the one she mainly needs, Nick. It's time to take off the blinders all the way and open yourself up again. Get those spiritual eyes open like I had to," Andi said. "She needs you to see *for* her because she can't right now."

Nick felt shell-shocked as he stared into Andi's eyes. He knew that no priest could have given him any better advice than she had and those blinders were indeed coming off as he sat there. He wasn't going to let Maura give up and he wasn't ready to give up, either. Not this time. Feeling better than he had in a long time, Nick stood up and held out a hand to Andi.

"Thank you. You've helped me more than I'll ever be able to tell you. When Maura and I get married, I want you to help officiate. I'll talk to Father Carini about it."

Andi laughed as she shook his hand. "Wow! A Protestant lady pastor officiating at a Catholic wedding! Aren't you afraid that God won't approve?" she teased him.

Nick chuckled. "If that was the case, He wouldn't have sent me here to talk to you. You're a sneaky lady. You sure got a lot out of a guy who didn't wanna talk about it. Free lunch for you and Arliss today, or whichever one he is at the time. In fact, he can be my guest waiter."

"You may regret that, but you'll be entertained," Andi said. "I'm just glad I could help you, Nick, and I'm here if you need me."

"Thanks again," Nick said, leaving her office.

Chapter Twenty-One

"There you are!" Sylvia exclaimed as Nick entered the kitchen at home. "Where have you been? Are you all right?" Her dark eyes roamed anxiously over him.

He hugged her. "I'm fine, Mama. I was at the church."

She gave him a quizzical look. "All night?"

"Yeah. I went to Spike's. I was gonna get drunk, but I didn't," Nick said.

"Nicky!" she said. "You've been doing so well. I know you were upset, but—"

"Mama, listen to me. I *didn't* drink. Just let's get breakfast on the table and I'll tell everyone what happened all at once," Nick said.

"All right, but this better be good," Sylvia groused. "It's almost ready. You can help me finish up."

"Yes, ma'am."

"You're really going to keep me in suspense, huh?"

"I really am, Mama," Nick said, smiling.

As she watched Nick move around, Sylvia saw something different in her son—a buoyancy that hadn't been there for a long time. He was always happy when he was in the kitchen, but this happiness seemed to come from inside him. She hadn't seen that in him again until recently, but it was even stronger now.

The rest of the family greeted him, plying him with questions, too, but he gave them the same answer as he had his mother.

"Well, we know he didn't stay out all night with some woman and he doesn't smell like booze," Sal said, smiling. "So whatever it is, can't be too bad."

"He said he was at the church," Sylvia said.

Nick got a kick out of the way they carried on their conversation as if he wasn't there.

Sal laughed. "Well, unless Pastor Andi turned the church into a brothel, then we *really* know it can't be bad."

Alfredo smacked his arm in passing and Sal almost dropped the plate of sausage he carried. "Don't talk about church like that!"

"Ow, Pop! I said she *didn't* turn it into a brothel!"

"Still, don't say things like that about church," Alfredo said. "Now quit causing trouble and go put that on the table."

"How is that that me, the reformed womanizer, always comes out the bad guy, when *he's* the alcoholic? I swear, it'll always be that way," Sal said.

Arrow snatched a piece of sausage from his tray. "That's because you are bad in many, many ways," he said, then left the kitchen.

"What's that supposed to mean? Hey, get back here! Here, Noodle, hold this while I go kill your husband," Sal said.

Vanna took it and laughed. "Don't kill him before we have a baby, Sally!"

Arrow popped his head back into the kitchen, giving her a displeased look. "But it's all right if he kills me afterwards?"

Sal tackled him from behind. "Never underestimate an angry Italian," he said, getting Arrow in a chokehold.

Nick let out a loud laugh at the sight of his little brother wrestling in the dining room with an Indian. "God sure has a sense of humor," he said, succumbing to a long fit of laughter before he went upstairs to see if he could get Maura to come down to eat.

She opened the door when he knocked and he smiled at her. "Good morning, *dolcezza*. Are you hungry? Breakfast is ready."

Maura's heart was filled with happiness to see him at first, but then she remembered all that was lost to her. "No. Not hungry. I will go soon."

His smile faded. "I don't want you to go, but I understand. I love you, Maura and I'm not gonna give up on us. I'm not gonna give up hope that this will somehow work out for us, so don't you, either. And if you can't find hope, that's ok. I know what that's like. I'll just hope for us both."

She shrugged a little.

"You know, since Allie got married, she's not living at home anymore," Nick said. "I saw Thad last night and he said that you could come live with them and use her old room until this gets straightened out. You know Jessie, Keith, and Molly. You'd be safe there and you wouldn't be alone. What do you think?"

Maura decided that since she didn't have any other options it was as good as any. "I will get job to pay them."

Nick said, "Ok. I don't think they're worried about that right now, though. I'll take you over after breakfast. Are you sure you're not hungry?"

She shook her head. "No." She wanted to believe Nick, but she didn't want to get her hopes up only to have them crushed again. She wanted him to hold and kiss her, giving her the comfort she desperately wanted. However, there was no guarantee of anything and having him hold her would only make it harder to do the right thing and leave.

Nick briefly let her see his disappointment, but then he brightened. "Ok. I'll let you know when I'm done and have the buggy hitched."

"All right."

Nick gave her a small smile and left to go back downstairs to fill his family in on where he'd been and what had happened.

Two weeks later, Maura came home from working at her nanny/housekeeping job that she'd picked up thanks to Molly, who'd informed her of the position. It was still strange to her to be living with the McIntyres. Although she enjoyed them and they were kind to her, she greatly missed the Terranovas, the people she'd come to think of as her family.

One of the things she missed the most, apart from being with Nick, was working in the garden with Alfredo. They'd had such a good time and she longed to work with the plants. She wanted to sit down to their noisy, argumentative dinners and greet Nick when he came home at night. They'd played cards a lot and she'd gotten pretty good at rummy.

The McIntyres were also noisy and Thad's grouchiness in the mornings before he'd had his coffee and cigarette made everyone laugh. Little T.J. was such a happy baby and Maura loved playing with him, Liz, and J.J. She'd even made friends with Killer, Thad's big black stallion. The horse and he had made quite a crime-fighting team back when Thad was still a bounty hunter. Killer now helped to keep the peace around Echo.

Nick came over several nights a week to spend time with her, trying to instill hope within her that they'd be able to get married at some point. He wasn't accepting her breaking off their engagement. She saw a new strength in him and she was proud of him for not going back to drinking. He made it difficult not to have fun when he was there or to keep her heart from reaching out to him.

Eventually he would go away and that was what was best for him. She loved him so strongly that she wanted him to find someone worthy of him and who didn't have anything keeping her from marrying him. She'd looked into getting a civil divorce because she no longer wanted to be tied to Red. It would require his signature and if he wouldn't give it, she'd have to go to court about it. Evan and Shadow were both prepared to testify on her behalf about Red's abusive behavior towards her. She was grateful for the help of her new friends.

She was tired that night and her only thought was to eat dinner and go to bed. She slept a lot these days and her fatigue weighed on her. Therefore, she was surprised and dismayed to see Captain Spencer sitting on the back porch.

"I already told you what I know," she said.

He nodded. "I know. I'm not here to question you anymore. I just felt so badly about what happened that day that I wanted to apologize to you in person."

His friendly manner put her at ease. "You did not know it would upset me. You were doing your job."

"Yes, but I could have been a little more sensitive. I didn't realize what the situation was between you and Red," he said. "It's really none of my business, but I hope you're going ahead with divorce proceedings. You really do have grounds and I'd be happy to put in a good word for you, too. I know the judge in Helena who deals with the divorces around here."

She was touched by his generosity. "Thank you. Yes, I will divorce him. I will let you know if I need your help."

"You're welcome. Now for the other reason I came. When you're ready to go see Red for him to sign the divorce papers, I'd like to be there to make sure he cooperates. I was wondering if you could go the Friday after next. I'm free that day and I could meet you at the state prison," Captain Spencer said.

Maura was even more grateful to him. "Yes. I will set it up."

"Good. I'll meet you there at one o'clock. I won't keep you, ma'am. Have a good evening," Spencer said, tipping his hat and walking to his horse. He mounted, waved at her, and rode away.

Jessie hadn't been eavesdropping, but she'd stayed in the kitchen to make sure that the soldier didn't upset Maura. When Maura came in the kitchen door, she asked, "Is everything all right?"

"Yes. I am going to go have Red sign the divorce papers. I will go next Friday if I can find someone to take me. He said he would make Red sign them. It will be good to be rid of him for good," Maura said.

Jessie smiled sympathetically. "I'm sure it will be."

As a woman who'd been trapped in a loveless marriage for a number of years before meeting Thad, she knew something of the relief Maura would feel at being free of the man who'd abused her so much.

Maura helped Jessie finish making and serving supper. It would just be her, Jessie, Thad, and the three older McIntyre kids. Molly must have been working late at the paper and Maura knew that Keith was working at the restaurant. She felt a pang of pain when she thought about Nick. She longed for him and sometimes woke up from a nightmare, wanting desperately to have him wrap her up in his strong arms and make love to her.

Used to holding in her pain, she did her best to smile during dinner. Thad said he'd be happy to take her to Helena the following Friday and Maura warmly thanked him. He and Jessie had grown fond of her since she'd been with them and they wanted to help her in any way they could.

Nick came later that night after the restaurant closed and they took a walk.

"I'm glad you're getting that part taken care of," Nick said. "We'll get the annulment, too. It's just a question of time."

Maura stopped walking. "Why are you doing this to us?"

He frowned. "Doing what?"

"Trying to force something that will never happen. You need to stop. My dreams of happiness have died," Maura said.

Although it pained Nick to hear that, he smiled softly. "I know that you're not in a place where you have any faith that we'll have a future together, but I'll keep praying and hoping for the both of us."

Maura grew angry. "Stop it! You are living in a … dream! Wake up. Do not come to see me anymore. It hurts too much!"

Before he could respond, she ran back to the house, rushing inside and going up to her room, locking the door. Nick walked slowly back to Thad's to retrieve his horse. As he did, he worked on quelling his disappointment, telling himself that it was just another hurdle that he would have to jump and to remain determined to reach his goal.

Thad came outside as he walked up to his horse.

"What the hell happened?" he asked.

Nick said, "She's mad at me because I won't give up. She said she doesn't want to see me anymore, but I'm not gonna take no for an answer. I've already written to Father Carini about starting the proceedings for an annulment and he's going to send me the paperwork. She's getting a divorce and that's great, but we won't be able to get married until the annulment comes through."

Thad didn't share the views of the Catholic church on such matters, but he wasn't going to disparage it to Nick. "Why does it take so long to get it done? I mean, all they gotta do is read the report or whatever to see that the marriage should be annulled."

Nick said, "It's a little more complicated than that. Some people lie about the facts to get a quick annulment. A Catholic annulment isn't like a divorce. A divorce just means that the marriage is over, but in our eyes, once a couple is married and their relationship was good at the beginning, they're to be joined until one of them dies. There are requirements that a marriage must meet to be considered valid, though."

Thad grunted. "Ok. That sounds really complicated, so I won't ask any more questions. I like things simple."

Nick chuckled. "Most people do. The point is, I know that the tribunals will grant the annulment based on the fact that Maura had no idea what was happening and because Red was so abusive to her. In the eyes of the Church, there was never any valid marriage. It's just getting it through the channels in a timely manner. The problem is that the tribunals are backlogged a lot. Too many people are trying to get annulments instead of working things out."

Thad nodded. "I'll agree with you there. If you don't really wanna get married, don't. See? Simple. Of course, like you're saying, if there's abuse or a lot of adultery and you've really tried to work it out, I don't have anything against divorce. It's better than staying together when there ain't love there anymore.

"But it seems like people don't wanna work at it. Marriage is about commitment since it ain't always easy. You have to *want* it to work to keep a home together. My parents were a good example of that. They had hard times, sure, but they didn't just give up and their marriage was all the better for it. It's a shame more people don't do that sort of thing."

"Your parents sound like wise people," Nick said. "My parents are the same way. They've had their share of spats, but the love has never gone anywhere, thank God. Well, I won't bend your ear about it anymore. Thanks for everything you're doing for Maura—and for me, too."

Thad smiled. "Don't mention it. We like having her here and you're not too tough to take. You're welcome anytime. I'm glad you're not giving up on either her or staying sober. You doing all right with that?"

"Some days better than others, but I'll be danged if I'm gonna let it win," he said.

"Good man."

Nick mounted up. "Thanks again. Goodnight."

"'Night, Nick."

Thad walked with Maura into the Montana State Prison, a place he'd been many a time when he'd delivered all kinds of criminals to them. He kept a hand on her shoulder, trying to lend her comfort and courage. She was terrified about seeing Red again but determined to get him to sign the papers. Maura had decided that she might not be able to marry Nick, but come hell or high water, she was going to get the divorce. It was something she wanted to do for herself.

Although the time away from Nick had been hard to bear, it had helped her become more independent and stronger. She was making her own money and her language skills had improved. A couple of times, she'd gone to visit with Alfredo, Gino, and Sylvia during the day, but it was so hard to leave them again. She also saw Lulu and Vanna a lot in town and they kept trying to convince her to move back home. So it wasn't just the loss of Nick that she mourned, it was the loss of the people who had shown her such kindness and taken them into their home.

Maura and Thad waited in the lobby and he chitchatted with the guard there. It didn't take long for Captain Spencer to show up, however, and then they were taken to a visiting area. It was a small, damp brick room with only one little window in it. A beat-up, wooden table stood in the center of the space with a chair on either side.

Maura's hands shook as her dread intensified, but she called upon more strength so she could face him. She knew he couldn't hurt her any longer, but she was still afraid.

When he was brought in, he gave her a leering smile. "Missed me, huh?"

Thad stepped forward threateningly. "Watch your mouth or something might just run into it."

Red sneered at him. "This ain't got nothin' to do with you, so back off."

"This young lady is my friend, so it's got everything to do with me," Thad said.

Maura wanted to get out of there as quickly as possible. Her heartbeat throbbed hard in her chest and she started to tremble upon seeing the man who'd heaped so much pain and humiliation upon her.

She cut into their exchange. "I am only here to have you sign these divorce papers." She unfolded them and pushed them across the table to him.

Red took them and looked them over while he rubbed his chin thoughtfully. He flipped through the thin packet and then gave her a perplexed look. "I don't get it. Why are you bringing these to me?"

"Because you married me and I do not want to be married to you." Maura said, her dark eyes meeting his steadily.

He let out a bark of laughter, which turned into a chuckle and then a full belly laugh. His mirth was such that tears stood out in his eyes.

Hot fury pumped through Maura's veins. "Stop laughing at me! Sign the damn papers!"

It was the first time Thad had heard her swear and he smiled, silently urging her on.

Red finally calmed down. "You don't understand. We were never married. Where'd you get that idea?"

Maura pulled out the marriage certificate that Captain Spencer had given her. "This has our names on it and it is real."

One look at the document sent Red off into gales of laughter again. Captain Spencer backhanded him. "Knock that off and sign those papers!"

Holding his face, Red glared at Spencer. "I'd be happy to be rid of her, but she ain't my wife! That certificate ain't real. Well, the paper itself is, but the ceremony was just for show. My friend, Bob Milner, used to dress up as a priest when we went to the Indian camps. He distracted them while the rest of us stole stuff. I already admitted to all this, so I don't care about sayin' it again if it'll get her out of my hair. That signature at the bottom is a fake. We ain't married. If you don't believe me, go see Bob. He's here, too."

Maura clutched at Thad's arm as a rush of relief and a thread of hope washed over her. Was it really true? Had she never been married to Red? *Oh, Great Spirit, let it be true!*

Thad asked, "Are willing to sign a paper saying you were never married to Maura?"

"Sure," Red said. "She's caused me enough trouble. If that's what it takes to be done with her, I'll do it."

Captain Spencer said, "I'll go have it typed up and be right back. There's a notary here on staff who can witness it."

He left the room in quick strides as Thad hugged Maura. "Looks like Nick's prayers were answered, sweetheart."

Burying her face in Thad's chest, Maura said, "I cannot believe it yet. Not until we talk to this Bob. I need to be sure he is the priest I remember."

Red snorted. "It's him, all right. I should know."

"Shut up!" Maura snapped. "You would do anything to make me miserable! I do not trust you at all!"

Thad gave him a warning look and Red slumped back in his chair, putting his arms over his chest sullenly. Captain Spencer soon returned with the notary and the document. Red wasted no time signing it and then demanding to go back to his cell. The guard took him and then brought back Bob Milner.

Maura recognized him immediately. "Yes! That is him! He is the priest!"

Bob remembered her, too. "Well, I haven't seen you in a while. I ain't a priest, though. Never was. What's this all about?"

She showed him the certificate. Like Red, he laughed. "Father Suggs was the name I used, but that was just an alias. I filched some certificates one time from the Catholic church in Helena and this was one of them. It ain't worth the paper it's printed on. We just did that fake little wedding that day to give our cronies a chance to steal stuff."

Maura fought the urge to dance around with joy. "Will you sign a paper saying this?"

Bob shrugged. "Yeah, sure."

Thad grinned at Maura. "I don't often see a miracle happen, but I'd say this counts as one."

She nodded. "Yes. I must go see Nick right away."

"You better believe we will as soon as we get back to Echo," Thad said. "We won't waste any time gettin' there, either."

Nick hummed like usual as he worked over the hot stoves at Mama T.'s in the early afternoon. He sometimes sang out loud at a part in the song he particularly liked. Sylvia smiled and laughed when he did this. Her mother's heart was thrilled to see the life back in her son's eyes and to hear it in his voice.

He'd just put some trout in a frying pan when Maura rushed into the restaurant.

"Nick, Nick!" she cried, practically attacking him.

The joy in her voice made him curious as he embraced her tightly. It had been so long since he'd held her that he wasn't going to miss the opportunity no matter who was around.

"What's going on?" he asked her in a strangled voice as her arms squeezed his neck tightly.

She released him and said, "I am not married! I was never married! The certificate is fake!" Her excitement was so great that she'd been speaking in Comanche.

"English, Maura. I don't speak Comanche," Nick said.

Maura took a breath so she could calm down enough to coherently explain everything to him. As she spoke, Nick's face registered confusion gave way to disbelief and then elation. He picked her up, spinning her around and around as her lips found his lips to celebrate with a fiery kiss.

When they parted, Sylvia and Keith joined in their happiness, hugging them and laughing with the couple. Nick was so happy that he ran out into the dining room and shouted, "She was never married!"

Only a few people present in the restaurant understood what this meant to him, but his enthusiasm was contagious, and they cheered despite not knowing why they were. Vanna had come over to pick up lunch for her and Lulu. When she heard his announcement, she ran through the tables, into his arms. Nick pulled her into the kitchen with him so he and Maura could explain it to her.

Then Sylvia shooed Maura and Nick out the restaurant so they could spread the good news. As she took over the cooking, happy tears flowed down her face and it felt as though the world had righted itself again.

Epilogue

A couple of days after Nick and Maura's reunion, Arliss stopped over at his carriage house after working with Lucky that day to clean up. He found a note from Andi laying on his kitchen table. Smiling, he picked it up.

Wash up and put on one of R.J.'s suits. You all have plans tonight. Come to the church at 7.

"What are you up to now?" Arliss asked aloud. "Did we forget some service? Nah. Even if I didn't remember, R.J. would."

Looking at the wall clock, Arliss saw that he'd better get going so he didn't keep his lady waiting. After a brief argument with R.J. over which suit was the better choice, he put on a navy blue suit and the new tie that Andi had given them. He put on a little cologne and tamed his hair. Ready, he hurried over to the church. Going in the front door, he saw that Andi's office door was closed. The sanctuary was dark except for the Eternal Flame and one wall sconce. He knocked on her office door.

"Andi? Are you in there?"

"Yes. Come in."

When he opened the door, he saw that the room was suffused in candlelight and that her desk had been turned into a pretty table complete with a red table cloth and an elegant setting. His gaze found her where she stood beside the desk and his heart thudded in chest. She wore a soft, lilac, satin dress that accentuated her fine, tall figure and showed off her pretty neck. He reined in the urge to nibble it, knowing she'd pick up on it.

"My goodness, darlin'. You're lookin' especially fine this evening and I love your redecorating. What's the occasion?"

She came to him, kissing his cheek. "Dinner. You're looking especially fine yourself, Mr. Jackson."

He smiled. "Thank you."

He seated her and then sat down himself. "Um, I hate to point out the obvious, but there's no food here. What are we eatin'?"

Andi chuckled and rang a little dinner bell on her desk, making his forehead crinkle in confusion. He jumped when Gino Terranova entered the office with a bottle of wine. Grinning and winking at Arliss, he poured the nice red Cabernet into their glasses and then left the bottle for them.

Arliss laughed. "Well, this sure is a surprise. A very nice one. So we're being served tonight, huh?"

Andi giggled. "Yes, we are."

Sal showed up with the antipasto and Arliss said grace for them after he left. They shared the events of their days with each other and then during the *secondo*, Andi said, "Arliss, I'd like to ask you something, and while I'm a little nervous about the answer, I want you to be honest with me."

Arliss arched an eyebrow at her. "I'd never lie to you, Andi. You can ask me anything. You know that."

She nodded. "So far, no enemies have shown up in Echo. Do you think any ever will?"

He knew what she wanted to hear, but he would be honest, as she'd requested. "I don't know. There's no way I could say one way or another. It's promising, but there's no guarantee."

"You're old life will never be completely over, will it?"

Arliss halted cutting his herb roasted beef, meeting her gaze. "No. I've been wanting to talk to you about that, but after what happened last fall, I just didn't know how to bring it up. Preston said that in exchange for helping us with Wild Wind and Arrow and the school, he might need me in the future. So I can't rule out having to go on a mission at some point. I know what I promised you, honey, and I never meant to go back on that. I feel terrible about it."

Andi could see the remorse in his eyes and feel it coming off of him. "I know that when you made that promise to me that you meant it at the time. I understand how situations can change and while I hate the thought of you going off like you did last year, I've come to accept that this is a part of who you all are. It's your path, what you were meant to do. You've always said that I was sent back from Heaven to do great things and I said that me, you, and your brothers have a lot of great things to do together."

Arliss said, "I believe that, too. One of the great things you were meant to do is to love us, Andi. No one else could the way you do. No other woman is strong enough to love and accept us."

Her smile was so beautiful that it almost brought tears to his eyes. "I do love you and accept you all. But I also accept what you were all born to do—protect people. All of your individual talents and gifts combine to become a force to be reckoned with and let's face it; the world can certainly use those sorts of forces. I accept that you might have to leave again and—" She had to swallow back her tears. "I accept that you might not come home to me." She put up a hand to halt his response.

"I dread that, but I accept the possibility that it could happen. After believing that I'd lost you all, I did so much praying and contemplating and that was the answer I received in response to all of my questions. It was your path and even though I detested it, I had to accept it and go on to do what God wants me to do. So, if Preston calls upon you or someone else, please don't feel guilty about going. It's what you were put on Earth to do, so do it as only you can. I'm so proud of you for all that you are and knowing that you're helping protect other people will help see me through until you come home again."

Arliss tried to collect his thoughts to come up with some sort of elegant response to that and he called up R.J., but he was so stunned that even he didn't have words. Finally, Arliss said, "No man could ask for a more understanding, generous woman than you, Andi." He shut his mouth, wiped it, and put his napkin aside. "Come with me."

Startled, Andi said, "What?"

He stood and held out a hand to her. "C'mon. Right now, woman."

She smiled at his insistence. "Ok."

Taking his hand, she let him lead her into the sanctuary. He made her stop at the second pew back from the altar. He sat in it and slid over, patting the space beside him. When she sat, he put his arms around her.

"You're my angel, Andi. No, don't laugh. You are. The night I came here after killing Williams out at Lucky's, I was so lost. I don't know what made me come here except to say that it was God's will that we were supposed to meet that night. You comforted me, extended me friendship, and helped me even though you didn't know me at all.

"And since then, you've continued to do all of that and so much more. We could search from now until eternity and we'd never find a more beautiful, kind, generous, smart, funny, or sweeter woman than you. You're ready now."

She searched his eyes, but for once couldn't get a read on him. "Ready for what?"

He knelt on the floor, leaned forward, reaching up under the pew in front of them, and manipulated something. In the dark, she couldn't see what he was doing.

"Andi, this spot right here is where it all began for us. It's where we met the woman we fell hopelessly in love with. I'm not usually sappy like that, but it's true. We couldn't do this until now because we knew that you weren't ready. We prayed every day for a sign that you were and you just gave us that sign."

Looking into the eyes that they thought were the most beautiful in the world, Arliss said, "We couldn't love you any more if we tried. Andrea Catherine Thatcher ..."

R.J. picked it up. "will you do us the great honor of marrying us... "

"and making us the happiest men in the world?" Blake finished, opening a ring box.

Andi's smile seemed to light up the sanctuary. "It will be a privilege to be your wife, my three-in-one men."

Blake picked up her left hand and said, "Then allow us to give you this," as he slipped the ring on her finger. "R.J. told me to say that. It's a good thing, too, because I'm not good at this stuff."

R.J. said, "It's true. I wanted this to be momentous since it's the only time we plan to ever do it."

Arliss said, "We'll always cherish you, Andi. We love you so much."

They kissed her then and it was a kiss unlike any they'd given her yet. It was sweet, sensual, fierce, and lingering, and Andi knew what it was like to be kissed by all three of them at once. It made her feel deliciously dizzy and her heartbeat ran faster by the time they let her go. Then they gathered her close and they sat in happy silence for a little, savoring the moment.

Andi jerked. "Oh! They're waiting to serve us dessert."

Arliss laughed. "That's right. Oh boy. I guess we'd better get back to dinner. I'm sorry, honey, but we couldn't wait anymore."

They hurried back to her office and she rang the bell for the next course. When Nick himself came upstairs from the kitchen with it, they told him their good news and he congratulated them before calling downstairs to his brothers. The other two Terranova men also celebrated the couple before the three brothers went back down to get everything cleaned up.

When their dessert of lemon cream cookies and cappuccino was finished, Andi and Arliss helped them despite their protests. They expressed their gratitude to Nick and his brothers before the Terranovas left. Andi and Arliss went back to their spot on the pew, planning their wedding and talking about the future they would share.

Vanna and Lulu had their hands full keeping Maura calm as they helped her prepare for her and Nick's September wedding. She wasn't nervous about being married to Nick, only the ceremony. She was petrified that she would trip while walking down the aisle or make a mistake while saying her vows. She'd been practicing them every day so she didn't embarrass herself or Nick.

Once she donned the lovely, cream-colored dress that Lulu had designed for her, Vanna went to work on her hair. Maura hadn't wanted to wear white because she wasn't pure and she knew that white was usually worn by virgins. During her and Nick's preparatory talks with Father Carini, they'd told him everything, wanting to be completely honest with him so that he completely understood the situation.

It was essentially a joint confession and the priest felt that it was cleansing for the both of them. Although he'd initially been very disappointed in Nick and had given him a stern talking to, he'd also had compassion in his heart for the young man he'd come to love like a nephew. Nick had been through a terrible ordeal, one that not everyone would come back from, especially if they didn't have the love and support of a good family like Nick did.

He'd liked Maura right off, admiring her strength in surviving all of the horror she'd seen in her young life. As she'd told her story, he'd had tears in his eyes and he also understood why Nick and Maura had been intimate even though he didn't approve. He wasn't naïve or so rigid that he couldn't comprehend human nature or how traumatic situations could steal away a person's good sense.

When Nick requested that Andi be allowed to help officiate, he'd balked. Nick hadn't backed down and the men had discussed it, argued, and finally compromised.

"Nick, it's not me necessarily that would object. Our church has a rich history of women who've held very powerful positions in the church throughout the ages, but not during a wedding mass. I'm sorry, but the most I can allow is for her to do the readings. I'd like to meet with her beforehand, of course," he'd said.

Nick had known that Father Carini couldn't be pushed anymore on it and since he'd been willing to baptize Maura and help her become a full Catholic the same way he had Arrow, Nick didn't want to press his luck. Before he would marry them, the priest made sure that Nick was strong enough to stay sober.

Many people would have been put off by all of the restrictions and requirements placed upon them, but Maura and Nick looked at it as a new beginning. They were starting out fresh, cleansed by their faith—his a renewal and hers newly-found—and they were able to be patient because they were building a solid foundation for their relationship and they wanted it to last forever.

Maura had continued to live with the McIntyres and she'd formed a close bond with them. She'd asked Thad to give her away and he'd grinned, saying, "I'm getting good at this. Maybe I oughta hire myself out or something."

Once Vanna and Lulu were finished, Maura was amazed at the transformation in herself. She'd gone from being a lowly slave to a woman who now had people in her life who loved her. No longer was she the orphan-like little girl, who'd known so little joy in her life. She had a family now and she had a man who'd loved her enough to be strong enough for both of them when all had seemed lost.

As she looked at the reflection of the reborn woman in the mirror, Maura promised God and herself not to ever let hope completely die again. It might dim now and again, but she would always keep hope alive in her heart.

Her thoughts were interrupted by Thad coming to collect her.

"Seems like I just did this not too long ago," he said. "I keep having to give away all the women in my life that I love."

She smiled at his joke. "You know you haven't really lost us," she said.

"Yeah. There's this really handsome guy out at the altar who's ready to marry you. Think we oughta go get you hitched?" he asked.

"Yes. I think we should," she said.

Thad offered her his arm and waited as Vanna and Lulu went ahead of her. "Noodle, this is your second Catholic wedding this year. How do you stand it? They're so long."

Vanna laughed softly. Thad had started teasing all of her family about being Catholic and they in turn teased him about his heathenish ways. "Why don't you just sit back and have a cigarette to pass the time?"

Thad laughed. "That's a good idea, but I think the padre would kick me out. Then I couldn't come to the reception and eat that terramee soup your ma makes." He always butchered the word on purpose.

The women laughed and then the music started. As they watched Vanna and Lulu go ahead of them, Thad patted Maura's hand where it rested on his arm. "Don't worry; I won't let you fall. I know you've been worrying about this, but you'll do great. Just relax and enjoy it."

Maura took in a deep breath and then nodded. "All right. I'm ready now."

She couldn't quite squelch the butterflies knocking around in her belly as she held Nick's gaze. With every step she took, she knew she was taking one more closer to forever with the man God had given her. A man who loved her completely, even knowing her past. Nick held nothing against her, didn't see a Comanche slave when he looked at her. She knew that in his eyes she was simply the woman he loved and she was grateful beyond words for all that he was to her. He was her comforter, her confidant, and her best friend.

Thad being Thad couldn't help razz Nick a little once he'd delivered the bride to him. Leaning close, he whispered to him, "Treat her right or there won't be anywhere to hide if you don't. Got it?"

Nick smiled and nodded. Satisfied, Thad saluted Father Carini, which perplexed the priest, and sat down. Maura and Nick somehow kept straight faces when the priest gave Thad a quizzical look before starting the ceremony.

Andi performed her readings beautifully and Father Carini was impressed with her again, as he had been when they'd first met. He'd teased her that it was too bad that she wasn't Catholic because she would have made a good abbess. Sal performed the Ava Maria for them and did a splendid job.

As they said their vows and exchanged their rings, Nick and Maura felt that they were exchanging their old, tarnished, tragic pasts for a bright, shining new future. They sealed the new covenant between them with a restrained kiss that was a promise of the love and passion they would share later on.

Their family and friends watched with smiles and some shed tears of joy. At the conclusion of the ceremony, while the wedding party filed out to the music, Sylvia said to Alfredo, "Poor Gino. Always the best man and not the groom. I told him to start writing letters again, but I don't know if he will or not."

Alfredo sighed. "I know. The whole thing with Chelsea sort of soured him on the whole idea. We'll keep working on him."

Sylvia nodded and then she and Alfredo filed out behind the wedding party, hoping that their only single child would find his mate soon.

When Nick and Maura made love in their hotel room that night, they took their time, savoring the experience. It was the first time they were doing so for reasons other than comfort or sheer lust. They were celebrating their love for one another and further strengthening their bond. With every kiss and whispered word of love, their commitment deepened.

The man who had lost his way, going far off the right path, had found his way back through the fiery-haired beauty who had given him her strength and kindness. The woman who had been an orphan, who had lost her hope in the face of what had seemed like insurmountable odds, had found in her handsome, Italian chef, her home.

Their passion for each other was reignited, but with the addition of love, it was even more heady and satisfying than before. Every one of their senses were filled with the other and they knew nothing else during those hours. As they held onto one another, their hope was strengthened, faith was confirmed, and their love solidified into the kind that would sustain them throughout the rest of their lives.

The staff of the Echo Canyon Indian School introduced themselves to their new charges, who stood uncertainly in the huge parlor of the new building. A couple of the older boys glared defiantly at them while one little girl cried. Edna took her in her arms to comfort her. The others looked around and fidgeted anxiously with their clothing.

Wild Wind smiled encouragingly at them. "You do not have to be afraid," he said in Cheyenne, which surprised the students who spoke the language.

They'd all been severely punished for speaking their native tongue, so to be addressed in it was startling.

"Our school is different than what you are used to, as you can see. You must still speak English for those who do not speak Cheyenne, but you are allowed to speak in your own language, whatever it may be. You are allowed to wear traditional Indian clothing, and we have some clothing for you to start with for those who wish to dress that way. You may grow your hair out again or keep it short. That is up to you. We do have rules that must be followed or you will be punished."

One of the older boys, Skyhawk, said, "I knew it. Will you beat us? Starve us?"

Wild Wind smiled kindly, understanding why he might think that. "No. There will be no hitting, spanking, or making you go hungry. We will work much like a tribe. You will have privileges, but when you misbehave or are disrespectful of your elders or any of the townspeople, you will lose those privileges. You will have a schedule to stick to and you will work hard at your schoolwork."

Lance said in English, "You're expected to do chores and keep your areas neat. You'll help cook meals and learn other skills. There will be playtime and you'll be allowed to go over to Wild Wind and Roxie's farm. The Quinns and Earnests have also said that you're welcome there as long as you don't cause mischief.

"You'll learn farming and we'll plant our own garden so we can grow some of our own food. Most of the people around here are happy to have you here, but there are some who are not. If anyone says anything mean to you, let us know, but don't argue with them. You'll have one of us with you when you go into town, so it shouldn't be a problem. We'll fill you in more as we go along, but for now, how about we get you settled? Then we'll have lunch and show you around."

Adam had given the school kids the day off since a lot of them wanted to meet the Indian children. Porter, his sisters, and Henley approached the new kids, introducing themselves and offering to help them settle in. Otto, having inherited his father's charming ways, quickly had a couple of young female admirers, which amused the group of adults.

Many of the townspeople had come out to welcome them, too, including Evan and his deputies, Jerry and the town council, and Erin and Win, who wanted to look the kids over after lunch. The Indian children didn't know what to make of all the kindness and lax rules. It was a whole new world for them and it would take some getting used to.

Once all of their belongings had been stowed away, the kids who wanted to were allowed to change into traditional Indian clothing. Skyhawk and his best friend, Dog Star, grinned, feeling better just with the familiar feel of the soft buckskin against their skin again.

Skylark said, "It might not be so bad here."

Dog Star nodded. "It seems like it."

Henley said, "You fellas look good. A lot better than in those stuffy suits and all. Do you play baseball?"

Dog Star frowned. "Baseball?"

Porter and Henley grinned at each other and Henley said, "Allow us to introduce you to the greatest sport on the planet. Come with us, everyone. The girls can play, too. We have a few girls who are really good players."

They trooped outside and set up a rough ball diamond, using large rocks as bases. Molly had come to do a huge write-up for the *Express* and she loved playing baseball. She put aside her writing to help teach the kids how to play and to participate herself. Some of the staff and adults joined in. Teams were picked and a game ensued until lunch was ready.

As soon as Andi said grace, they all dug in and a celebratory atmosphere developed. The Indian kids began relaxing as the Echo kids teased and talked with them and the adults also conversed with them. Some of Roxie and Wild Wind's dogs had ventured over and the kids gave them little tidbits of food, making friends with them.

Wild Wind and Arrow exchanged a long look. Wild Wind signed, "This is what we were meant to do, brother."

"I agree," Arrow signed. "Our parents would be proud of what we have helped build. I believe they are watching us and perhaps they even helped us."

Wild Wind nodded. "I think you are right."

They smiled and then went back to eating and visiting.

Molly had hired Dan Griffin as a part-time photographer for the *Express*, and he took pictures of everything pertaining to the school. He snapped photographs of all the rooms inside, took several shots of the outside from various angles, and had taken pictures of the baseball game. He'd taken some group pictures of the students alone and then several more with the staff.

When the special edition of the *Express* came out, the pictures showed a large, beautiful log structure situated in the center of some tall trees. There was a large front porch lined with rocking chairs. Flower beds had been planted around the house along with shrubbery.

In the first pictures of the Indian kids, their expressions were serious and nervous, but when their lunch was over, Dan took some more pictures. This time, their faces showed big smiles and a couple of them were caught in the middle of a laugh. Then he took pictures of the town kids with them and caught one of the little girls, Dewdrop, kissing Otto's cheek while he grinned.

Edna drew Andi off to the side. "I want to thank you for your special prayers. It's because of them that I'm so much better now. I'm grateful to you for using your talents to help me."

Andi smiled. "I'm always happy to help, but I know that Win's treatments help, too. I'm so glad that you're able to get around so well now. I know that being in so much pain and cooped up had to be hard for such a vital woman like you."

Edna hugged her. "You've helped give me back my freedom and I wouldn't have this job if it weren't for you. I'm going to love working with these children. I'm proud to be a part of something so positive."

"You're going to be wonderful for them," Andi replied. "They're lucky to have you and everyone. God has certainly done a great thing here."

"Yes, He has," Enda said.

Jerry stood back watching Dan take the pictures. Marvin appeared beside him.

"I would say this is a success," he said.

Jerry said, "It sure is. Look at how happy those kids are now. It makes it all worth it, doesn't it?"

"I agree."

"And it's good for the town, too. If only we had a telegraph office. It would make it easier to keep in touch with Preston about things and it would help Evan and Molly, too," Jerry said.

Marvin rocked back and forth on his feet a little. "Well, I actually have an idea about that."

Jerry smiled to himself. "Really? Where are we going to get the money? The left over money from the school is earmarked to help improve the town roads."

"I'm aware. I think we should take up a donation towards the telegraph and our family is willing to match whatever is collected," Marvin said.

"Are you sure?" Jerry asked.

Marvin said, "I would say so if we weren't. Also, if we bring it over Creasy's Pass, it'll cut off a lot and decrease our costs greatly. In fact, the men in the area can start taking down the trees."

Andi heard him. "I'll help, too. I'm very handy with an ax."

Arliss took her hand. "She sure is, and she looks great in pants, too."

Marvin laughed. "Yes, she does."

"Marvin!" Andi objected.

"I'm only being honest," he said with a laugh.

Jerry chuckled. "Always causing trouble. Whatever trees we chop down, we should keep some to make boards to replace some of the ones on the town hall. The rest of it we could donate to some of the poorer families around the area for the winter. That way they wouldn't have to worry about buying wood for a while."

His wife Sonya came over, holding their two-year-old daughter, Ginny. "That's a great idea, honey. I'm sure they'll appreciate it."

"I'll start organizing a work day," Jerry said. "We'll need to make sure that we have enough logging chains…"

As the large group of them stood around making plans on that September day, everyone felt hopeful that they could make the town a better place for everyone to live in. It seemed that they were on their way to making sure that it didn't become a ghost town. Through their collaboration, ingenuity, and generosity, they were shaping the future of Echo for the better and doing their best to assure that it would stay on the map.

The baseball game resumed and, as the new kids played and made friends, the youngsters, who had essentially been made orphans when they'd been forced to leave their families, felt that just maybe they had found a home where they could flourish and where they would be loved. They grew hopeful that the Great Spirit had brought them to a place where they could have a future full of happiness. They had prayed for it to be so and the Great Spirit had heard their silent pleas and smiled upon them.

The End

Thank you for reading and supporting my book and I hope you enjoyed it.

Please will you do me a favor and review "Montana Orphan" so I'll know whether you liked it or not, it would be very much appreciated, thank you.

Linda's Other Books

Echo Canyon Brides Series

Montana Rescue
  (Echo Canyon brides Book 1)
Montana Bargain
  (Echo Canyon brides Book 2)
Montana Adventure
  (Echo Canyon brides Book 3)
Montana Luck
  (Echo Canyon brides Book 4)
Montana Fire
  (Echo Canyon brides Book 5)
Montana Hearts
  (Echo Canyon brides Book 6)
Montana Hearts
  (Echo Canyon brides Book 7)
  Montana Orphan
  (Echo Canyon brides Book 8)

Montana Mail Order Brides Series

Westward Winds
  (Montana Mail Order brides
  Book 1)
Westward Dance
  (Montana Mail Order brides
  Book 2)
Westward Bound
  (Montana Mail Order brides
  Book 3)
Westward Destiny
  (Montana Mail Order brides
  Book 4)
Westward Fortune
  (Montana Mail Order brides
  Book 5)
Westward Justice
  (Montana Mail Order brides
  Book 6)

Westward Dreams
(Montana Mail Order brides
Book 7)

Westward Holiday
(Montana Mail Order brides
Book 8)

Westward Sunrise
(Montana Mail Order brides
Book 9)

Westward Moon
(Montana Mail Order brides
Book 10)

Westward Christmas
(Montana Mail Order brides
Book 11)

Westward Visions
(Montana Mail Order brides
Book 12)

Westward Secrets
(Montana Mail Order brides
Book 13)

Westward Changes
(Montana Mail Order brides
Book 14)

Westward Heartbeat
(Montana Mail Order brides
Book 15)

Westward Joy
(Montana Mail Order brides
Book 16)

Westward Courage
(Montana Mail Order brides
Book 17)

Westward Spirit
(Montana Mail Order brides
Book 18)

Westward Fate
(Montana Mail Order brides
Book 19)

Westward Hope
(Montana Mail Order brides
Book 20)

Westward Wild
(Montana Mail Order brides
Book 21)

Westward Sight
(Montana Mail Order brides
Book 22)

Westward Horizons
(Montana Mail Order brides
Book 23)

Connect With Linda

Visit my website at **www.lindabridey.com** to view my other books and to sign up to my mailing list so that you are notified about my new releases.

About Linda Bridey

LINDA BRIDEY lives in New Mexico with her three dogs; a German shepherd, chocolate Labrador retriever, and a black Pug. She became fascinated with Montana and decided to combine that fascination with her fictional romance writing. Linda chose to write about mail-order-brides because of the bravery of these women who left everything and everyone to take a trek into the unknown. The Westward series books are her first publications.

Made in the USA
Monee, IL
14 July 2020